The Dyke and the Dybbuk

Ellen Galford

Seal Press

For Ellen Kelly,
and for all the aunts and cousins
of the Lowenstein clan

Copyright © 1993 by Ellen Galford

This U.S. edition first published in 1994 by Seal Press, 3131 Western Avenue, Suite 410, Seattle, Washington 98121. Published by agreement with Virago Press, Ltd., London.

Cover art and design by Kris Morgan

Library of Congress Cataloging-in-Publication Data

Galford, Ellen
The Dyke and the Dybbuk.
1st Seal Press edition.1. Women film critics – England – London – Fiction. 2. Spirit possession – England – London – Fiction. 3. Taxicab drivers – England – London – Fiction. 4. Lesbians – England – London – Fiction. 5. Mysticism – Judaism – Fiction. 6. London (England) – Fiction. 7. Dybbuk – Fiction. I. Title.
PR6057.A383D94   1994   823.'914–dc20   94-10567
ISBN 1-878067-51-6

First printing, October 1994
10 9 8 7 6 5 4 3 2 1

Distributed to the trade by Publishers Group West

1

Before the Beginning

If planet Earth slips off its axis tomorrow, put the blame on Rainbow Rosenbloom.

If we are smacked by a rogue asteroid, ingested by a black hole, or poisoned by something dripping through our tattered ozone canopy, feel free to lay it at her door.

For the melting of the polar caps, the disappearance of the snow leopard and the souring of the seas, Rainbow must take the rap.

Not fair? Well, life isn't.

Note the ground rules: there are 613 commandments that must be obeyed by every Jew alive in the world at any time. To breach even one of these disturbs the universe, and sends the whole of Creation out of kilter. Step on a crack, and break your mother's back.

How's that for a heritage of guilt? Bum raps over child murder, plague-spreading and a political execution in Roman Judaea seem, in comparison, small potatoes.

Just look at Rosenbloom – thirty-odd years old, devotee of forbidden fruits, not a skirt nor a husband to her name.

By neglecting to get married, Rainbow has done worse than cheat her relatives out of a party: she has cocked a snook at the Law, as laid down in Leviticus. The way Rainbow lives and loves (when opportunity arises; it hasn't, lately) involves unspeakable acts that rank right up there with throwing your children into the fire as a sacrifice to Baal.

And, speaking of children, she has flouted that quintessential

1

obligation upon the female Jew to be fruitful and multiply, to replenish the tribe. She has done nothing to replace the legions that have lately fallen through a hole in history.

Rainbow has not put her foot into a synagogue in twenty years; instead, you'll find her at the cinema. As the film critic for *Outsider* magazine, Europe's leading journal of lesbian and gay culture, she's turned her passion for graven images into a vocation.

But what kind of job is that for a Nice Jewish Girl?

Lots of fun, a little glory, but pays *bubkes* (beans, to you).

Which is why we now find her driving a taxi through the streets of London. Not your typical NJG occupation either, but perhaps it satisfies some inborn nomadic yearning for this daughter of a wandering tribe.

Enough, already, of this gossip. We're about to hail her cab.

After dropping off a pair of Jesuit priests in Farm Street, Rainbow crawls through gridlocked Mayfair. She's decided to call it quits after a heavy day. To get the kinks out, she has some vintage Ozark banjo-pickers banging and twanging from her tape deck, she's beating time on her steering wheel, and alarming nearby drivers with the sight, if not the sound, of her loud 'Yahoo!'s.

So she almost doesn't hear the message from Radio Control. When she does, she wishes she hadn't. It runs: 'Ring your aunt. Extremely urgent.'

This is not as simple as it sounds. Which aunt, for a start? She has five. All of whom live life at an operatic pitch. Cliffhangers and crises are their meat and drink. Rainbow runs through an inventory of possibilities: uncles with heart attacks, burglaries, cars crumpled into brick walls, a giant south-coast tidal wave swallowing up the Oceanview-Bellavista Kosher Hotel and all its guests as the Red Sea swallowed Pharaoh's armies . . .

This last vision does the trick.

She smacks her forehead. 'Oh God, no . . . Passover! Aunt Becky's seder!'

2

At a pay-phone, trying to get a word in between outraged gabbles: 'Sorry . . . I thought it was next week – You know I never remember the dates . . . All right, I said I was sorry, sorry, sorry. Anyway, I couldn't have rearranged my hours . . . OK, I'll be there as fast as I can. No I won't speed, I promise – you think I want to lose my licence? Yes, I do know the quick way through Walthamstow . . . What? My black cords and a red shirt. Why? *Of course they're clean*!!. . . No, I will not go home to change. You wouldn't like anything I could change into, anyway. I told you, I don't own a dress . . . Listen, Aunt Becky, if I stand here talking any longer, I won't get there till bloody midnight!'

Unimpeachable logic. She wins the argument, but loses the game. In this traffic, she'll be lucky to make Ilford in an hour.

Never mind. We're heading for Aunt Becky's house, too. But it will take us a little longer to get there. Say about 200 years.

For I must bring you first to another time and country. A grey, low-lying land, of mud and marshes, a strip of plain and the beginnings of a forest that goes on forever. The sea is not far away: you can almost hear it behind the dunes. You will certainly catch a whiff of rotting fish.

Between the forest and the plain there is a track of sorts, and today it is full of traffic. Oxen or bony horses drag laden carts, women trudge with bundles on their shoulders, heading towards a wooden steeple and a huddle of roofs on the horizon. Below them, the market square.

This is where journeys end and begin again. The pelts of forest creatures who have failed to evade the hunters lie in heaps, waiting to be made into hats for holy men. Amber and salt herrings, travelling south and east, cross paths with silks moving westward. Hands visit pockets other than their own. Coins, of a brittle and corrupted metal, flow in rivers through the crowd, trickling through the palms of the peasant women, pooling around the tavern keeper and the tax collector, until they disappear in an underground stream that leads to the prince's strong-room.

Behind the square, in a narrow street, another journey is beginning. From around the corner comes a tootling band and a bevy of wedding guests, escorting a bride. Suddenly the mule that carries her stops dead, halfway between a shrine to the Virgin and the bathhouse of the Jews.

A tall woman, lounging against the bathhouse wall, takes this opportunity to cast a leisurely look at the bride. The girl's face lies hidden under its veil; the onlooker's is marked with lines and shadows that have to do with sleeplessness and poor feeding, not with age. She has been chewing on a flat disc of poppyseeded bread, but suddenly spits out her last mouthful, narrowly missing the mule, and throws the remainder to the ground. She tramples it into the dirt.

Someone taps the animal's rump, and the procession moves on. The woman follows at a distance, gnawing on her lower lip until it bleeds. Then she stops, stares at the back of the disappearing bride, and mumbles. She speaks only in a whisper, far too low for anyone in the wedding party to hear. But the girl on the mule suddenly arches her back, as if she's been shot by an arrow. Now the damp air is stirred by a sudden beating and fluttering. From eaves, knotholes and chinks in chimneys, all the birds of the town rise up as one, and fly, in a body, out to the invisible sea.

Now, that's what I call a curse with a bit of style. Don't ask me the rights or wrongs of it. She may be only a humble market-woman – you can see her in the square most mornings, killing chickens to order – but she is a veritable Michelangelo of maledictions. You should see the one she's cooked up this time.

But who is this woman? Why is she so angry?

She is twenty years old, her name is Anya, and she is neither one thing nor another. According to ancient Mosaic law, she is, by virtue of her mother's blood, a Jew. According to the priest of the church in the market square, she is not. Her father was a woodcutter, named for the local saint. She was orphaned early: the recruiting officers swooped and took her father, who never came back again; her mother, quite sensibly, died of shame.

She drifts between the hamlet in the forest, where her father's people live, and the Jewish dorf half a mile away, on the edge of the plain. Children on both sides throw stones and insults: 'Anya Christ-killer' in the forest; 'Anya the Apostate' in the dorf.

Their fathers and elder brothers, after one or two ill-starred attempts, prefer to find their fun elsewhere. The market town has plenty of girls more willing, and better looking too.

Anyway, Anya doesn't need their trade. She owns – or has stolen – a rooster and some hens. They thrive and multiply: rumour has it that she knows a charm for paralysing foxes.

And who's the bride? What's she to Anya?

Her name is Gittel. She comes from a hard-scrabbling household in the Jewish dorf.

And Anya the Apostate cannot forgive her for what she has just done.

For Gittel and Anya have sworn undying sisterhood. They have pierced their palms with a sharp twig, and let the blood blend. From Anya, Gittel has learned how to swim in the stream, found out where babies came from, and received the shocking news that God is not necessarily the only God (there is also Christ, and the Corn Mother, and the old Lord of Thunder). Sometimes Anya has slipped her hand under Gittel's clothing, and spent quite a while there. Gittel, liking it, has done some searching and squeezing in return.

She has also reciprocated by giving Anya things to dream about.

For Gittel has told Anya how the road into the market town also leads out again, towards places beyond imagining. A traveller with sufficient time and endurance need only cross seven rivers, then traverse a range of mountains that rises high enough to bite the sky. On the far side lie other countries, each one stranger than the next. There is a kingdom of wise men, a kingdom of fools, a kingdom where women rule the roost and men bear the babies, a kingdom where people walk upside down, and one where even the noblemen are Jews. This last is also the realm of King Solomon the magician, who sits in judgment over birds, snakes and demons, as well as humankind.

In one of these lands, Gittel once promised, she and Anya would find happiness together.

But all that's a dead issue now. There is a bridegroom in the picture. He represents a social coup: the boy is not only a good Torah scholar, but the son of people who own a shop in the market town. Not a stall in the square, a mere board on a trestle; not a pedlar's pack; not even a pile of wares in a wagon, but a proper set of premises, with a shelf, a door and a painted sign. The bride's family bask in their neighbours' congratulations; Gittel herself is thought to be delighted.

Anya the Apostate, needless to say, is not. This morning, while hauling her cage of live fowl to market, she has wailed at every devil and angel whose name she knows, and called upon all the old spirits of forest and plain.

She says that Gittel has stolen her life.

So I have arrived, in response to her cries. My assignment is to even the score by stealing Gittel's soul.

And who am I? A dybbuk – a demon of all shapes and no shape. My profession is forced entry into the minds of mortals; my speciality is Jews.

I go by many names. Most of them impossible to twist a human tongue around. Apart from Kokos. So that one will have to do.

Anya's curse on Gittel, as I've told you, is a masterpiece. What we have here is a verbal edifice of Byzantine intricacy, a little palace of hate, with mirrored galleries, secret cabinets, poisoned gardens, torture chambers, and a number of underground passages burrowing into the distant future.

The gist of it, once I hack my way through the luxuriant, toxic undergrowth, is a wish that Gittel should be possessed by

6

a dybbuk; that she should disappoint her husband by bearing only daughters; and that the surviving first-borns of the female line should be similarly afflicted unto the thirty-third generation.

Phase One of my task seems straightforward enough. I initiate the usual procedures: slip into Gittel; speak gibberish out of her mouth in a horrid, raven's croak; stare wildly out of her eyes; cause beds, heavy tables and the fire from the hearth to fling themselves across the room. This scares the daylights out of her friends and relations, although I sense that Gittel, deep down, enjoys the fuss.

I don't know what all these people are worried about. It's not as if I were trying to kill the girl. That would put me out of business before I started.

Unfortunately, I have underestimated the opposition. Gittel's loving bridegroom may be a mere slip of a thing himself, but he is the star pupil and teacher's pet of the redoubtable Shmuel ben Issachar, most learned of the learned, most pious of the pious, known to his fans as the Saintly Sage of Limnititzk.

Who, as every little yeshivah-mouse knows, can quote any randomly selected page of any book of the Talmud and its commentaries backwards, upside down, diagonally across, or expressed purely in terms of numerical values, in eleven different ancient and modern languages. He also knows the names and numbers of every star in the sky, its shifts in position around the clock and across the seasons, and is able to determine the correct birth-dates of a man's grandparents just by counting the subject's eyelashes.

In spite of, or perhaps thanks to, his prodigious virtue and volcanic sanctity, the Limnititzker Sage is a dab hand at card tricks, and at putting fretful babies to sleep with a single, whiskery 'Sha!' As you would guess, he also knows how to walk between the raindrops.

When his distraught young prodigy comes begging for help, the Sage immediately promises to do his utmost. Carried on the shoulders of his joyful followers, he accompanies the boy back to his own town – a perilous three-day journey through wildernesses infested with wolves and robbers, all of whom fall instantly into a deep and dreamless sleep when the Limnititzker party passes by.

Because of his extreme purity, Shmuel ben Issachar will not enter the same room, or even the same house, as a woman (apart, of course, from his own equally saintly wife). He is installed, therefore, in the home of the bridegroom's parents, next door to the young couple's love-nest. Despite the longing looks of his travel-weary disciples, he refuses all offers of food and drink. (This devastates Gittel's mother-in-law, who has been up since dawn preparing a feast in the Sage's honour, and has now obediently decamped to Gittel's house, where she awaits dispatches from her own.) He commands that some garment belonging to the afflicted woman be brought to him: nothing immodest, heaven forbid; a shawl or perhaps a shoe will suffice. Yes, he thinks a shoe would be best.

The combined efforts of the young husband and six female relations are needed to hold Gittel down and pull off her slipper. Gittel and I are not going to give in to the old foot-fetishist without a fight.

The object is conveyed from one house to the next in a closed basket, for fear that it, like Gittel, will start leaping and growling. Shmuel takes the shoe in his left hand, holds it close to his nose, and sniffs it all over, in the manner of an inquisitive cat.

'Aha! I thought I recognised the spoor. It's her again . . . Kokos. The Unspeakable.'

Perhaps I should explain. We are lifelong sparring partners, ben Issachar and I. In fact, our prickly relationship goes back to the very day of his conception.

It is a well-known fact that a pious matron, heading home from her monthly purification at the ritual bath, should count herself lucky if she comes face to face with a scholar. If she does so, she must memorise his features, and keep his image firmly fixed in her mind when she and her spouse next make love. You might think that the average husband would be a little miffed to share centre stage between the sheets with some stranger, no matter how well-read. But there's a pay-off: the fruit of such a union will be a scholar, too. We're in the days when doctors are merely jumped-up barbers, remember: in this era, 'My son the sage' carries more cachet.

Therefore, the mother of ben Issachar was overjoyed to collide with a white-bearded fellow with his nose in a book. So absorbed was he in his text that he did not even notice the woman coming in his direction. Had he done so, custom would have demanded that he cross at once to the opposite side of the street, lest random contact with a member of the dangerous sex besmirch him. But his lips never stopped moving and his eyes never lifted from the page.

Oops! Too late! Before she could swerve, they were knee to knee. The poor woman tripped over him, and fell to the ground. From this vantage point, she struggled to look upwards, to record his learned features before they passed from sight. But all she could see was the motion of his lips, and a quick glimpse beneath his gown, as he lengthened his stride to step over her, meanwhile never missing a syllable.

Still, she did what she could with what she was given. From the fleeting underside view, he was quite a well-endowed scholar, which ensured that she would not easily forget him. However, the book in his hands was a treatise on the names of female demons, and the one he mouthed, at the fatal moment, was mine.

The result of that night's coupling was the boy ben Issachar. Sure enough, he grew up into a sage unequalled in breadth of knowledge and depth of understanding. But, with my name branded on his infant soul, our fates became entangled. Nothing I could do about it – rules are rules. All his mother's fault, of course.

I teased him, piqued him, stage-managed his nightmares, hovered in the shadows cast by the study-house candle when he bent over his scrolls in the depths of the night.

Mostly, my interventions were harmless. I practised a bit of ventriloquism, so he was wished good health in the street by a tethered goat; sat on the rim of his cup to ensure that his wine would taste sour; made his bride fall out of bed on their wedding night.

I suppose the final straw, from his point of view, was my little musical interlude at the time of Chanukah, the festival of lights, when I forced him to sing Christian hymns for seven days running. You'd think the dear boy could have seen the fun in that. But I guess some people have no sense of humour.

In response, he turned the bright beam of his intellect on the arts of mastering and exorcising demons. From the texts of ancient Babylonia to the Latin recipes of Christian monks, through every syllable in the occult writings of his own faith, there was no word on the subject he did not memorise. He knew how to inscribe 700 different protective pentagrams and sacred circles, could make amulets out of anything from a dragon's testicle to an old kitchen spoon, learned words of power hidden since the days of Solomon, to entrap us, paralyse us, make us appear, disappear, or generally jump through hoops for his greater glorification.

So, though we go together like – you should pardon the expression – eggs and bacon, there isn't a lot of love lost between ben Issachar and me.

Back to business.

Shmuel places the shoe in the centre of the table, orders many candles to be lit around it, and begins to sway back and forth, muttering in a tongue that is neither the Hebrew of the study-house nor the Yiddish of the streets.

In the bedroom, guarded by her phalanx of in-laws, Gittel opens her eyes wide, snorts contemptuously and, in a voice no one has ever heard before, bellows, 'Come on, ben Issachar, you can do better than that!'

The challenge is clearly audible in the adjoining building. (The intervening walls are no thicker than two slices of rye bread.)

Shmuel's disciples cluster around the Master, watching

anxiously; beards quiver in the smoky air. He calls for a scrap of paper, inscribes some characters upon it, rolls it into a tight pellet and orders it to be fed to Gittel, washed down by a glass of wine over which he has intoned an exorcistic formula.

She/we swallows the pellet, but spits out the wine with considerable force. Next door, the disciples flinch at the explosive 'Ptui!', which rattles half the windows in the town. Nor is any go-between required to convey our next roared remark: 'Won't you ever learn, Shmuel? *White* wine with fish, *red* wine with incantations!'

The holy man calls for a little satchel that he has brought with him from Limnititzk. He opens it and draws forth a parcel bundled up in several layers of cloth. He unwraps this slowly, revealing a small book, no larger than the palm of a child's hand, bound in some kind of mottled purple hide, and clasped shut with a rusted lock. At a word of command, all onlookers close their eyes. When they are permitted to open them again, they find the Sage holding a tiny key between thumb and forefinger. He presses it, with considerable difficulty, into the lock. With a sudden snap that makes the observers' earlocks stand upright, the book flies open.

The pages flutter back and forth, as if flicked by an invisible hand, then lie flat, exposing a faded diagram of impossible intricacy. Pursing his lips, ben Issachar extends a forefinger, and begins to trace a course around this labyrinth.

As he does so, a nerve twitches on the cheek of Gittel, crouched like a cornered fox on the floor next door.

Shmuel moves further into the maze. Gittel flings out an arm, which vibrates at astonishing speed.

He reaches a hexagon, deep within the design, and a shrill whistling emanates from her ears and navel.

At the Sage's barked command, his senior disciple reaches into the satchel, and produces three small mirrors on pewter stands. These are propped up around the open volume. Shmuel, finger still planted firmly on the hexagon, moves the looking-glasses about with his free hand, fussing over their angles and relative positions.

He's bringing in the heavy weaponry. I redouble my efforts. Gittel bursts into song – a rude, amorous ballad in a language she doesn't know, chronicling activities that neither she nor her attendants have ever in their most outrageous dreams envisioned.

Responding to a silent signal from Shmuel, the boys next door start chanting. Their low murmur gathers volume and rises until it fills the room, the house, the town, the midnight sky.

In one of the mirrors, gleaming in the candlelight, appears the face of Gittel. In the second, Anya the Apostate. The third is empty. Until I feel the words of Shmuel's next incantation, pulling at me like a tidal undertow.

Deep inside Gittel's belly, the letters of the swallowed charm glow molten and break apart in fiery shards. Dazzled by their light, I am drawn into a vortex, whirled about, and cast out into something that feels like an icy pond. I see where I am: trapped in the third mirror.

With a swift movement, the Sage – eyes averted – snatches up the glass, thrusts it into a black velvet pouch, pulls the drawstring tight, drops the bag into an iron casket and bangs down the lid.

Damn, he's good. And he's got me.

In this round, Sage: One, Dybbuk: Nil.

Just before sunrise, Shmuel and his disciples enter the forest. The iron box is no larger than a pillow, but it takes four men to carry it, all of them panting and sweating. Oblivious to his minions' difficulties, the Sage wanders for some considerable time, pausing before various trees, kicking at their roots, looking up at the spread of their branches in the half-light, examining their bark. Finally he finds one, a fat old oak on the verge of a stream, that seems to satisfy him. Gratefully, the four bearers place their burden at its foot. He brings his mouth to the oak and whispers something. Its boughs rustle in a breeze that stirs no other tree.

He crouches down, and a hole opens in the bark. He bids

his disciples heave the coffer into this breach. As they do so, they are deafened by shrieks and roars from inside the box, and a seepage of foul vapours. The men shrink back, terrified. But he laughs, and points. The box has been swallowed up into the wood, and the hole now seals itself, leaving no scar.

A few oak leaves drop into the water, though it is not the proper season for their falling. They float away, but come to rest a mile or two downstream, trapped against a stepping-stone near the hut of Anya the Apostate. She wakes up scratching, plagued with a fiery and inexplicable rash that will bedevil her for the rest of her life.

Confinement in a tree, depending upon species, may last for several hundred years. But raging is useless, a waste of resources. And I wouldn't give old Shmuel the satisfaction. He'll be more than smug enough by now: the little anecdote of my defeat at his hands will add lustre to his legend. Around the Sabbath tables of his cult, generations hence, they will still amuse themselves with the tale.

So, bowing to the inevitable, I follow the standard procedure set down for such emergencies. I slip, cat-like, into a trance to wait out time's passage.

A mere 200 years later, lightning bisects the oak.

Together with a stream of bewildered refugees – outraged crows, some squirrels, legions of woodlice, and the snake that nested beneath the roots – I am flung out into the open air.

Ready to resume my mission, I head for the dorf. It isn't there. Not a stick of it.

Next, I try the market town. Unrecognisable. The Great Synagogue, still standing, has been turned into some kind of warehouse, but it's locked. Behind it, in the old cemetery, crammed with 500 years of burials, the tall stones tilt at impossible angles. They are sinking into the earth. Wisps of fog float between them – outraged ghosts.

They tell me their grievances. For a long time, no one has come to visit them, not so much as a pebble has been laid on their graves. And the anniversaries of their deaths have gone unnoticed: where are the memorial candles that should have been lit by their children's children, who have been named with their names? Some have sallied forth, to visit their anger upon these neglectful descendants, and have come back frustrated, finding no one to haunt. No one.

Where has everybody gone? I have no answers.

2

report without delay to the Head Office. The capital city looks much the same as always. Spires and pinnacles jab at the sky, gates are barred and windows shuttered against the yellowish smog. As usual, the streets are empty. But something has changed. Headquarters isn't there any more.

The building, a once-handsome mansion in the old Diplomatic Quarter of the town, stands windowless and gutted. A fire burns somewhere inside; I can see the flames through a ground floor window. Even as I stare, a high crane swings its wrecking-ball and smashes through the roof.

It doesn't take me long to find out what's happened. My company, I am relieved to hear, not only survives but flourishes. It has recently relocated to a new plant – winner of architectural prizes – in an industrial park on the western outskirts.

The security guard in the gatehouse keeps me waiting for some time: my old ID card doesn't function in the new electronic access system. It takes a lengthy and suspicious interrogation, several telephone calls and passage through a sequence of scanners and screening devices before I am allowed to proceed.

Under the gaze of a dozen mounted cameras, I make my way down the long walkway to the Administration Module. As instructed, I wait between two sets of sliding doors until I am collected and delivered to Ms Topaz, of Personnel. Hardly what you'd call a heroine's welcome.

'Well, yes,' admits Ms Topaz, 'there have been quite a few changes.'

She has made a valiant attempt to infuse her office with a home-like atmosphere. On the window ledge, cherished pot plants climb, spread, curl, flow, trail, creep and twine into a jungle that almost screens the vista of the junior managers' car park. She offers me coffee from a pot bubbling gently on a hotplate, and opens a canister of ginger biscuits.

'Now, help yourself – they're quite good, my mother makes them – while I just call up your file.'

She taps a keyboard, and my entire history twinkles into view. 'Hmmm . . . Not really an auspicious time, careerwise, for you to have been *hors de combat*. Your department was completely restructured, after the takeover.'

'What takeover?'

'Of course. Silly old me, how could you have known? We were Acquired.'

'Acquired?'

'Don't look so upset, dear. It's been very good news. Increases our domestic market share, allows for all sorts of hitherto impossible expansion, opens up a whole slew of new overseas possibilities. And, in staff terms, it has perked us up like anything – higher professional standards, enhanced promotion prospects, increased facilities for in-service training. Not to mention the new Company Health Club. And I am sure you'll be glad to know your existing pension rights are unaffected.'

'Who owns us?'

'We prefer not to put it that way,' she smiles, pouring me a second cup of coffee. 'Try to think of it as who we have become.'

'Well, who are we then?'

'A wholly owned subsidiary of Mephistco Industries!'

Topaz preens. I spill coffee all over my lap and her tasteful carpet. She vaults over her desk, with the agility of a dedicated Company Health Club regular, to clear up the mess.

Mephistco?!?

The last time I checked the trade press (admittedly, some

time ago, when it was still composed in black-letter Gothic and typeset in hot metal) Mephistco was a rank outsider, a minor third-division player in the field. Whereas our firm – in its now apparently vanished days of glory – was a small but superior organisation, steeped in tradition. Purveyors of little red forked devils to the Christians, of djinni to the Arabs, of dybbuks to the Jews.

'How could they? Compared to us, Mephistco was nothing but a minnow.'

She's at my ankles, mopping. 'Well, now it's a leviathan. Move your foot.'

I ask Topaz about my current project. I have just spent 200 years in a tree for the sake of this assignment, and would not be too pleased to discover the enterprise had been aborted.

She reassures me. According to the terms of the takeover, all existing contracts are to be honoured.

'And, since your little – ah – mishap occurred before the new rules came in, you shouldn't lose any pay.'

'What new rules?'

'Downtime caused by operational errors – which, I'm afraid, includes being overpowered by the Opposition – is now chargeable against the sum total of hours worked.'

My response to this is an expletive so potent it makes even the minty-cool Ms Topaz blush.

She decides that I have had enough of her coffee, biscuits and attention, and sends me off, in the care of a minion, to report to my department.

I am led along moving walkways, across glazed and gardened atria, up via bubble lifts, and down corridors floored with marble. My guide pushes open a pair of swing doors marked CONTRACTS.

Changed days, indeed.

No massive ledgers bound in the hides of long-extinct species. No plumed quills trembling over a vellum page. No padlocked book-chests labelled Destinies A through Z.

Instead, a broad indoor plain dotted with facsimile transmitters, state-of-the-art printers, computer screens. We thread our way between cluttered work stations, towering in-trays, and shirtsleeved colleagues whispering or shouting into telephones. Arriving on the far side of the floor, we stand before a little glassed-in cubicle; inside, a man swigs from a green bottle of mineral water as he shuffles mounds of printout. He is fat and furious.

At my guide's timid knock, he glances up, stares right through us, snorts out a little puff of steam, and bends again to his papers.

'By the hairy bollocks of the blessed Beelzebub, I ought to march down to Personnel right now, and murder that boss of yours. If I told that Topaz woman once I've told her ten thousand times – I will not take on new trainees in the month before the quarterly reports are due.'

'She's not a trainee,' blurts the minion. 'She'll explain.' And bolts.

The fat man scowls, looks up blearily, then – half a beat later – breaks into a full moon of a grin.

'You're a little late.'

'Nick, you old bastard! Head of department! What idiot promoted you?'

To the amazement of the outer office, we spin each other around in a dance of greeting.

'Do you know you hold the divisional record for length of time on the Inactive list? Another century and they would have shifted your file to Eradicated.'

'I was treed.'

'So we heard. One of those old Polish wonder-rabbis, was it?'

'Ben Issachar.'

'Aha. A master. There aren't many like him these days.'

'That's good.'

'My dear girl, once you've had a taste of what currently passes for talent in that area, I guarantee you'll miss him.'

'Things not what they used to be?'

'You bet your boots. Now, let's find you a work station to call your own.'

'A work station? One of those little cluttered desk affairs out in the middle of the traffic? What about seniority? I've had an office of my own since the Albigensian heresy.'

'Hard luck. Nobody's entitled to a private room any more. Unless you're so far up in the hierarchy that your heels dangle somewhere over Alpha Centauri. Then you get a whole suite, a personal toilet, and your own choice of colour scheme.'

Some things, fortunately, never change. Nick insists we celebrate our reunion with an early lunch. The canteen food also adheres, with reassuring consistency, to the eternal verities – it remains as inedible as ever.

Over an indeterminate soup, Nick takes me through the last 200 years of upheavals. Sales decline, consumer expectations alter, new technologies sprout like dragon's teeth. Our own firm, encrusted with precedents and hoary protocols, drowns in its own fat. We miss boats, neglect opportunities. Hungry outsiders, like Mephistco, grow lean and mean, eventually outrun us. Our shares slip in price, are nibbled first, then guzzled, and we are theirs.

I'm not entirely astonished. The rot set in long before my little contretemps with ben Issachar. Personally, I blame the quaintly misnamed Age of Reason.

However, as I remind Nick, I still have a job to finish.

'*Festina lente*, sweetheart. Don't rush in headlong. They'll be putting pressure on you soon enough.'

'So what? I've been stuck on hold since the Third Partition of Poland. I'm raring to go.'

'Just wait till you see the latest production targets. You might wish yourself back in the wood.'

I shake my head emphatically, begin to protest. He cuts me short.

'Don't interrupt. Do yourself – and me – a favour. Phase in gently. I want you to take some time for reorientation. For a start, there's been quite a bit of action out in your territory, one way or another. You have a lot of history to catch up on. And, tough as you are (and I'd be the first to admit it), you're bound to suffer some kind of delayed reaction to the stress of incarceration. Not to mention all this corporate culture-shock.'

'Been on a management course, have we, Nick?'

A little jet of steam rises from his pate. I must be on target.

'Don't be so cocky, sister. Just take care you don't crack under the strain. You want to turn into a clapped-out hack like me?'

There is no answer to this. Nick was once the hottest field operative of our cohort. A mad genius, temperamental as a typhoon, but he always got his way – and got results. I don't need to see the files to know exactly what happened after the takeover: Nick tried to buck the new system, and it bucked him back. They're very clever, Upstairs. Let the rebel run himself straight over a cliff, then promote him out of trouble, into a bureaucratic cul-de-sac. We both know he will sit in that glass cage, shuffling papers, until the end of time.

Nevertheless, I do what I'm told, and find my way to Archives. What a treat. The new library puts our old one to shame – all soft lighting, ergonomically designed armchairs, state-of-the-art information retrieval systems, open access to the stacks. And the video facilities are a dream. No more crouching over a worn-out crystal, or queuing up to get a shot at the scryers. It's all fingertip controls, instantly adjustable fine-tuning, direct voice-link to the projectionists.

The collection, of course, remains second to none. And in addition to every text in every tongue since Sumerian scribe first pressed wedge to clay, we have a few tasty rarities. I'm glad to see Mephistco hasn't sold them off as part of some asset-stripping strategy.

My first stop, for sentimental reasons, is the alcove that houses the great lost library of the Ptolemaic kings at Alexandria, that wonder of the ancient world. Human historians think it was burnt to cinders. But they happen to be wrong. When the flames engulfed the building, a passing dybbuk (modesty forbids me to name her) snatched the contents out of harm's way, and brought them back to base for safe keeping. So if anyone wants a peek at the love letters between Solomon and

Sheba, dictionaries for the lost language of the ancient Minoans, or the architect's brief for the Hanging Gardens of Babylon – complete with the relevant planning applications and objections by local residents dreading sightseers and greenfly – here's where to find them.

Now down to business. I settle myself at a computer, and give myself an intensive course in humankind's last 200 years. I soak up data without stopping, for three days and three nights, and emerge feeling queasy. It seems that these so-called moderns, when they really get going, are capable of deeds that would make a demon blush.

During the course of my research – somewhere between an unnecessary famine and an equally avoidable little war – a shadow falls over my VDU. Two small female figures, in the regulation blue boiler suit of Engineering, hover at my shoulder.

'There's an urgent meeting. Your presence is requested.'

I hate interruptions. Almost as much as I hate meetings. I tell them so.

They shrug.

'Don't shoot the messenger,' says one. 'Up you get.'

Slip of a thing though she seems, this tiny technician knows a wrestling hold or two. And her friend's a dab hand with the old Carthaginian wrist-burn.

'Hands off, girls. I outrank you.'

'Sez who, old-timer?'

Things definitely are not what they were.

I swallow my wrath, demand explanations.

'How about some details? Whose meeting is it? What's it about?'

'Wait and see,' is all I get. And am led through miles of corridors, into a lift that descends for a very long time, and along a succession of underground passageways lined with pipes and cables. There's a faint whiff of burning.

'This is where the real work gets done,' one of my escorts informs me.

She opens a metal door, marked DIVISIONAL CHIEF ENGINEER, and we are almost washed away by a flood of loud rock music.

The room flashes, pulsates and buzzes with information from the screens, gauges and digital indicators lining the walls.

'All right,' comes a command from the far end of the room. 'All right, thanks, you two. She won't bolt. So piss off.'

My guides award me identical smiles, exposing multiple rows of serrated shark-teeth, and sidle out.

The voice's owner – also in Engineering blue – propels herself between the control panels, banging key-pads and flipping switches, reaching out to kick a lever with a black-booted foot. Without turning round, she jabs a button to kill the music, and roars into the sudden silence, 'About bloody time!' before rushing over and flinging her arms around me.

It's Lil. A close friend and enemy from way back when. She looks me up and down. 'Thinner, I'd say, but fitter. Maybe your little enforced sabbatical did you some good.'

'And you,' I reply, looking round the control room, 'don't seem to have let the grass grow under your feet while I was gone. Not bad. From a Grade 6 technician to Divisional Chief Engineer in a mere two centuries. I'm impressed. What can I say?'

'Well,' she huffs, 'you could at least start by saying thank you.'

'For what?'

'For springing you from that tree.'

This stuns me into silence. I've always known that Lil has carried a torch for me, but I never expected her to convert it into a bolt of lightning.

I think about it. 'You took your time.'

'No choice,' she replies. 'Office politics.'

'What's that supposed to mean?'

'Wait and see.'

'I'm not sticking around this mausoleum to find out. It's back in the field for me a.s.a.p.'

'Enjoy it while you can. There's a faction in senior management that doesn't even think we should run field operatives any more. And we certainly shouldn't waste any money bailing you lot out when you come a cropper.'

'*Whaaat?*'

'Don't scream. Or old Hatchet-Face next door will accuse me of having another sex orgy during working hours. Anyway, I had to choose my moment, didn't I? First I had to wait until I'd risen high enough to function without some supervisor snooping over my shoulder. And even now, running my own department, it hasn't been easy to sneak in a rescue job that wasn't in the budget.'

'Since when does that matter?'

'New company policy.'

'I don't like the sound of that.'

'Take this as a friendly warning: make the most of that famous outstanding contract of yours now. Your forthcoming trip into the field will probably be your last. Everything's in flux: by the end of the year, nobody in this place will be doing the job they did before – if they're still around at all.'

Not what you want to hear when you've spent your last 200 years watching bark dry. Nevertheless, I make suitably grateful noises.

'So how did you swing it?' I ask.

'I've been running a little experiment for Research and Development on meteorological phenomena as omens of geopolitical upheaval. Lucky for you, one of the bolts went haywire somewhere over the Baltic. At least that's what I said in the report. So I got away with it. So don't think I don't stick my neck out on your behalf.'

This puts me in a tricky position. Does in her debt today mean in her bed tomorrow?

I suspect Lil has thought of this already. That smile has more than teeth in it.

'What are friends for, Kokos? You and I go back a long time together.'

I'll say we do.

Right back to the Great Succubus Strike of 943. When demons of the female gender met in mutinous cabals, and resolved that the sexual entrapment of male mortals should no longer be a compulsory condition of service. Those who liked that sort of thing could get on with it; the rest of us wished to be recognised for our other talents.

It was one hell of a fight. Before we were finished, we shook the firmament to its foundations. Sit-ins outside the celestial courtrooms, the odd Molotov cocktail through the windows of Azazel's palace, activists chaining themselves to the gates of Erebus, a work-to-rule on curse-fulfilments and a ban on all responses to invocations (unless conducted by a female sorceress known to be on our side in the struggle).

Many's the policy statement Lil and I hammered out together, to hand round at stormy public meetings. Many the runs for flyposting, or daubing graffiti. Many the potential schisms we papered over to forge a united front. And many the nights we found ourselves sharing the same mattress in some temporary base camp.

But nothing ever happened between us.

Not that Lil didn't make the occasional thinly veiled offer: 'Hey, why don't we give ourselves a night off from the struggle, and go back to my place for a hot bath and eight hours in a proper bed?'

All right, so I was almost, for a nanosecond, tempted. But at the time I was dabbling in Eastern philosophy (a recent assignment had taken me the length of the Silk Road, choreographing nightmares for an itinerant merchant on behalf of a wronged wife), and I believed that sexual energies should be dammed and rechannelled into other forms of power. Besides, whatever Lil's undoubted attractions, we had a war on. And I felt sure we'd never win it between her scented sheets.

I know, I know. I was younger then.

And, whether it was my abstention for the sake of the Cause, or the fact that some temporary glitch in the cosmic equation allowed justice to triumph for a change, we won the day. Management surrendered.

Succubus assignments would henceforth be allocated on a purely voluntary basis, and – once we females had done all the fighting – incubus activities too were made optional for males. (In fact, that whole area of operations eventually became the special province of the tumtums – the brigade of demonic androgynes – who quite liked the chance to put their particular gifts to use in all imaginable directions.)

'Remember the victory celebrations?' Lil's obviously been riding the same train of thought. 'You really stopped traffic on the dancefloor.'

'And you almost killed the party stone dead,' I replied, 'with that arse-licking speech. About mending fences with the Opposition, wasn't it?'

Ha. Watch her flinch. She thought maybe I'd forgotten. But Lil's saved by the bell. More precisely by a screaming klaxon.

'Angel dung!' she mutters, bashing keys on the console as red lights appear. 'Sulphur overload in Area Nineteen!' Then she leans over and screams into a microphone.

'Get moving, you grease-monkeys! There's another hot one down below! 185 units to saturation. Alarm is Alpha Yellow! Alpha Yellow!' She waves me away. 'Sorry, Koke, we'd better finish the reunion later.'

The corridor is full of blue boiler suits, scrambling purpose-fully out of a ready room, bellowing incomprehensible orders and responses.

If I didn't know how dangerous an Alpha Yellow was, I'd say she'd triggered the alarm herself.

I'm not going to let Lil's little warning deflate me. I'm itching to get back into the field. And if changes are coming, I'm going to make sure that – whatever else happens – I get some fun out of it.

Back in Archives, it takes me a lot of rummaging in very old directories (only recently transferred from manuscript to disc) to discover what happened to Gittel. The main obstacle is the annoying habit, common to most earlier archivists, of leaving women's destinies out of the running record.

But I finally manage to track down the file, by starting with *ben Issachar, Shmuel, Miracles of* (see also *Limnititzk, Second Sage of*, and *Wonder-rabbis, Polish and Lithuanian*) and chasing up various footnotes and secondary references.

There was little detailed information, but I found the bare essentials. Gittel did indeed produce daughters. So if the female line has lasted, I'm still in business. At least until the thirty-third generation.

As I scroll forward in time, the face of Gittel Number One recedes until, at the vanishing point, only the sheen of her auburn hair remains. Her descendants preserve this, and other features, but I have no leisure to linger over the generations that lived and died while I was in captivity. As it happened, history played them some far nastier tricks than anything I could have invented.

But Gittel's girls, like Gittel in the old days of sneaking off to her assignations with Anya, have a knack of making their escapes. When their native territory – to call it a homeland would raise their Christian neighbours' hackles – becomes more hellish than Gehenna itself, they transplant themselves to safer ground. In some chink of time between pogrom and cholera and Holocaust, Gittel-plus-five packs up husband, baby and a pair of brass Shabbos candlesticks and conveys the family genes – via wooden wagon, railway carriage and passenger steamer – to London.

The Jews who have come before – Hispanic and Iberian grandees; German bankers and merchant princes who, by their manners and education, could almost pass as Christian whites – are not particularly thrilled to see her. Or the thousands like her, trooping in with their thick plaid shawls and smells of alien cooking.

Gittel-plus-five clutches a scrap of paper, directing her to some distant cousin or friend-of-a-friend from the old home province. He steers her to an East End cellar where she can sew to scrape a living. Gittel-plus-six stands behind the till in her husband's bagel bakery, marshalling the takings so prudently that Gittel-plus-seven marries well enough to stay home all day. Her principal occupations – besides the tireless purging of grime from all domestic surfaces – are charity work and family worries. But she takes enough time off from these pursuits to bring up Gittel-plus-eight.

Gittel-plus-eight practises faithfully on a suburban piano, then discovers sex, jazz and her own sultry voice, and breaks her mother's heart. Bye-bye Schubert, Liszt and Mendelssohn to lend a cultured tone to family parties; hello gigs in urban cellars and The Road. Some time later she reappears with a fiancé who plays the saxophone.

Her parents are edgy, until they discover he is, beret and goatee notwithstanding, just another Nice Jewish Boy. And, best of all, the newlyweds immediately desert the jazz circuit in favour of bookings at weddings and bar mitzvahs.

I'm sorry I didn't make it out of the tree in time for this particular Gittel. But Plus-Eight's left the scene early, with her saxophonist in tow, because of someone else's folly on a motorway. Lucky for us, she's also left a daughter, old enough to fend for herself.

Which brings us into the life and times of Gittel-plus-nine, better known as Rainbow Rosenbloom.

And, by the by, we've also – at long last – arrived in Ilford, just in time for the seder, the ritual meal that inaugurates the festival of Passover.

As far as I'm concerned, our timing couldn't be better.

Of all the Jewish calendar's holy days, anniversaries and other excuses for colossal communal meals, I must admit that Passover is my favourite. You work with a single people long enough, you acquire some kind of shared history. And, for those of us who specialise in this particular client group, Passover marks a turning point in our own chronology. For, when Moses bested Pharaoh's magicians in the contest of snakes and wands, he released us from enslavement to those dank-smelling, jackal-headed gods of the Nile. And when the Red Sea parted for the Hebrew slaves, we came along with them – invisibly, in an excited, chattering horde. From that day forward, we could set our own agenda, without reference to our necrophiliac ex-bosses.

*

As far as Aunt Becky's concerned, Rainbow Rosenbloom's timing couldn't be worse.

'Hurry up! Everybody's starving!' barks Rebecca as she opens her front door. 'Uncle Jack was just about to start the service without you. What took you so long?'

'What do you think?' mutters Rainbow, who has had it up to here. 'The Romford road was hell on wheels.'

3

Ma-nish-ta-na ha-lila ha'azeh?
'Why is this night different from all other nights?'

Thus the first of the ritual Four Questions sets the stage. Over 2,000 years or more, the seder's script has hardly varied. Over and over again, in first and second person – this happened, to me, to you, to us – the answers are given, the reasons provided, the tale is told. But at this particular seder, on this particular Passover night, we may come up with a few new answers.

Ma-nish-ta-na ha-lila ha'azeh . . . ?
Why is this night different from all other nights?

Because on this night, Mrs Rebecca Rosenbloom Litwak, sister of the late Cy 'Silvertones' Rosenbloom, has once again played her trump card and commanded the attendance of her difficult niece Rainbow, orphan of Cy, at the family's Passover seder.

On every other night of the year, Rainbow may do what she damned well pleases, but on this night she will turn up – out of respect for the memory of her parents, or simply to get Aunt Becky off her back.

'We are,' as Becky reminds her yet again, 'all the family you've got.'

'Thank goodness,' Rainbow retorts, but not out loud.

*

Ma-nish-ta-na ha-lila ha'azeh . . . ?

Because on this night the five Rosenbloom sisters have marshalled all surviving spouses and any offspring still sufficiently under their control, and assembled to relive the Exodus. While doing so – though only Rainbow, who takes a mild interest in such matters, knows it – they also celebrate much older rites of spring.

Here they are, in the glowing flesh.

(1)Aunt Lila, contemplating the candlesticks' patina and the sheen of the tablecloth with an expert's eye. She is the Rich Sister, who has married more shrewdly than the rest. She has a skin like Spanish leather, acquired on the sun-decks and balconies of various time-shares.

Because she travels (merry widow), the rest see little of her. 'Just as well, she's such an interfering old boot,' say

(2) Becky and (3) Minna, who spend half the evening away from the table, in Becky's kitchen, sparring: over the amount of salt needed in the soup, the right size for a portion of gefilte fish, the most appropriate serving dish for the carrot tzimmes, and whether or not Lila is beginning to look . . . well, a little old, maybe. None of these details concern

(4) Aunt Goldie, who gazes benevolently around the table, at her sisters, her brothers-in-law, the 'young people' (anyone under sixty), and their infant progeny. Her place is set with dishes, cutlery and glassware that differ from the rest.

She is a spinster of exquisite piety, so kosher that she will only eat with implements from her own scrupulously policed kitchen, rather those tainted by Rebecca's much laxer approach to the dietary laws. Needless to say, she has brought her own food with her as well, which stands ready on the sideboard, hermetically sealed in Tupperware against contamination.

'All that holier-than-thou business of Goldie's is nothing but showing off,' mutters

(5)Aunt Molly, who would like to think she could outrun Goldie in the kosher Olympics any day, but 'can't be bothered with all the palaver'. She has retired, with easy-going husband Saul, to the Oceanview-Bellavista Kosher Hotel at the seaside, and trusts the kitchen staff not to seethe the kid in its mother's milk.

Ma-nish-ta-na ha-lila ha'azeh?

Because dinner will not be served tonight until history repeats itself. The Hebrews must be slaves in Egypt, Moses must out-conjure Pharaoh's magicians, Jehovah – who is not a moderate – must send down twelve plagues to scare the daylights out of the master race of the moment, the Children of Israel must – not for the last time – pack up fast and get out of town; the Red Sea must part; and Rainbow Rosenbloom's people must be let go, just in time to make the copy deadline for the Ten Commandments.

Ma-nish-ta-na ha-lilah ha'azeh?

Because on this night, as on every Passover, the Four Questions are asked by the youngest male at the table. In this case, the questioner is a thirty-two-year-old dermatologist named Noah, live-in lover of Aunt Becky's adored only son, the Crown Prince Michael.

There are, as it happens, two much younger men present at the feast, but both are asleep in their carrycots, and incapable of speech.

Ma-nish-ta-na ha-lilah ha'azeh?

Because on this night, Rainbow's other aunts keep their mouths firmly shut when Becky – as every year – congratulates her Michael's lover for his word-perfect Hebrew (once and always, the bar mitzvah boy), prints a lipstick tattoo on his cheek, and calls him 'my son-in-law, the doctor'.

With a mighty effort of will, they refuse to be shocked. They Say Nothing. But here and there, a nostril quivers, an elbow nudges its neighbour, a nerve twitches in a jaw.

Ma-nish-ta-na ha-lilah ha'azeh?

Because on this night, the homophobes sit down with the homos, the Zionists with the anti-Zionists. Labour sits down with Tory, capitalist with community worker, militantly child-free with the frantically philoprogenitive, vegetarian with carnivore. And the uncles, who would – to a man – prefer to be in the other room, with beer and sandwiches, watching Tottenham Hotspur's match on the box, are on this night sitting, without complaint, in jackets, ties and skullcaps, beside their wives.

Ma-nish-ta-na ha-lilah ha'azeh?

Because Rainbow has been struggling to keep sanity and temper in the presence of a full complement of Aunts.

But her patience is tried. After the symbolic foods of the seder itself and the all too real ones that follow – the gefilte fish, the chicken soup with matzo-balls heavy enough to repel Sennacherib's siege, the pot-roasted meats, the special kugel, the three kinds of tzimmes – we pause for breath.

Uncle Saul lifts his wine-glass for the time-honoured plea: 'Next year in Jerusalem!'

Too much for our Rainbow. She lets rip with a speech. On exile, conflicting interests, entitlements to homelands, power struggles and fights over the water supply. She is not short of an opinion on these or any other issues – she is, after all, a London taxi-driver.

Crown Prince Michael backs her up with an intervention on behalf of the Palestinians. His mother Becky, who clings to her socialism as she does her yellowing wedding dress, backs him up.

Aunt Minna bridles, and lays down her version of the law. Lila quotes from a leader in last week's *Jewish Chronicle*. Molly plays it safe by keeping up a constant chorus of tsk, tsk, tsks. Goldie announces, not for the first time, 'You're all talking rubbish. There's no such thing as a Jewish state until the Messiah comes.'

The uncles, knowing themselves mere onlookers at a Rosen-bloom convention, stay silent. Rainbow's married cousins, further along the table, contribute little; instead, they police small scrums of toddlers underfoot, and rescue endangered pieces of Becky's good Passover china.

32

Becky's Jack – remembering his role as Master of Ceremonies – bangs on the table to restore order; only quick work from Lila spares the cloth from a Red Sea of kosher wine.

'We're not finished with the seder yet,' Jack bellows. 'So let's cut the crap, and get down to business. We have some songs to sing.'

Aunt Goldie snaps to it. '*Dai-dai-yenu . . . dai-dai-yenu . . .*' in a sparky, if throat-cracking, soprano.

The others plunge in at the second '*yenu*'. '*Dai-dai-yenu, dai-dai-yenu . . . dai-dai-yenu . . . daiyenu daiyenu-u-u-u,*' muddling up the verses, but making up in verve and volume what they lack in fidelity to the text.

Then comes the moral tale of the little goat that Father bought for two *zuzim*.

Again, the chorus is all they can manage, without a crib . . .

'*Chad gad ya-a-a-a, chad gad ya . . .* A single kid . . . a single kid my father bought for two *zuzim . . .*'

But listen to Rainbow. She suddenly takes a breath and carries the entire cumulative, circular saga of crime and come-uppance all the way through to the climax, when: Along Comes the Holy One, Praised be He, who stops the Angel of Death who kills the butcher who slaughters the ox who drinks the water that puts out the fire that burns the stick that beats the dog that bites the kid, the one little kid, that my father bought for two *zuzim*. *Chad gad . . . ya-a-a-a, chad gad ya.*

Unlike her sainted mother, Rainbow is 100 per cent tone deaf, but tonight she sings like a canary. And in word-perfect Aramaic, too.

The company, silenced by this aberration, sits spellbound. Cousin Michael recovers first. 'My dear, I didn't know you had it in you.'

Neither did Rainbow.

But before she has leisure to ponder this, Rainbow is marched out to the kitchen for her annual ordeal before the Rosenbloom sororal court.

Who will come to her rescue?

The uncles nod in armchairs. The cousins with small children prepare for departure, packing up the wagonloads of supplies, scouring the house for lost coats, stray crayons, one missing three-year-old, and a Barbie doll's stiletto-heeled slippers.

Even Michael and boyfriend Noah have no power to intervene. They have extended their ritual offer to help with the dishes, safe in the knowledge that it will be politely rejected. Never mind that both are tidier and more obsessively hygienic than a whole houseful of Rosenbloom aunties. They lack the right chromosomes or attitude; they'd only get in the way.

For this is woman's business.

To a drum roll of dinner plates being scraped into the kitchen bin, the guilty party is lined up against the larder door. She has apparently refused a blindfold; instead, she clutches a tea towel printed with coloured reproductions of the Stately Homes of Hertfordshire and rubs compulsively at a succession of dripping utensils passed on to her from Molly and Goldie, at the sink.

Minna's first up, with bow and arrow.

'So, how's the taxi business?' An apparently innocent question, but wait for the dart to land. 'Nobody tried to rob or rape you yet?'

'I always wonder,' says Molly to Goldie, aiming her slingshot sideways while scouring a pot, 'how a girl with all her education doesn't get bored driving around in traffic all day long. What kind of life is that for a young woman? How does she expect to meet people?'

'I'm not so young,' retorts Rainbow, shielding herself with a crater-sized salad bowl. And I meet people all day long, Aunt Molly. Hundreds of them.'

'That's not what I mean, darling . . .'

En route to the refrigerator with kugels in clingfilm, Lila sees the minefield coming and alters the route of march. 'You know, I saw in the paper they have some lovely little one-bedroomed flats up in Hendon. Going for a song.'

'I hate Hendon,' sulks Rainbow, viciously shaking the drips from a sieve. 'And I don't want to buy any – '

'Don't want to or can't, I wonder?' Minna skewers her. 'You know, if you'd put what your parents left you into bricks and mortar, Rosalind, instead of into that ridiculous taxi . . .'

'Rainbow! Rainbow, Rainbow, Rainbow, Rainbow!' sighs Rainbow, banging her head with a baking tray in desperation. 'For twelve years I've been Rainbow. Legally, by deed poll. How much longer will that little item take to sink in?'

'Rainbow, schmainbow,' Molly counters, torturing a frying pan with a Brillo pad. 'By me you're always Rosalind. You are named for our Bubbeh – your great-grandma, Rachel-Malke Rosenbloom. You were not called after a meteorological phenomenon.'

Minna pops out of a gun turret, flaps a fresh tea towel, swings around her tank and opens fire.

'You know, as she gets older, she's even getting to look a little like Bubbeh Rosenbloom. Now that was a handsome woman. She had natural elegance. But even Rainbow could improve if she took herself in hand. You should make more of your good points, darling. Treat yourself to some smart clothes, for a change. Maybe do us all a favour and get rid of that dreadful leather jacket of yours, that makes you look like the president of the Hell's Angels Ladies Auxiliary. Get out of London, go on a nice foreign holiday. Soak up some sun . . .'

Rainbow tries a parry. 'Sun? You want me to get skin cancer?'

'God forbid! Bite your tongue.'

'Anyway, I went away on holiday last summer . . .'

'Oh, so you did. To that Greek island whose name I'd rather not mention. And whatever happened to that girl you took with you? Is it true you paid for her trip? That was extremely kind of you . . . She must have been a very, very good friend . . . But I haven't heard you say anything about her for some time now . . . What's the matter, some kind of falling out?'

Rebecca, slamming the cutlery drawer, interjects on behalf of the accused, 'Mind your own business, Minna.'

Minna considers ordering up the firing squad for this traitor in her own ranks. 'Becky, she's our flesh and blood. Poor Cyril's only child. Someone has to keep an eye on her.'

Goldie now takes aim, if only with a rubber bullet. 'And, if you ask me, she's looking a little pale and peaky.'

'From the traffic fumes,' is Minna's diagnosis. 'And when she's not sitting in them, she's sitting in the dark, in the cinema, ruining her eyes.'

'Oh, she's still writing film reviews, is she?' asks Lila, switching on the water cannon. 'For that dreadful little magazine, *Outlandish*, or whatever it's called . . . If only she could break into proper journalism, get to be a critic on one of the quality papers, now that would be something . . .'

'Rainbow,' interrupts Becky, 'I'm putting some of the soup and *knaidlach* into a plastic container for you to take home . . .'

'Give her a little of the tzimmes, too,' Goldie urges. 'She shouldn't go hungry.'

Lila examines her niece with a rueful eye, and lobs in a grenade of her own. 'With the stored fat on those thighs of hers, and that belly she's getting, she won't starve to death so fast, so don't worry. And, if you don't mind my saying so, Rainbow darling, it wouldn't kill you to shed a few pounds. There was a marvellous diet in last month's *Harpers & Queen* . . .'

Rainbow decides that the moment for radical action has come. For the past five minutes she has been drying and redrying a single item – an empty horseradish jar, part of her Aunt Rebecca's recycling campaign. So she makes a choice between saving the earth and saving her sanity, and drops the jar with a crash on to the quarry-tiled floor.

'Oh God! What a fright!' shrieks Molly.

'Don't worry about it, Rainbow. I have six dozen more of those in the larder,' Rebecca assures her.

'Anyway, a little broken glass means good luck . . . so *mazel tov*!' adds Goldie.

'I'd rather say *mazel tov* at Rosalind's wedding, please God,' declares Minna, detonating a small tactical nuclear device.

AAAARGH! HISSSSS! NOOOOOOOOOH!

With the groan of a soul in torment, the dishwasher announces the end of a cycle.

'Rainbow, darling, go in and ask the men if they want some tea and almond macaroons.'

She is tossed aside, a well-picked bone. Guilty as charged, but free to go.

'Minna,' says Lila, 'Maybe this is the wrong time to bring that up, but aren't those the earrings you borrowed from me last Rosh Hashanah? . . .'

For the roasting of Rainbow has only been a small appetiser. Now the moment has come for the main course. The Aunts have bigger fish to fry. Each other.

Blood will run in the Avenue before the night is done.

But Rainbow's evening isn't over, either.

We find her back in town, an hour later, taking deep restorative breaths of Soho air.

She peers into a window filled with racks of hanging ducks, curly entrails and mahogany slabs of barbecued pork. Behind them, she sees her friend Naomi alone at a table, turning the menu's many pages with mounting excitement.

'My God, Rainbow, I thought you'd never get here.'

'Sorry. Blasted seder went on and on.'

'Ours ended nice and early. My parents started their punch-up along with the soup this year. She got him right smack in the jaw with a matzo-ball. I had to get Grandma back home riding pillion; almost had to tie her down to force the helmet on . . . She didn't want her holiday hairdo spoiled. "And what do you think is going to happen to your hairdo when we get up to sixty going round the park?" I said. So she gave in.'

'Well, at least the early exit let you off the hook from the usual barrage – '

'Are you serious? My career plans, living arrangements and haircut were all shot to pieces before we got as far as the first blessing of the wine . . .'

'Fast workers, your lot. Mine need a while to get warmed up.'

A waiter hovers.

'Ready?'

'Right, Naomi, you first.'

'OK. Number 3: Wafer-paper prawns; Number 19: Barbecued spare ribs . . . Number 53: Mixed Chinese sausages and preserved duck . . . How am I doing, Rainbow?'

'It's a start. Right, Number 49: Crispy pork and fried oyster in hotpot; Number 27: Baked crab with ginger and black bean sauce. And why not go for broke? It's a holiday, after all. Number 45: Braised lobster, Cantonese style.'

Why is this night different from all other nights?

Because Rainbow isn't even hungry.

Because Naomi claims to be a vegetarian.

Because barely three hours ago they were both force-fed dinners on a scale to gobsmack Gargantua.

But this is a special case. An all-out emergency. They have done their familial duty, as Nice Jewish Girls, and look what has befallen them. Antidotes are called for.

Forbidden Fruit Gluttony Shock: Jewish Lesbian Renegades in Midnight Lisle Street Mercy Dash.

The food arrives. Chopsticks flash.

Aaaaaaaaaah. That's better. Injunctions maternal and commandments Levitical dissolve into the smoke of sacrilegious burnt offerings. And who knows the effect of each mouthful of *traif*? Trains are late, a child falls out of bed, a star goes nova . . .

All their fault.

And why else is this night different from all other nights?

Because I, Kokos, am finally back in business.

She does not know it yet, but Rainbow Rosenbloom now has a dybbuk sitting on her shoulder.

4

Much later that night, while Rainbow tosses and turns in her bed (Hah! Divine retribution for those gastronomic sins) and finally rises to seek out powders for her indigestion, I assess the situation.

Dybbukry, as my mentors drummed into me during my long-ago apprenticeship, should always be a spontaneous exercise. Only the humdrum go into an assignment with a rigid game-plan. This is guerrilla action: stay loose and flexible. But never lose sight of your ultimate objective.

Which is: to take control of the subject, to possess her in mind, soul and body. To transform her into something Other than what she was before.

But by any conventional standards (and there is no one more conventional than the Accounts Department at Mephistco), this rather eccentric individual is pretty Other to begin with.

As to outward appearance, I've seen more promising specimens. I prefer my potential subjects to be damsels in distress – slight, intense and doe-eyed. Not built like the gates to a rich man's house – broad, solid and topped with a grating of spikes. (This she calls a haircut?)

Nor am I much encouraged by shrewd eyes that – when awake – hide behind sinister spectacles, nor by the cheekbones of a Siberian shaman, nor by a mouth that always wants to have the last word (and often gets it, except when in the company of aunts).

Tonight, asleep, she is a vision in a faded purple T-shirt

bearing a clenched fist and a washed-out political slogan. The clothes she favours by day lie heaped on the floor: boots that would not disgrace a hod-carrier (although, granted, they seem well polished). A leather jacket buffed and faded, suggesting a history of several previous owners. A chequered scarf to indicate solidarity with the Palestinian struggle.

As to the subject's place of residence, it's as eccentric as its owner. I know I'm a little out of date, and they don't all live in wooden cottages in Polish Galicia any more, but Rainbow's is not exactly your typical Jewish nest.

Her flat – three rooms above a Cypriot bakery in north London – smells pleasantly of honey and cinnamon, but looks as if it has been ransacked by a troupe of amphetamine-crazed whirling dervishes. No point in trying any poltergeist pyrotechnics: the dear girl will never notice.

Magazines, newspapers and books stand in ready-to-topple columns against every wall. A quick survey of their subject matter proves most enlightening.

1. *Cinema* – from post-Lacanian savants deconstructing Westerns to Hollywood gossip queens trashing reputations. Marginal snide remarks by Rainbow scrawled on many pages, turned-down corners (what an outrage for the People of the Book) mark the location of interesting ideas and quotes she plans to steal or borrow.

2. *Self-improvement* – Someone, not a million miles from here, has apparently made a resolution to understand the new mathematics, learn Italian, dabble in creative paint effects, do windowbox gardening, contemplate the links between nuclear physics and Tantric Buddhism, rediscover German Mannerism and complete the whole of Proust's *Recherche du temps perdu*. This pile seems practically untouched.

3. *Mind-candy* – Dyke-detective thrillers, biographies of self-destructing female rock stars, science fiction tales of intergalactic sex wars, and one very racy lavender bedtime story from an obscure transatlantic press.

A major fly in the ointment, as far as I'm concerned, is the fact that Gittel-plus-nine's sexual proclivities do not augur well for the creation of the future Gittels I need to keep my contract alive. No secret that our subject is a dyed-in-the-denim dyke. Gittel One may have ventured on to Sappho's island as a tourist, but Gittel-plus-nine has clearly come to stay.

Not that there's much action between the sheets at present. Rainbow's last inamorata ankled off the set last summer, shortly after the holiday on Lesbos to which Aunt Minna has already alluded. Things had been going badly between the lovers for some time. The last nail was hammered into love's coffin when the lady in question – an ambitious sound technician – went to work for the film industry's most homophobic director on his big budget female-as-victim thriller-diller.

('You should have seen it coming,' tut-tuts Rainbow's friend Naomi. 'Eighteen months of hell. Why can't you be half as intelligent about relationships as you are about Scorsese's camera angles, Szechwan cooking, and the quickest rush-hour route from Hammersmith Broadway to Highgate Hill?')

Now, it's plain as day that I'm the last one to be prejudiced. Indeed, when I myself feel the urge – every hundred years or so – for a fit of passion, my appetites run in precisely the same direction. But how am I supposed to make this contract last until the thirty-third generation unless I can actually persuade the dear girl to succumb to a broody fit and procreate?

Our heroine is not one of your self-propagating Amazonian Earth Mothers, who does it all with a test-tube and a turkey-baster. So I contemplate the feasibility of inspiring fits of baby-lust, of implanting just the sneakiest bit of heterosexual inclination at precisely the wrong (for her) moment in the month.

But, if what Lil says is true – and one of her least attractive features is the fact that she is rarely wrong – I won't be out here in the field long enough to reap the benefit. I have to face the fact: after Rainbow, no matter what rabbits I pull out of hats, this contract may well expire before its time.

Now we come to an even thornier problem. I like her.

If she were a dybbuk, I'd ask her out to lunch.

I've finally met a human I find interesting. Does this mean

that our client group has changed, since I've been in the tree, or that I have?

Such favourable bias towards a subject is absolutely, totally, unequivocally against the Rules.

And that suits me fine. Let the Ms Topazes of the world choke on their gingernuts, let the Lils conspire, let the Nick Thumbs fume with envy. And let Mephistco's senior management, with their long-term strategies and operational reviews, disappear up their own pin-striped fundaments.

Who cares?

For if this is the swan song of my long career, I'm going to sing it my way. To hell with the rulebook (or, more precisely, those pages I don't particularly like). Whether she knows it or not, my new pal Rainbow and I are going to have some fun.

So let's begin the dance.

A human's mind is a densely populated city, full of winding streets, endless confusing suburbs, second-hand shops, building sites, museums and libraries, rubbish tips, traffic jams, secret shortcuts and blind alleys. It takes a while for a new arrival to get to know the place, move in and take charge. Lucky for me, I'm a quick learner.

Next I set to work inside her dreams. Which, even with a dybbuk in the director's chair, are of interest only to the dreamer.

The next day is one of those Rainbow reserves for her other life. Someone else will drive her taxi, while she indulges her cinema addiction by seeing the films she wants to review for next month's *Outsider*.

But a hellish night has made its mark. She is not in the most receptive of moods at the day's first screening. Several million dollars' worth of production budget passes, to little avail, before her bleary eyes. On the menu, a tale of blood and ballistics, of gangland betrayals and unpleasant acts of revenge. She doesn't like the script, has little time for the pretensions of the director. We're barely into the second reel and her mind is already wandering.

Meanwhile, in the shell of a burnt-out factory, a hired killer points a gun straight at us; the camera stands in the victim's place. The director tries an arty shot: we zoom in close enough to see the subject's terror, reflected in the mirrored sunglasses worn by the assassin.

Rainbow snaps to attention, pinpricked. The frightened face in the glass shifts from male to female, and seems to be a dead ringer for Rainbow herself.

Rainbow blinks, rubs her eyes (time to visit the optician!), and looks again. But all she sees is the twinned reflection of the doomed man, praying that his next incarnation will bring a juicier role, perhaps in some plush costume drama for the BBC.

BANG!

We fade to black.

I found that little trick quite easy to do.

Isn't cinema delightful? I'm quite smitten.

Over the next few hours we immerse ourselves in an American war film (male bonding in the battle zone), a frothy French romance (Rainbow spits like a cat when the young tomboy walks misty-eyed up the bridal aisle), and a lavish documentary on drag queens at the Carnival in Rio (even in her present, petulant mood, she warms to this one, especially when a battalion of ninety maraca-shaking Carmen Mirandas all turn out to be clones of her cousin Michael and his sweetie, Noah).

I also make my inaugural visit to the editorial headquarters of *Outsider*.

The spiritual heirs and heiresses of Marlowe, Wilde, Sappho and Stein operate out of two rooms above an Indian takeaway in the Holloway Road. Let me tell you this: Mephistco Plant Number Three it isn't. Whoever claims that inside every homosexual there beats the heart of an interior decorator is whistling Dixie. We have here a nest of radical intellectuals: the place is a slum.

Rainbow scuffs in, bringing fresh supplies of chaos.

An armload of press-kits from the last three weeks' screenings, dumped on the floor beside her desk.

A ham sandwich, which will be abandoned to moulder while she struggles to finish her piece in time for its deadline.

A bottle of ginger ale which will spill, hissing, to soak the pad that holds all her working notes.

(Never mind, dear, I'm writing the reviews this time.)

And I do. When Rainbow has pounded out her 2,000 words and tries to read them back, she finds they have been inscribed in Hebrew characters: the letters glow emerald, like the divine warning to Belshazzar, on the screen of her VDU. Incomprehensible. And for her, three hours of wasted work.

(Sorry, Rainbow, you've only yourself to blame. Who was it threw the tantrum of the century, at age eleven, when her parents threatened to send her to Hebrew classes after school? If you could but translate what you see before you, you would find not only a crisply written cracker of a piece, but a completely fresh perspective on the art of cinema. Serves you right.)

'Whatever is going in inside this frigging machine,' roars Rainbow, 'is nothing to do with me. Which of you creeps has buggered up my open file?'

'*What* did you say, dear? Beg pardon? *Buggered*? Oooohhhh. Shame . . .'

A ticking-off from the Sub-Editor In Charge of Ideological Purity is not what she wants to hear right now.

She takes the only sensible course of action, which is to damn, blast and smack her computer terminal. As an act of solidarity, the entire office network immediately shuts down in an electronic huff.

Colleagues look up, say nothing. They've seen her in these sulphurous moods before. Best to keep your head down, they've all learned. The features editor flinches when he sees her shadow darken his desk.

'Look, Philip, about my bloody copy . . . Something's happened. I can't figure it out. But you'd better ring the computer people again, because my software is absolutely fucked. So much for your nifty discount price on that word-processing program. Anyway, I'll have to cobble the bloody thing together from my notes. You'll get it tomorrow. Can you live with that?'

He'd better. No one else on the staff has a clue about movies.

When she's stomped off, taking her thunderstorm with her, there is a palpable lightening of the atmosphere. Bleeps break the silence; half-edited copy, invoices, love letters and spreadsheets twinkle back on to the screens.

Just after she has escaped death at the hands of a motorbike messenger near Highbury Corner, sod's law goes into operation. It takes the form of a sudden electricity blackout over London and the whole of south-eastern England. That's my bleep. An urgent summons back to base.

'Piss off,' I say to Nick Thumb, as I walk in. 'Things out there are just beginning to get interesting.'

'They've been having another budget review. They don't want any more resources allocated to this contract. You're about to be redeployed to the new General Pool.'

'Bastards! I just won't stand for it, Nick. What are they playing at? This assignment is supposed to run to the thirty-third generation: I've barely started. Anyway, why didn't you say something last week, before I went out into the field?'

'Nobody tells me anything, sweetheart. And yesterday we had a little management reshuffle. The new Top Gun in the division spent all afternoon looking over my shoulder. Demanded to see all the current project files. And pointed out, after scrutinising yours, that the contract couldn't possibly extend to the specified termination point. Even if they allowed it, which they won't. Your present subject is the last of her line.'

'And how does this red-hot new broom presume to know that?'

He snorts a cloud of steam, and momentarily disappears behind it, all but the scarlet flicker of his tiny eyes.

'Don't play games with me, Kokos. You know as well as I do – Gittel-plus-nine is hardly the marrying kind.'

'Get out of cloud-cockoo-land, Nick. Whoever said she had to be a wife to be a mother?'

'She is, according to the data, a thirty-five-year-old lesbian. She has never been known to have the slightest interest in parenthood. She does not smile at women pushing prams, never pauses before shop displays of sweet little socklets. As far as our records show, she has not even possessed sufficient maternal instinct to keep a cat. So the probability of her taking the trouble to produce even one more generation of Gittels is rated slightly less than a snowball's chance in our Accounts Department.'

If there's one thing I hate, it's being told what I already know.

'Well, you can tell that nosy little *arriviste* to stuff his shiny new MBA up his dorsal vent.'

'Don't make sexist assumptions,' says Nick, emerging briskly from his cloud, straightening his tie, rising from his seat and flashing an ingratiating smile over my right shoulder. 'You can tell her yourself.'

Outside his glass cubicle, the entire population of the outer office has scrambled to its collective feet.

I turn to meet our new superior. Its seven heads are crowned with aureoles of magenta flame, its skin is luminous, and its tail is nearly three scaly metres long. Nevertheless, despite these insignia of higher office, there's no mistaking the bearer's identity. I am only dumbfounded for a nanosecond, and don't let it show.

'Well, hello there, Lil! I hear that felicitations are called for. Didn't Engineering provide enough scope for your talents?'

This breezy greeting does not go down well. There's nobody as authoritarian as a newly promoted anarchist. I hum a favourite song: 'The working class can kiss my ass, I've got the foreman's job at last.'

'You watch yourself, sister,' she mutters, for my ears only. 'Or you'll find yourself retraining as a software virus.'

*

Nick's booked a conference room. We are going to thrash all this out in an organised manner. Present: Nick, myself, Ms Topaz, three smartly dressed strangers to whom I shall no doubt be introduced, a pert secretary (he looks about twelve years old) to pour the coffee and take the minutes, and, at the head of the table, Lil.

The trio of unknowns turn out to be from some organisational nook entitled Corporate Strategies. I have no idea what role these Strategists play in the higher scheme of things, but two of them spend most of the session avoiding my gaze. The third gently dozes, obviously one of that happy breed who are never any good at meetings after lunch.

Lil kicks off, for my benefit, with a somewhat patronising summary of the latest internal reorganisations, new corporate objectives, altered economic climate, need for flexibility, the disappearance – not before time – of the old narrow lines of demarcation. I don't think I like what she's driving at.

Just before she makes her pitch for the new general pool of remote-control demons (I can see it coming, a mile off), I interrupt her.

'Hang on a minute,' I say. 'I do Jews.'

Everyone blinks, in perfect unison. Even the sleeper appears to wake.

Lil takes breath, to call me to order.

I raise one finger: 'Hear me out.'

To my surprise, she subsides, and I continue. I think she is trying to impress the others with her managerial sensitivity and finesse. But I take my time: just this once, I think before I speak.

The silence is so deep you can almost hear the screams from the factory floor.

'I have every respect for the work of my colleagues in this organisation, who have perfected the techniques for possessing the souls and haunting the psyches of those brought up in other tribes or traditions. And, no matter whether we specialise in Protestants or Papists, Muslims or Hindus or devotees of

Iamanja, we all share certain fundamental skills, and adhere to the same standards of professional conduct.'

Everyone nods their assent. Nothing controversial here.

'In an emergency, if called upon, I'm sure I could step in to tempt a Saint Anthony or negotiate an existential pact with a Lutheran alchemist. If you've checked my records, you know that I have undertaken three successful joint ventures with Islamic djinns and affrits, in medieval Spain, when Jewish and Arabic magicians explored forbidden ground together . . .'

Approving nods all round. I haven't said anything to rock their boat yet.

'But this new set-up . . . what a waste! Thousands of years of experience – down the pipe! With all due respect, no one who has ever been out in the field could have come up with such a hare-brained scheme. If you want to run us like a global hamburger franchise, go ahead. But don't be surprised when the customers laugh our whole operation off the streets.'

I think I'm pretty impressive. Nick goes so far as a surreptitious wink. Even Topaz stops nibbling at her chocolate biscuit.

One of the strangers looks a little huffy. Probably because, as I find out later, his last job was with a hamburger multinational, forecasting swings in the price of Styrofoam and sesame seeds.

Lil is not going to be shown up by an underling in front of the Corporate Strategists. She turns to me, and all seven heads display a condescending smile.

'With all due respect, Kokos dear, the profession has progressed during your little stint in that tree. Your attitudes are, if you'll forgive me, just a tiny bit dated. The old narrow specialisms are out the window. You may notice that people – thanks to jet travel and mass communications – have mingled their beliefs and bloodlines. What would you do, say, with a subject whose mother was a Polish Catholic, whose father was an atheist from Nigeria, and who herself has embraced some Californian amalgam of Taoism, cabbalism, science fiction and Polynesian cargo cult?'

48

'I'd do my homework. Use the library. Pick the brains of workmates who knew about the bits I didn't,' I reply. 'Just what we've always done, without benefit of deskbound busybodies trying to justify their inflated salaries, since the days when our clients worshipped stones!'

I bang the conference table for emphasis. The little secretary jumps and upsets the coffee tray. There is a pause for urgent moppings up.

For the first time, one of the pin-striped wizards deigns to speak. He has a military haircut and a booming baritone.

'First off, we've been studying your file . . .'

(That's never good news. And that obsequious smirk of his means trouble.)

'And I would like to say how impressed we are with your past achievements and your obvious dedication to the work. But money doesn't grow on trees any more. The old palmy days, when we did things handsomely and never had to ask how much, are over.'

He pauses, pulls a few folders of expensively bound reports and glossy flowcharts from his attaché case. 'Here's a little bedtime reading for you. Glance over it, and I think you'll see what we're driving at. Fighting-fitness, cost-effectiveness, lean and mean . . .'

I shove it into my case without a glance. 'So instead of the Four Horsemen, the Apocalypse comes via motorcycle courier?'

They chuckle.

'Forget the wage bill,' says Strategist Number Two. 'And scrap the messenger. We'll deliver it by fax. Ho, ho, ho.'

While all this business school bonhomie rolls round the table, I shoot a glance at Nick. It says, plain as day: why aren't you supporting me, you craven coward?

He fidgets, shifts his bulk, checks the clock below the magnificent portrait of the Founder. Creep. He turns to Lil.

'Umm, sorry to cut short this exchange of views, Madam Chair, but we've only got the room until four o'clock.'

A compromise is reached. As I point out, it will look very sloppy on the Annual Report if this particular project, which

49

has been carried forward since seventeen hundred and ninety-something is expensively and abruptly written off.

The good news: I get to complete the contract on Gittel-plus-nine before joining the deskbound labour pool.

The bad news: 'You have a lunar month.'

'WHHAAAAAAAAT?????'

One of the windows, looking out on the Sculpture Court, shatters. Unfortunately, none of my colleagues is injured. I suppose they'll dock the repair costs from my next pay packet.

OK, so I don't exactly win my case. But I resolve to take full advantage of this last buccaneering fling, before I am shunted over to the demonic equivalent of a mass-production assembly line. The only alternative they've offered is a chance to find out, after nearly 3,000 years of job security, what life is like for an unemployed dybbuk out on the streets.

'The end of an era,' I sigh, as we rise from the table.

'Lighten up,' says Lil. 'Think of it as a beginning.'

She aims seven simultaneous grins at the Corporate Strategists, to make sure they know whose side she's on. But they are far too busy trying to wake their somnolent Number Three.

Lil takes hold of my arm. 'Hang on a minute. I'm still your old friend under all these fancy trappings. So what about our dinner date?'

I am seething, as the full implications of what has just passed come home to me. And when I'm cross, I'm afraid my good manners desert me.

'No thanks. I couldn't stomach the sight of you talking with your mouth full, multiplied seven times.'

My arm is abruptly handed back. Nobody can accuse me of sucking up to my superiors.

'You know, I'm beginning to wish I'd left you in that tree.'

We file out past the party-in-waiting. Topaz flashes them a deferential smile. The group is dominated by another bunch of suits from Finance, plus one of the very Highest of the Higher Ups. He is showing the paintings that line the corridor – mostly works by old Flemish masters – to a quintet of Japanese guests: two businessmen, with Visitor badges dangling from their impeccable lapels, and three Fox Ghosts, magnificent with their silver swords, shimmering kimonos and bushy tails. They salute us with abbreviated bows, and glide into the conference room. The double doors shut behind them.

'And what's all that about?' I ask Nick, as we hive off from the rest and head for Contracts.

'Something's in the wind.'

'Like what?'

He cuts me short. 'Can't stop to chat. Not now. Too much coffee . . . the poor old bladder's bursting. Sorry.' And scuttles away.

I don't hang about. It might be a good idea to get out of here and back to work before the brainless bureaucrats send me straight down to the spook-pool without so much as a chance to kiss Rosenbloom bye-bye.

And, with this completely ridiculous and totally unrealistic deadline hanging over my head, there's not a minute to lose.

The petty-minded will now assume that I will revert to some imaginary type and turn into a raging cosmic pervert avenger from hell. Scarlet-skinned, with spitting vipers curling in ghastly locks that frame a wolfish visage, rending my own and everybody else's garments. Letting rip and taking it all out on hapless Rainbow. Well, don't make any assumptions.

Right now, I feel considerably warmer towards my victim than I do towards my employers.

5

I catch up with our quarry at the optician's. She sees
the world through metal-rimmed spectacles, and
something (I wonder what?) has convinced her it is now time
for a new prescription.

'Right,' says the woman in the starched white coat, oblivious
to the erotic potential of sitting knee to knee with an important
lavender culture critic. 'If you'd just like to read me the letters
on the chart, starting with the top line.'

'B U N A Z E L
B E L I A L
H A Z I E L
K O C H B I E L
KOKOS KOKOS KOKOS'

'Pardon?' says the optician. 'I don't think I quite heard . . .'

'Shall I do it again?' says Rainbow, edgily.

'If you would, please.'

'B U N A Z E L
B E L I A L . . .'

'Excuse me, dear. I didn't think your eyes were that bad. But
you haven't got any of the letters right at all . . .'

'You must be joking,' bristles Rainbow. 'They're all sharp as
a knife . . .'

'Look, I'll just slip in a stronger lens on the left-hand side –
that's always been your weaker eye – and we'll see what
happens . . .'

'B U N A Z E L . . .'

'Hmmph. Very odd.'

'That's what's there, damn it.'

'No, I'm sorry, love, it's not!'

They try again. Stronger right lens. Weaker left one. Modifications for astigmatism on one side, then another. Every permutation known to optometry. Finally the optician leaps up and marches straight to the chart. Reads out the letters, one by one, with a sigh. Completely different.

Rainbow leaps up, marches across the room, elbows her aside and jabs a forefinger up against each character: B, U, N, A, Z, E, L . . . B, E, L, I, A, L . . . H, A, Z, I, E, L . . . K, O, C, H, B, I, E, L – So there!!

'Miss Rosenbloom,' says the optician. 'I think we should make a new appointment for another day. Perhaps when you're not under so much pressure . . . less tired . . .'

'I am not under pressure. I am not tired!'

'Then I suggest it's not your eyes that need examining, dear.'

It's high season for celluloid gangsters. Watching another new release (it's never too soon to start next month's column), Rainbow wishes she'd worn her bulletproof vest. Stately Mafia dons exchange meaningful kisses; Bronx loan-sharks float downstream in concrete boots; next year's Best Supporting Actor falls dead into his bullet-peppered cannelloni.

Even failed *film noir* (and, believe me, Howard Hawks has nothing to fear from the last of the week's offerings) packs a punch for Rainbow. Images of cheap hotel rooms, flickering neon, midnight streets and threatening footsteps make her feel tense and lonely. Or that's what she tells herself, when she stumbles out into the watery sunlight.

Personally, I think it was the morgue scene that did it for Rainbow. The Unidentified Jane Doe in the bottom drawer could have been her double. Easy to organise, once you know how.

Oh, I do love the movies.

*

The next day, we're back in the taxi and on the road again. Finsbury Park to Angel, City Road to Swiss Cottage, Finchley Road out to Heathrow, no airport pick-ups allowed but there's better luck at Hounslow, although it's three small eastward jumps before she's back in town, via Acton, Chiswick, Shepherd's Bush, then in to Queensway and down to Battersea, Battersea to Waterloo Station, Waterloo back to Lavender Hill, from there to Harley Street.

Then several short but lucrative West End lunch runs: art director and copywriter to *dernier cri* Vietnamese vegetarian; boss and new secretary to fraudulent *nouvelle* French; ex-spouses to a pizzeria (access during the school holidays negotiations); publisher and author (poetry) to pub lunch; agent and author (blockbuster) to this week's starry wunderkind chef (witty tricks with wild boar consommé and truffle vinegar).

Like every London taxi-driver, Rainbow is a creature of shifting moods. Sometimes she is uncommunicative, offering her passengers nothing but a view of her indifferent neck. But when she picks up someone whose face, dress or likely attitudes displease her, her captives find themselves on a cab ride straight to hell.

'I had the manager of a big sausage factory in the back of the cab, once,' she tells one party of eager lunchers. 'You wouldn't credit what he told me about mechanically recovered meat. First they drain out all the . . .'

'Pity about that famine in Africa . . . Did you see the pictures of those starving kids on telly . . . ? Crying shame . . .'

'Sorry about the potholes, sir! Do you know how much money each of the councils in the Greater London area lopped from their road-mending budgets this year . . . Well, I'll tell you. In the borough of Kensington and Chelsea, for a start, they cut exactly . . .'

'Too hot for April, isn't it? Probably all that atmospheric pollution. If you want my opinion, they should start by banning . . .'

'Well, I was going to take you round by Archway, because that would usually be the shortest route, now, wouldn't it.

Except they've had five-mile tailbacks up that way all morning, something to do with a royal visit to some hospital (very nice, but it might be nicer if that lot paid their taxes), so I'm going to have to cut through Tufnell Park, or we could chance the Brecknock, but the radio said there was a warehouse fire near there about an hour ago . . . I don't know. Probably arson. Somebody trying it on with their insurance or something, usual stuff . . .'

Just to round off her morning, I arrange a little gift. It consists of a right-wing MP. He is rushing from the Mother of Parliaments to an impatient mistress with stiletto heels, rubber bikini and cat-o'-nine-tails. Just as a false-alarm bomb scare gridlocks all traffic between the river and Hyde Park, Rainbow recognises him as the father of a particularly vicious little Immigration Bill. For half an hour, pinned to the spot, he reaps the benefit of her wisdom.

Rainbow takes seven minutes for a bacon roll at a friend's café in Holborn. Then a frantic woman with two petulant moppets hails her and produces an address, faintly pencilled on a matchbook, on the farthest fringes of south London. According to the rules, Rainbow is not required to accept a fare going such a distance, but she is feeling unaccountably soft-hearted. (What could have got into her? Whatever it is, it hasn't stopped her from wolfing down a slice off the hindquarters of some poor innocent pig.)

The traffic is diabolical (I must admit to making things even worse, just to try my hand, by introducing a minor fault into the taxi's steering mechanism), the junior passengers restless. It takes forever for Rainbow to locate the address, argue over the fare, and get back to town through a miles-long gauntlet of garden gnomes. When she does so, she discovers that her last passengers have left a souvenir: the acrid proof that at least one child really couldn't wait to get wherever he was going.

She climbs into the passenger compartment to attack the damp patch, loses her balance.

'Shit!'

While she scrubs and curses, a message seems to be coming

over her radio. No interference, no crackles. Everything crystal clear. It's the sound of maniacal laughter, growing shrill and ever louder. Somebody out there must be having a whale of a time. Me, as it happens.

She hands over the taxi to her driving partner, who's taking the Friday evening shift, and who doesn't think Rainbow has done quite as wonderful a cleaning job as one might have hoped for on the passenger seat. Then home again, after this busy and – for me – delightful day.

The flat smells overwhelmingly of last night's kung-po prawn and chicken in black bean sauce takeaway. The post is nothing but a final notice electricity bill, a chain letter from persons unknown promising her untold wealth if she sends £5 to the name at the top of the list and certain death if she doesn't, and a note from the unsound sound woman, reminding Rainbow that she still hasn't forwarded sound woman's tape of Tibetan lamas' chants and the Grand Old Opry T-shirt, both inadvertently left behind.

'Too bad, pal,' scowls Rainbow. 'I'm keeping the Himalayan hip-hop because I like it, and I tore up your Nashville T-shirt to bandage mah pore ole broken heart.'

At that moment, her tape deck starts up of its own accord and regales her with Patsy Cline's rendition of 'Walking after midnight'.

She jumps sky-high, and then does what every modern Nice Jewish Girl does in moments of crisis. Reaches for the phone.

Naomi, to Rainbow's relief, answers on the second ring. Rainbow makes her pitch. 'Are you two in tonight?'

'Is the Pope Catholic, sweetheart? It's our sacred Friday night ritual: beer and pizza and a video. Even now the luscious Mary-Catherine is gliding in the front door with . . . what is it? . . . fabulous! *Arsenic and Old Lace!*'

'Can you stand a gatecrasher? Strange stuff's been happening. I just don't feel like being alone right now.'

What sort of strange stuff? Naomi wonders.

Rainbow is unable to put it into words. Can you blame her? Faces that shouldn't be there grinning out of movie screens, computers with minds of their own, Aramaic songs popping out of her mouth, uncanny voices on the taxi radio, and so forth. Don't tell me this is business as usual, even for somebody with a PhD in Shoving Things under the Carpet.

'So Greta Garbo's had a personality transplant, has she? Come round right this minute.'

Naomi lives off the far end of the Seven Sisters Road. Tonight, Rainbow can't get there fast enough. Especially since she's not behind her own wheel, and the bus ride takes forever. Lorries break down, minor accidents block one-way systems, crews of workmen excavate a major junction, traffic lights freeze on red.

I find it all quite entertaining to organise: perhaps, when this assignment ends, I'll apply for a temporary secondment to Automotive Demonics. They should be thrilled to have me: Personnel is always after them to iron out their gender imbalances.

Twitchy (she's not a patient lady, is she?), Rainbow abandons the bus, and continues the trip on foot. Just as well. She needs a bit of time to review the little oddities of the past few days, don't you, dearie?

We're on a wide street of Victorian terraced houses, tall three-storeyed piles of crumbling yellow brick, front steps slanting sideways or sinking into overgrown front gardens. A district that's come down in the world, but one where – even in its heyday – no one ever did a lot of smiling. Dour plaster gods hang over the doorways, minus the noses that a century of leaking drainpipes has washed away. I feel right at home: we have districts just like this in our own capital.

I feel even more at home when I see what's walking towards us.

Between a mighty headpiece of astrakhan fur and a long silk caftan, with earlocks curling down to join a magisterial beard, a face out of my own lost world approaches. Around him, an entourage of more sparsely-bearded younger men, holding their sons by the hand. The little boys have embroidered skullcaps and skin as pale as milk, and clutch the velvet bags that hold their fathers' prayer-shawls. The procession, without giving any sign that Rainbow has been noticed, swerves and crosses, as one, to the other side of the street.

So where are the women? Of course, silly of me. It's Friday evening, after all; pious ladies are busy indoors, laying the Sabbath table. The whole street smells of simmering soup. In one of the houses, I see several men clustering near an open window, bent over prayer books, swaying back and forth. The words almost reach me. A brush with danger. Just as well I had all the necessary inoculations before this latest round of fieldwork.

Nevertheless, I find the district curiously restful, and quite nostalgic. Rainbow fights off a twinge of homesickness for a world she never knew. A stirring in the blood, from all the Gittels, a sense of tasks undone, candles to light, plaited loaves of bread to bless. She hears someone chanting, and stops, trying to trace the sound to its source. Then a black-coated teenage scholar, with a wistful attempt at a beard, hisses something at her as he passes. The insult is not in English, but the syllables drip acid in her ear.

Soon we are even more rudely interrupted.

'Rainbow! Hey there, Rainbow! Rainbow Rosenbloom . . . Yoohooo, darling!!! Over here!'

Rainbow's Aunt Goldie waves from a doorway. She wears a white headscarf, about eighteen strands of pearls, a riotously flowered silk dress and a clashing but equally botanical apron. And she's far livelier than she was at our first encounter. Full of the skittish joys of spring.

'Oh, shit,' mutters Rainbow, 'that's all I need.' But obediently crosses over the road to greet her.

'Hello, darling. Fancy seeing you here. I thought you lived over by Green Lanes somewhere, with all those Greeks.'

'And what about you, Aunt Goldie? You're a long way from Ilford.'

Now that's what I call good manners. Here's Rainbow

teetering on the edge of an abyss, and what does she do? Makes social chit-chat with an aged relative.

'Every so often I come down here to see some people. Do a little cooking for them, stay overnight. You know me, dear. I'm very strict about not travelling on Shabbos . . . I hope you don't mind my saying, but you're not looking so good today. I thought you looked a little peaky at the seder. Are you coming down with something? There's a lot of flu going round . . . You work much too hard. It isn't healthy, really. You want to come into my friends' house for a little while? Have a little supper. There's plenty of food . . .'

(Surprise, surprise.)

'. . . and they would love to meet anybody in my family. They've heard all about the Rosenbloom clan.'

(Oh, terrific. Dining out on you lot, is she?)

'I'm sorry, Aunt Goldie. I'd really like to . . .' (Aha, I t⟨ you so – Rainbow may be wearing a Friend of Lesbian Line ⟨ shirt, but she's a well-brought-up Yiddishe *maydl* inside he. skin.) 'but I'm on my way to my pal Naomi's place for dinner.'

(Notice she mentions the friend with the Jewish name. Notice she doesn't say that the house and the dinner also belong to Naomi's lover, Mary-Catherine, ex-Sisters of the Holy Name, from County Cork. Rosenbloom, you're a hypocrite.)

'. . . But thanks very much all the same.'

'That's nice. I wouldn't like to think of you spending Friday night alone, dear.'

What a relief. We are just about to be let off the hook with an A for Effort. And not a moment too soon. Because you have to watch these pious old birds. They sometimes have an instinct about things that makes me a little uncomfortable . . .

But just as Rainbow's about to be dismissed, with a queenly 'Good Shabbos' from her aunt, the door of the house swings open and a naked toddler, carrying a large blue sponge in the shape of a duck, bolts down the steps. Two women rush after him.

Goldie, slow on her swollen ankles, fails to stop the giggling fugitive, who runs smack into Rainbow's knees. Rainbow tackles him, passes him to her aunt, who kisses him on the forehead and hands him back to the forces of law and order. The older woman, laughing and scolding, wraps the rebel in a bath-towel and disappears.

The younger one stops to say thanks.

Our reward is a ravishing, radiant smile.

Take note of those eyes – like blue-black plums. And hair even blacker. She is dressed with becoming modesty – longish skirt, full sleeves, high collar and demure pearl earrings, piercing tiny lobes. A pretty sight.

Hoo-ha! Now this is what I call a Nice Jewish Girl. She and the Rosenbloom might as well belong to different species. Our new acquaintance is four or five years younger than Rainbow, and two or three centuries older. They observe each other, obliquely, too cool or too uneasy to let curiosity show.

I have no access to the newcomer's thoughts regarding Rainbow, but I know how Rainbow reacts to her.

It's the moment when the spaceship gangplank drops down in *Close Encounters*. Except the alien says 'Good Shabbos', and kisses the mezuzah on the UFO's doorpost as she disembarks.

For all either of them know, they're thirteenth cousins, seven times removed, sharing common ancestors in Krakow, Magdeburg, Avignon, Granada, Tbilisi, Salonica, Babylon. Their cradles may have been rocked to the same lullabies, and tied with the same red ribbons to ward off the same Evil Eye. They may both have cut their milk teeth crunching mandelbrot, and both licked drops of honey off a page on the day they learned to read. They may have dressed up in the same Queen Esther costumes on the feast of Purim, and shaken their noisemakers to drown out the name of the racist vizier in the three-cornered hat.

What is certain is that they are the descendants of restless, wary people. Who may have sniffed blood on the wind, or may have been looking for the golden city, but who, for whatever reason, took their future generations out of danger's way in time.

Otherwise, they are as much alike as a coral snake and a canary, who are also, according to some theories, long-lost cousins.

Aunt Goldie performs the introductions, thrilled by this miraculous chance meeting. Each party is identified, biblically, in terms of clan and kinship: Riva as daughter of Goldie's hosts for the weekend; Rainbow as 'my poor late brother Cyril's only child'.

Having oiled the wheels of social intercourse, Auntie folds her arms and waits.

Go on, Rainbow, say something. Hurry up. We don't have all night.

'Don't I know you from somewhere?' is the best she can do.

Oh come on, Rosenbloom, not that old chestnut. Where do you think you'd know this baby from? Browsing through the lesbian romances in that feminist bookshop in the Charing Cross Road? Burning up the dancefloor at some Friday night disco? Do me a favour.

'I don't think so,' smiles the little bird of paradise. 'But anyway, you know me now.' (How's that for witty repartee? See, not only beautiful, but smart.) 'I suppose I'd better go in and help my mother or we'll never get the dinner on the table. Good Shabbos.'

Goldie, duty done and honour satisfied, waits until the young woman has disappeared into the house. Then she squeezes Rainbow's hand, and gives her a parting pat on the cheek.

'Well, maybe another time you'll come for a visit when I'm here. I'll tell your other aunts I saw you. Won't they be surprised?'

I hear skylarks singing. Taste manna. Smell all the perfumes of Punt. For I have received just the inspiration I need. Let us now fulfil this final contract in a blaze of glory.

With strange emotions churning round inside her, Rainbow has no memory of anything else until she finds herself at

Naomi's. An untouched pizza congeals on a plate on her knee; the beer in her glass has gone tepid and flat.

'You really are in a peculiar mood tonight, Rosenbloom.'

'Everything's peculiar tonight. Why should I stand out?'

'And you've hardly touched your food. What a waste. Don't you know there are children starving in the Third World?'

'You sound like my Aunt Becky.'

'So what's wrong with that? I always said that woman was a closet dyke.'

This, for once, gets no rise out of Rainbow.

'OK, Rosenbloom, what's bothering you? Don't you want to talk about it?'

'I thought I did. That's why I came over. But now I'm not so sure.'

'No talk, no movie.'

'No movie, no talk.'

'It's our house.'

'I'm the guest.'

'You may find yourself disinvited.'

'OK,' says Rainbow. 'I give in. I promise, Ms Florence Nightingale Freud, I'll let you practise your DIY first-aid psychotherapy on me later, after the video. But if you really want to help me, what you'll do right now is let me slump in this armchair and watch Cary Grant making an ass of himself, *capisce*?'

It's a deal.

But when we're well into *Arsenic and Old Lace*, just as the sweet old ladies complete their efficient disposal of a gentlemanly corpse, Naomi jabs a button and puts the tape on Pause.

Blast her, I was really enjoying it. However, this also means I have allowed my attention to wander from my subject. What on earth has she been up to?

Naomi stands with her arms akimbo, blocking the screen. 'For God's sake, Rosenbloom, stop muttering to yourself.'

I'm aghast. Here we have someone who believes that capital punishment should be compulsory for people who rustle sweet papers during movies . . . What's she doing gibbering?

'Well, do you want to watch this movie or not?'

'Sorry.'

'I thought this was one of your all-time subversive favourites.'

Indeed. Has Rainbow not produced an essay entitled 'The Labyris and the Knitting Needle: Maiden Aunt as Movie Maenad' for the last *Outsider* but two?

'Maybe I'm not really in the right frame of mind tonight. I didn't mean to spoil your evening. I probably should have stayed home and gone to bed early. I'm feeling sort of . . . distracted. It'll pass. Come on, let's see the rest.'

Naomi shrugs, hits the Play button. The film continues.

Rainbow may have seen this picture before, but I have not. Uncle Teddy, blowing his trumpet and leading the charge of the Rough Riders up the stairs, reminds me somehow of Nick Thumb. No matter how often the joke is milked and repeated, it still makes me laugh. Louder and louder and louder. I just can't stop; in fact, I forget myself entirely.

When I finally recover my professional *gravitas*, Rainbow is on the floor, gasping for breath. Naomi and Mary-Catherine cling to each other, their eyes and mouths agape, forming perfect circles. A vase of freesias has fallen from a shelf; two pictures on the walls tilt sharply sideways.

I seem to have made my public debut.

If these weren't politically idealistic, socially conscious, historically aware late twentieth-century lesbian feminists, I suppose they would have stretched her on the rack to make her spill the beans, or shone a light in her eyes and played Good Cop, Bad Cop. But being who and what they are, Naomi and Mary-Catherine try to calm their own blasted nerves just sufficiently to organise restorative brandies (Naomi) and (Mary-Catherine) pots of camomile tea. Rainbow opts for the second. Pity. Camomile makes me bilious, but I could have done with a nip of old-fashioned slivovitz.

They finally get her talking, but she finds it hard to explain.

'. . . You know how it is, you're walking down the street with two people, say, and you keep feeling there's a third one just outside your field of vision . . .'

Well no, actually, they have to admit they don't.

Rainbow tries again. 'OK, you know that bit in every thriller when the star drives along a lonely country road in fog, and suddenly sees headlights, much too close, in the rear-view mirror . . . And then the car breaks down, and we're in a deserted house, all full of white-draped furniture and cobwebbed curtains, when a hinge creaks, and a trapdoor lifts, and Something slowly, slowly, slowly rises up from the depths beneath . . .'

I can't resist it. I make the lights fuse. NOW!

When the screaming stops, they hear a next-door neighbour banging on the door, and threatening to call the police. Mary-Catherine (much as it galls me to admit it, that convent training really counts for something) recovers first, and pops out to shut him up with a placatory fiction about power failures, dropped teapots, scalded guests, and so forth.

'I think I'd better go home now,' says Rainbow.

Nothing will induce her to stay. Mary-Catherine gets busy with a few candles (no bells or books, I'm happy to say) to light the room, and busies herself in the understair cupboard, hunting for spare fuses. Naomi offers a lift, which Rainbow refuses.

Her psyche may be dancing Strip-the-Willow on the sitting-room ceiling at the moment, but that doesn't mean she's suicidal. Naomi's ashen face and sweat-daubed brow do not inspire confidence in potential pillion passengers. Anyway, Rainbow insists, a long walk is just what she needs right now.

'We'll talk tomorrow, all right? I promise.'

There's no holding her. Off she goes. But her friends need not worry. The dangers of the midnight streets can't touch her. No one will rob her to feed his craving for drugs, no one will rape her to feed his lust for power. Tonight, she is under my protection. Rendered invisible, though too preoccupied to notice. And just as well. For there is a large black bear, broken loose from someone's dream of a Lithuanian forest, stumbling through the gardens of south Tottenham. A headless rooster, white feathers bloodied, lands on a roof after the long passage over oceans, delivering a tropical curse to terminate a lovers' quarrel. At Manor House, a banshee wails: the last of an old line of Celtic kings will die tomorrow, by his own hand, through a small error in the timing of a bomb.

But we have other concerns tonight, my subject and I. For I am planting seeds in her, that ache and tingle, and searching out the secret places where her ghosts hide. And she feels it, oh yes she feels it, though she cannot put a name to what is happening.

6

For the first time in many moons, Rainbow has the weekend off. And just as well. I allow her to sleep half of Saturday away, and wake in sheets that are soaked with sweat and the juices of her own excitement. How scandalous! In her dreams, she has been having her wicked way with that sweet, mysterious Riva. Who has proven, to the dreamer's surprise, to be a very dextrous hand with zips and buttons.

Rainbow Rosenbloom you should blush for shame. Catching sight of herself in the bathroom mirror, she has the grace to do so.

'What is wrong with you, sunshine?' she berates her own reflection. 'Stop scaring yourself to death. You know this house's party line on shrinks, psychobabblers, aura-masseurs and other expensive charlatans . . . So why are you trying to drive yourself into their arms? Get a grip, girl, get a grip!'

She decides that what she needs is an immediate purge of mind and body. She will mortify and cleanse the flesh by the ritual application of scalding steam and ice-water, in an old Turkish bathhouse near Bethnal Green.

Few people know of this place. Most of its clientele are elderly; the regulars are gradually dying off, or drifting away to the suburbs. A few of Rainbow's friends use the baths, on certain weekday evenings, as a rendezvous, but on Saturday afternoons it is quiet.

Today, as always, the cockney attendant and a select band

of her towel-wrapped cronies are sharing tea and jam doughnuts in a curtained cubicle. In the warm room, alongside the plunge pool, two young Asian girls take turns massaging each other with rose-scented oil, while a third subjects them to a personality quiz – 'Are You A True Romantic?' – from her magazine. On a lounger next to the hot pipes that feed the steam, a tiny black woman, full of years, lies sleeping, curled into a question mark. She is wrapped in an emerald green bath-sheet: on the Zimmer-frame parked at her side she has draped a kimono embroidered with turquoise peacocks.

And inside the steam room itself sits Rainbow, her legs drawn up on to the bench to avoid the geyser of hot vapour from a pipe underneath her, her sweat beginning to pearl and slide. She breathes deeply, remembering a long-ago yoga class, holding the air in and counting before she exhales it at the same measured pace.

Then she hears what seems to be an echo of her own breathing – the same pattern of inhalation and release, but half a beat too late. She is startled. She had imagined herself to be alone in the room, although suddenly – through a thick cumulus of steam – she sees the outline of someone who has been there all the time, sitting cross-legged on the floor in the far corner.

'Hotter than usual, today,' says Rainbow, by way of acknowledgement.

'Hotter than usual, today.'

'Whewwwww . . .'

'Whewwww . . .'

Rainbow falls silent, slips back into daydreams, allows herself a tiny smile.

'Thinking about her, are we?'

'What?'

'Your unattainable desire?'

'Sorry?' Ruffled, Rainbow gathers her towel about herself, prepares for a quick escape. 'I don't know what you're talking about.'

'Oh you do, Rainbow, you do. It's a matter of record that

you have had more than one entanglement with hopeless causes. What about that very straight cousin of Mary-Catherine's? Or your flatmate, final year of university, who received your confession of undying lust on the night before her wedding to good old Pete? Stop boggling; the list's as long as my arm. And we both know what you were up to in your dreams last night. And shame on you. With that sweet, virtuous creature, a young woman of valour, whose price is undoubtedly above rubies, the exotic little blossom from Stamford Hill?'

'Who the fuck are you?'

'I know who you are. Inside and out. I've been following you for a while.'

The steam turns reddish.

'Now look what you've done. Temper, temper. That's your anger showing. Because you've been caught out.'

'I'm getting out of here . . .'

'No you're not. Because you're dying to know who I am.' Oh, look, the atmosphere's gone bluish-white now. Blind panic. Rainbow drops her towel and, naked as a nymph, bolts for the door.

'It won't open, my friend, until I'm good and ready.'

Rainbow rattles the handle, then starts banging.

'Who's to hear you? The attendant is trading racy gossip with her pals down the end of the corridor, the three young girls are upstairs dressing to go home, the old lady's dreaming calypso dreams of her childhood, and anyway, her hearing aid's switched off. And though the committee's been talking for ages about installing an alarm bell, they've never managed it. Money's tight. So just settle back on that bench, and make yourself comfortable. It's time we were properly introduced.'

She spins round, fists clenching, ready for a fight. Chest heaving, eyes blazing, teeth bared, hair standing up in gunmetal spikes. Quite a formidable sight, if she weren't also shivering uncontrollably – no mean feat at 100 per cent humidity and 112 degrees Fahrenheit.

What can she see that alarms her so?

I've thought long and hard about what physical embodiment

to wear for this big moment. When you're dealing with heretics and heathens, you have to come up with something original. The traditional forms don't do the trick.

Many of my colleagues, in engagements such as these, favour the Doppelgänger Treatment, but personally I think the mirror-image routine has now been done to death. And the phantom countenance looming out of the ether may induce no more than giggles in someone whose first experience of cinema was *The Wizard of Oz*. So, since we are, conveniently and cosily, in a steam room, I opt for a modified Brocken Spectre look. A pale reflection, larger than life, shimmering out of the mist. I've used this before, on a smuggler carrying amber across the High Tatras. It works a treat in mountain snow. In a Turkish bath, however, it comes out a little blotchy.

Still, good enough to put the frighteners on her.

The door opens, very slowly. The attendant holds it wide, and the tiny old woman, wrapped in her emerald towel, enters at a slow and stately pace, leaning on her Zimmer.

'Sorry if I'm letting all the steam out, dear,' she says to Rainbow. 'I'm not so speedy as I once was.'

'It's OK,' gasps Rainbow, 'I'm going. I think I'm starting to hallucinate. The heat must be getting to me.'

Not to mention the stranger squatting on the floor.

Except, now that the steam has been so diluted, Rainbow can see there's no one there.

'Well you know what they say,' the old lady chortles. 'If you can't stand the heat, get out of the kitchen. Time you did the cold plunge, dear.' She opens her arms wide and stretches luxuriously. 'Aaaaaaaah, that's gooooood.'

The plunge pool is empty. Rainbow holds her breath and lowers herself into the cube of icy water. Shuts her eyes and dives below the surface to swim round in circles until her blood feels like it's begun to flow again. What she doesn't expect is to find herself entangled. Something slipping across her body like ribbons of seaweed, sliding under her arms and between her legs, a voice bubbling incoherently.

Then she hears a bellow and someone blowing on a whistle.

She bursts out of the grasp of whatever is holding her, and swings herself up the ladder out of the pool.

'Hey, hey! You there!' shouts the attendant. 'What do you think you're doing? Stop carrying on like that. If you want watersports you'd better go down the road to the Leisure Centre.'

Rainbow, fighting for breath, shakes her head. 'I wasn't . . . doing . . . anything. Something's . . . in there . . . Tried to . . . drown me!'

The attendant looks at her, then down at the plunge pool, then back at Rainbow, eyes narrowed. 'Listen you, there's nothing in there. Look, now that you've stopped churning up the water, you can see all the way to the bottom. Nothing there. Nada. Zero. Zilch. Are you on drugs? Because if you are, you're banned.'

Rainbow bellows a denial, then lets the side down by bursting into tears.

'Oh dear, oh dear, I do get all the nutters on my shift, don't I. Never mind, wrap up in your towel and come into my cubbyhole, and I'll fix you a nice cup of tea.'

There have absolutely positively never, the attendant assures her over a custard cream, been any reports of ghosts or poltergeists or anything else peculiar at this bathhouse.

'Spooks don't like soap and water, you see, dear. They're very dirty creatures.'

Bitch. Bigot. And not only offensive, but incorrect.

'Do you believe in them?' asks Rainbow.

'Well, I wouldn't say I did and I wouldn't say I didn't. But my next-door neighbour did once have a very odd thing happen when she went to see a medium after her husband died. He'd been sick for ages, and she waited on him hand and foot, and when he finally went, it was a terrible shock to her, and . . .'

Rainbow does not particularly want to hear the saga. She hands the woman the empty mug, and rises.

'Thanks for the tea. I really have to go now. But thanks for everything. And I'm sorry to have made such a fuss in there, but . . .'

70

'Are you sure you're all right now?'

'Yes, really. Fine. It was probably too much steam, nothing to eat all day, PMT, biorhythms off kilter . . . you know . . .'

The woman doesn't know. But she has a new story now, to match her next-door neighbour's Voices, of the Something in the Plunge Pool. About the presence in the steam room itself, Rainbow has chosen to say nothing.

In Stamford Hill, they have finished singing the songs that celebrate the day's mystic marriage of male and female godhead. The sun has set, the third star has appeared in the sky, and the bird of paradise, her mother and sisters, face a Mount Ararat of unwashed dishes. Aunt Goldie waits for her taxi back to Ilford.

Rainbow also waits, in her own house. The telephone rings, and she does not pick it up, but listens in silence to the message on the answering machine: it's Naomi, interrogating.

'Now what was that about last night? Do you want me to come round and talk about it? Damn it, Rainbow, ring as soon as you get in and tell us – what is going on???'

Rainbow bangs at the wrong keys on the machine, but misses Naomi. Rings her and, when Naomi answers, bursts into tears.

'Should I come round? Give me half an hour . . .'

She's about to say yes, I know she is, so she can pour her troubled heart out on her good mate's shoulder. But I cut right in there, and Rainbow hears her own voice say, 'Thanks, but no. I'll be OK. I'm just upset. No, tomorrow would be soon enough . . . Yes, I promise, I'll survive till tomorrow.' She smiles as she snuffles. 'And don't worry, you won't be disappointed. I promise. I won't let the crisis go off the boil.'

Naomi offers the best spiritual first-aid she can think of. A Chinese dim-sum lunch in Soho. Usual place and time.

I'm looking forward to it.

When Rainbow puts the phone down we immediately head off again, to prowl the night. She steers our steps (all right, maybe I help a little, but she doesn't fight) back to the Street of the Believers. But if Rainbow wants to spend the evening crouched behind a parked Talmud-Torah school minibus with one dodgy tyre and no tax disc, watching the lights go out behind a certain set of curtained windows, then who am I to argue?

Truly, a world of wonders. This thoroughly modern creature is now cultivating her unhealthy obsession with her own several-times-great-great-grandmother, or a reasonable simulacrum thereof. Whatever would all the long-gone Gittels say to that?

For a start, they would tell her to exercise some of the common sense she was presumably born with, and come in out of the rain. Water oozes down the back of her jacket, drenches the scarf, soaks through everything underneath. Oblivious, Rainbow stares at the blank face of the house, as if hoping that her gaze can split the brickwork and open the building like a book. What on earth does she think she's doing here?

Perhaps she'd be better off if she didn't think at all. For the roe deer never comes down from the mountain of spices: the garden stays locked, the spring shut up, the fountain sealed. But only when I get bored – and I can be wonderfully patient, when I choose – does she finally give up the vigil.

7

On Sunday morning the North London streets are relatively quiet; on this day alone it is almost possible to breathe the city's air. Unless one suffers from a head cold because one has unaccountably forgotten to come in out of the rain.

'Garlic,' announces Naomi, scrutinising Rainbow as the waitress brings their second pot of tea. 'What you need for a cold like that is garlic. And lots of ginger.'

'Braised duck webs,' says Rainbow, signalling to the young woman who pushes a cart of different dishes towards them. 'Sharks' fin soup in juicy buns. The little spare ribs . . . we'll take two of those please, Miss. Tripe with black bean sauce. A little congee. Thanks. I guess that will do us til the next cart comes round. Keep your eye out for trolley with the wafer-paper prawns, Naomi. And the deep-fried yam croquettes . . . And . . .'

I may be rearranging her psyche, but I've left the dear girl's appetite strictly *virgo intacta*.

Naomi raps Rainbow's fingers with a chopstick. 'Hey, you just nicked my crab-stuffed mushroom. I take it you did live through the night.'

'I'm not so sure.'

'Well, your ghost is doing pretty well on the crispy duck buns.'

'This is comfort eating. That's all.'

'Well?'

'Well, what?'

'So nu? as my grandmother says, when she's snuggling down to hear the latest scandal about cousin Rose's extramarital affair . . . What exactly is it you need comfort for? You were more than a little weird the other night. Now shut up and tell me everything.'

'I'm being – ' Rainbow searches for a word that will not compromise her dignity ' – haunted.'

'Haunted? Are we back to the other night? Old Gothic mansions? Bats and secret chambers and Vincent Price?'

'Naomi, if you're going to piss about, forget it. Let's just drop the subject, eat what's here, and go.'

'Sorry. I'm just relieved to see you acting what's, by your usual standards, normal. After that maniacal laughing fit . . . and last night on the phone. OK, so back to business.' She pours more tea, hails a passing trolley for some oyster-sauced bean curd and a dish of gingered meatballs. 'Now what do you mean, haunted?'

'Something is . . . getting at me.'

'Something? Who?'

'I don't know if it's a who.'

'Well, what's it like?'

'Do you know what a dybbuk is?'

'A dybbuk. Come on, I'm a nice Jewish girl with one grandmother who sat through *Fiddler on the Roof* twenty-seven times and another who used to scare me to death with bedtime stories about the Evil Eye. What do you think?'

'Don't laugh at me. You're going to say I've gone completely over the edge, but . . . I've got one . . . A dybbuk. Inside my head.'

Naomi looks at Rainbow hard. Her own face displays a rather interesting sequence of colour changes. What I find particularly fetching is the little flicker of alarm in the eyes. And, for a moment, she seems to grow distracted, as if listening to the faint voice of some witchy old ancestress from the shtetl, trying to broadcast a warning in her inner ear.

She shakes her head, then gives a rueful smile. 'That's ten

quid I owe her on this one . . . I hate it when she's always right.'

'Who?'

'Mary-C.'

'She knew? How?'

'Come on . . . She used to be in the business, didn't she? – well, sort of. Incense and holy ghosts and bell, book and candle, and the whole shebang. And, last year – don't you remember? – she went off to that place in Scotland for a weekend workshop in shamanism and psychic self-defence. As I recall, you took the piss out of her when you heard. Anyway, she's worried about you. Sends her love, and says, if there's anything she can help with . . .'

(Hoo-ha! I can hardly keep from laughing. What a touching gesture: an offer of free and and gratis exorcism services from ex-Sister Mary-Catherine, divorced Bride of You-Know-Who! How delightful . . .

It reminds me of that old chestnut about the maiden who wakes at midnight to find the traditional bat-cloaked figure aiming his bared fangs at her throat. To save herself, she holds up two fingers, in the form of a cross. So the monster sighs, shakes his head, and smiles, 'Oy vay, dollink, have *you* got the wrong vampire!')

Thanks for the offer, Mary-C. But you can save your breath and your incense.

Rainbow runs through the inventory of my manifestations to date. Starting with someone borrowing her vocal chords at the seder, moving on to the little interventions I made in the films she's seen, not omitting the Hebrew inscriptions in her computer, the voice on her taxi radio, the day when things went from bad to worse (not fair; only half my fault, and I was only doing a bit of gentle teasing), and culminating in the misty apparition and the phantom seaweed taking liberties in the plunge pool at the Turkish bath.

'Holy shit.'

I am gratified. I do like the spectators to be impressed.

'Holy,' says Rainbow, 'is not perhaps the precisely accurate adjective.'

'Pedant!' snaps Naomi.

'Defence mechanism,' mutters Rainbow, who is tired of being brave and cool. 'OK, I admit it. I'm a little worried.'

Naomi moves her chair closer, reaches out, starts patting. 'Don't shout at me for saying this, dearie, but I'm still not convinced, Mary-C.'s opinion notwithstanding. It's all heavy stuff, of course, but there has to be an explanation somewhere. Personally, I think you've let your life get out of hand. You're trying to do too much at once.'

Well-meant, but a blunder. Rainbow glowers. 'Are you trying to tell me it's all because I'm tired or something? Piss off . . .'

'All right, take it as read – the old saw about just because you're paranoid doesn't mean they're not out to get you. But look at you – you're a walking disaster area. You've practically turned into a hermit, don't see anyone but Mary-C. and me, have – according to your own testimony – turned into the office ogre at *Outsider*, and have given every movie you've seen in the last six months a bad review.'

'I told you, knocking copy is easier to write, and funnier . . .'

'Let me be like Lucy in Peanuts and offer you some Psychiatric Help, 5 cents. Deep down, I don't really think you're over Madam Unspeakable yet, however glad you said you were to be shot of her at the time.'

Damn and blast the little wretch – I hate these secular rationalists! Not a shred of imagination. What's the world coming to?

Rainbow opens her mouth for an outraged denial; Naomi plugs it with a wafer-paper prawn.

'You could afford to take a few days off work. You told me your driving partner's desperate for more shifts. So do yourself and the human race a favour. The state you're in, you'd be death on the road.'

'Thanks, pal. Just what I need to hear.'

'I'm serious. Treat yourself like a human being for a change.

Come and stay with us in sunny south Tottenham. We'll pamper you obscenely. Mary-Catherine does a sublime foot massage. And I'll cook. That should scare any ghost away.'

'Thanks. Maybe soon. Not now. I think I have to be on my own for a while. But I don't know. I don't know what I want. Because when I'm not being terrified, I'm kind of in a state of high excitement. Waiting to see what they – it – is going to spring on me next. I sort of . . . like it.' She peers at Naomi. 'You think I've slipped completely out of orbit, don't you?'

'I don't know what to think.'

'I want to go now. Let's get the bill.' Rainbow rises, abruptly, catches a waiter's eye.

'Isn't there more to talk about? We could go round to that café off Old Compton Street for cappucino?'

'No. It's late. I have to be somewhere. Family stuff.'

Little liar. Must be my pernicious influence. However, notice she did not spill the beans to Naomi about the other novelty in her life: her peculiar passion for our little *tsatskeleh* in full skirt, long sleeves and black stockings.

You'd imagine somebody who spent most of her working life on the streets of this city would avoid them like the plague on her afternoons off. But not our Rainbow. Something – me, actually – weighs down on her; in hopes of shaking it, she keeps on moving.

On foot and in buses, we roam from council estates on the slopes of Hornsey to the Edwardian grandeurs of Muswell Hill. From the parapets at Alexandra Palace we contemplate the distant ridge where London finally ends, and descend to watch a flotilla of ducks looking lost on the New River. We eavesdrop on an adulterous tryst being arranged in Ducketts Common by two heterosexuals pushing their respective toddlers on the swings. We stand on the edge of a crowd in an open-air market, while wide-boys auction crates of oranges. And we do all this in silence.

In Clissold Park we pause long enough to watch a pair of women's softball teams do battle. After the second innings, though, Rainbow has had enough. We're on the move again.

And you guessed it – here we are once more in Little Jerusalem-on-the-Lea, surrounded by bearded patriarchs in long black coats and children with pale, geriatric faces.

We pass the famous house, stand before it for a moment, then we're off again. We find a café in the main road, order tea and never touch it. Twice more, we approach the street, and veer back at the last minute, wandering in ever-decreasing circles. We've travelled miles and miles and miles. Even in her well-seasoned boots, Rainbow's feet are blistering.

Then back to the house of her heart's desire once more. But this time she opens the gate and walks up the ragged path. Stops at the foot of the steps, turns as if to change her mind, then climbs straight up them.

Will she?

Won't she?

Will she?

She does.

What chutzpah! Can you believe it? She's rung the bell.

A pregnant woman, with stiff, bouffant hair that is certainly a wig, comes to the door. A pair of snuffly toddlers hang from the hem of her skirt, dragging it even further towards her swollen ankles.

'Ye-e-s?' She does not seem to like the look of this caller. Her social radar may be tuned to an otherworldly frequency, but even she can tell this creature in corduroys is not collecting contributions for the Jewish Old People's Welfare Board.

'I'm Goldie Rosenbloom's niece. Rainbow.'

The portcullis rises half a chink. 'Ye-e-es?'

'I met her in front of your house the other day, and she said she was visiting for the weekend . . .'

'Oh, right, of course, you're the one who drives a taxi.' Warmer now, but is that not a slightly contemptuous smile? 'I'm sorry, but you've missed her. She went home to Ilford last night.'

Rainbow hesitates for a minute. 'Ahmmm, ah, well, right. I just thought, since I was in the neighbourhood again, I'd stop by on the off-chance she might still be here . . .'

As she speaks, she tries to sneak a look over the woman's shoulder, as if surreptitiously checking that no Goldie lies bound and gagged in the hallway behind her. Two pairs of suspicious eyes contemplate Rainbow from knee height. The owner of one set kicks her.

'Yossi, stop that! Sorry, dear. You'll probably get her at home tonight, if you phone.' And shuts the door.

Rainbow presses her ear to the stained-glass panel, as if trying to determine where the retreating footsteps might be heading. Then she scuttles down the steps and sets off down the road.

The terrace ends a few doors down, separated from the next run of houses by a paved alleyway. Rainbow darts down this passage, and dives into a narrow strip of waste ground, a jungle of weeds between the rows of back gardens. With unexpected agility, she clambers over fences, scrabbles through under-growth at the rear of flowerbeds and vegetable patches long gone to seed, counting houses under her breath.

'Six!' she hisses, and crouches down in high grass, next to a half-collapsed shed. Bent double, below the sightline of the ground floor windows, she makes a hobbling run to a grey-brick outhouse projecting from the rear of the building, hoists herself up on to the boundary wall beside it. An old apple tree, thick-limbed, untended, and almost growing into the rear wall of the house, provides a foothold for her to clamber on to the flat roof of a back extension. Crawling on her belly, she makes her way to the first of two windows that open on to this platform, and inches herself up just enough to peer over the sill.

The window is open, just a crack, not enough to alleviate the thick cloud of cigarette smoke, but sufficient to carry the sounds of passionate disputation. Several men, bearded and in skullcaps, sit around a table, riffling through thick volumes, shouting in triumph when they find the page that proves their point: 'Ha!'

Then someone else drags down another book from a high and heavy-laden shelf, licks a finger, hunts, wait, wait, wait, and finds an equally authoritative contradiction. Half the room

79

bellows its assent, the other half sniffs and maligns the author's soundness, schooling and parentage.

Summoned up from graves now lost, the shrines where old grandmothers once left coins and petitions, dead sages are drafted in to adjudicate. The fight, it seems, concerns the sexuality of demons. The issue's an old one. Do these entities have sexual organs? Of what nature? Do they partake of a fixed gender, or can they shift between female and male? Can they have congress, either between themselves or with ordinary mortals? Do they reproduce? Is procreation between human and demon possible? If so, what species is the fruit of such a meeting?

Arguments first overheard by Alexander the Great are pursued in letters between Persia and Khazaria and Spain, mulled over in ships' steerage between the sickening lurches, sewn into hems along with diamonds for the crossing of unfriendly borders.

Every question is interpreted three ways; every answer has a qualification; complications are sniffed out, tasted, sucked and savoured. Angels dancing on pinheads is not the half of it: how many centuries of rabbinical footnotes can dance in a right-to-left line of Hebrew letters? Theoretical palaces are built in clouds, celestial and infernal hierarchies named and counted, words dissected for the secret numerical codes inside them, mathematics whirled round the head and shot off into space, to return to earth as prophecy.

I can't fathom what Rainbow makes of it all, but I'm enjoying the show.

Until a sudden, gut-wrenching realisation smacks me right in the chops. These aren't just any old common or garden Chasidim in that room: I can tell by the vocabulary, the textual references, body language and shapes of beards. These are Limnititzkers.

And the boss disputant of them all, the one with all the answers, the head honcho with the bushiest beard, the longest sidelocks and the shiniest skullcap, has features that are not altogether unfamiliar.

Screw it. They're unmistakable.

The old boy may be the irresistible Riva's father. He may be Aunt Goldie's personal guru. He may be wiser than Maimonides, and more famous than Mickey Mouse. But to me – Kokos – he's not such marvellous news. Certain powers (as well as profiles, eyebrows and smug expressions) run in families: few royal successions have survived as long, or as secretly, as the bloodlines of the great wonder-rabbis. And, twenty to one, if the Limnititzkers have made it through the horrors and perils of the past ten generations, then the thread that's holding them together is the DNA of my favourite old sparring partner, Shmuel ben Issachar.

And it would have to be the current Sage's precious daughter I've got Rainbow fixated on. That'll teach me. Because once such a spell as I have made is set in train, no code will break the program.

In moments of extreme duress, self-control flies up the chimney. This is one such moment. I can almost smell the suffocating sweetness of the sap in that damned Lithuanian tree. I let out an almighty howl. In fact, what with Rainbow's cold in the head, it comes out as an ear-splitting sneeze.

The scholars glance out the window, to find the source of this annoying interruption. Quicker on the draw than Rainbow (whose throat has done the business on my behalf), I shove her down out of sight, and rustle up a diversion. Two huge crows flap out of the apple tree and past the window, yattering and scolding, no doubt over some question of ancient avian theology.

The men shrug and turn back to their discussion. Nature only interests them as parable. Otherwise, London birds are nothing but menaces to hats and car bonnets; city sky nothing more than smoke and weather. It's what's on the other side of the clouds that counts.

Rainbow, struggling to suppress a sneezing fit, will be deflected no longer. She moves across the roof with a speed that is quite impressive for someone travelling on hands and knees and trying to be invisible, to the other window.

81

Here we find her. Riva, the shy dove of Friday night's encounter, sits cross-legged and barefoot on a bed. She leans forward, her eyes wide, hands tracing shapes in the air. On the floor, on stools and rugs and cushions, an audience of children sucks in her stories.

Once there was an old *babushka* who hadn't even a penny to buy herself a Sabbath candle . . . once there was a werewolf . . . once there was a girl who knew what the wind said to the trees . . . once there was a man so wicked he was sent back to live again as an ox . . . once there was an angel . . . once there were some demons who . . . once there was a bride too poor to find a dowry . . . once no twice no twenty times there was a wicked king who tried to turn his people's anger from himself on to the Jews . . . once there was a thief who repented . . . once there was a scholar alone in the *schul* at midnight when the candle blew out and disembodied voices began to pray . . .

Once there was a woman looking through a window at another.

Rainbow, it's turning chilly. The wind's come up. We're in for another downpour. Rainbow, the light is going. The children have been taken away for their baths and their suppers. Rainbow, any minute now she will come straight over to draw the curtains. There will be nothing but the width of a course of bricks between you, a slice of glass, a fold or two of flowered cloth. No distance greater than the thickness of a book of laws.

Rainbow descends, more carefully than she arrived, and slips back into the dark place where some former inhabitant once grew grapevines and lilies.

8

Stuffed up and feeling sorry for herself, Rainbow spends the morning in bed. She has mustered enough voice to rearrange her shifts, and take the day off. To amuse herself, she leafs through an illustrated history of the cinema, a birthday gift from Michael and Noah. To be honest, I don't think she absorbs a single line of print; her mind's still juddering between the vision of bliss in a certain window, and the vision of something unthinkable in a certain Turkish bath. No wonder she's having trouble concentrating. I, however, take the opportunity offered by the open book to broaden my knowledge of the film industry.

I note, with some interest, that Hollywood, from its earliest days, has been a stamping ground of ex-yeshivah boys from Belz, Pinsk, Odessa and Etceteragrad. Next time I'm back at the office, I must check the old project files – did any of those moguls, with their fruity shtetl accents and pushcart-pedlar tactics, have dybbuks of their own? It wouldn't be the first time some great, allegedly human invention was actually the work of a demon whispering into a subject's inner ear. And Movieland certainly reminds me of home-sweet-home: tricksy phantasmagorias with lights and mirrors, plus lots of battles over the budget.

The doorbell interrupts our studies (mine) and mental moonings (Rainbow's).

'Oh shit,' snarls Rainbow to herself.

We face a small but unstoppable invasion of aunts.

Not the full battalion – Molly being back in Bournemouth, Lila still under a time-shared sun, Goldie off on her own mysterious business, probably knitting skullcaps for needy Limnititzkers – but a war party consisting of Rebecca and Minna.

More than enough.

'Get back into bed,' orders Becky.

'How did you know I was in bed?' snuffles Rainbow through a wad of paper hankies.

'Not even you, my dear, walk about the house wearing nothing but a T-shirt that barely covers your you-know-what. And look at the state of you!'

'I told you so,' announces Minna to her sister. 'We're just in the nick of time. That cold will go into her chest if she's not careful.'

'How did you know . . .'

'Radar.'

Minna produces an apron from a Selfridges carrier bag. 'You get her back under the covers, Beck. The paracetamol and the vitamin C and the cough linctus are in that Boots bag. I'll put the soup on.'

'I can get myself back under the covers, thanks, and I don't want any chicken soup!' rasps Rainbow.

'Do me no ethnic stereotyping, please. And give us credit for a little originality,' says Becky. 'It's bean and barley. You used to love it at Grandma Rosenbloom's when you were a little girl.'

Minna looks around the flat with a scornful and scandalised eye. 'Judging from the way she keeps this establishment, I think she's still a little girl . . . I ask you, what normal sane adult woman puts up a poster like that one over their bed?'

Rainbow ignores the critique of her décor. 'What do you mean, radar?'

'Your Aunt Goldie told us how you bumped into each other in Stamford Hill. She also told us you weren't looking so good.'

'So you knew to come running round here with soup and cough linctus three days later?'

'You have always taken three days to develop one of your full-blown colds, darling. So it wasn't hard to guess.'

'Swallow two of these,' Rebecca orders. 'What were you doing walking down a street in Stamford Hill?'

'Since when do I have to account for my movements? I was going to Naomi's for dinner.'

'Is that Jilly Goldstein's daughter?' demands Minna from the kitchen. 'The one who never married that lovely boy from Edgware?'

'I thought you told me Naomi lived in Tottenham now.'

'She does. So what?'

'So why were you walking? What's wrong with the cab?'

'It was one of my off-nights. And I like to walk. And what business is it of yours?'

'You don't need to shout. It won't do your throat any good at all.'

'I'm not shouting,' Rainbow replies in a deep, throat-rasping croak. Most satisfactory. A classic symptom, to the initiated, of demonic possession. Which is not, however, how Rebecca reads it.

'Blast, I wish I'd remembered to bring some Vicks for your chest. I don't suppose you have anything so sensible in your medicine cupboard, do you?' Rebecca wanders off to the bathroom. 'I thought not!' she sings out, and soon reappears. 'My God, Rainbow, you have enough exotic massage oils in there to open up your own bordello. And what, may I ask, are you doing with something called Aphrodisiac Compound?'

'Saving it for a Chanukah present for you and Uncle Jack.'

'Don't get fresh with me, young lady.'

I manipulate Rainbow's next sneeze into a cyclone that blows half a dozen postcards off the mantelpiece, and causes the bedside lampshade to fall from its base and spin across the floor.

'If you bought yourself some decent lamps,' observes Minna, advancing on Rainbow's bedside with tray, bowl, spoon and purposeful expression, 'things like that wouldn't happen. You pay rubbish, you get rubbish. You buy good you get good.'

'It was a gift.'

'From whom?'

'Aunt Molly, as it happens.'

Minna sneaks a wink at her sister Becky. 'I should have known.'

'So I understand you met Goldie's pet fanatics,' remarks Rebecca. 'Five minutes with that bunch of bigots would be enough to give anyone a cold in the head.'

'What's Aunt Goldie doing with them?'

'If you took more of an interest in whether your family was alive or dead, you'd know these things,' Minna chides her. 'Finish your soup.'

'Oh, you know your Aunt Goldie,' Rebecca sighs. 'Even God's not quite kosher enough for her. So she's got herself hooked up with some little ultra-orthodox sect or other, run by this extremist rabbi she calls the Maggid of Manor House. Goldie thinks he's the Messiah on wheels.'

'Maybe she fancies him,' Rainbow offers.

Rebecca snorts, collapses across the foot of Rainbow's bed, and laughs until the tears come.

Minna purses her lips – 'Such a thing to say about your poor Aunt Goldie' – and reaches out an auntly hand, which starts as a mock-slap but winds up assessing the heat of Rainbow's face and forehead. 'I knew it. Burning up with fever.'

This also counts as a classical sign of demonic visitation. But Minna's too blinkered to perceive it.

'Well, I'm afraid I don't share my sister Goldie's sentiments,' Minna announces. 'As far as I'm concerned, they're a *shondeh* for the goyim.'

'A what?' (Shame on you, Rainbow. Ignorant of your ancestral mother tongue. If Gittel Number One walked into this room right now, you wouldn't have the vocabulary to offer her a glass of tea.)

'A Disgrace in the Eyes of the Gentiles.'

'Oh dear, oh dear, oh dear,' jeer Rainbow and I. 'Letting the side down. And if they didn't exist, would our white Anglo-Saxon brethren think the better of us?'

Becky jabs an admonitory finger. 'Don't you be so sarcastic, young lady. When the day comes in this country that a Jew, or a black, or any other minority can commit a crime without everybody else nudging and winking and saying What else did you expect from that lot?, then you come and talk to me about letting the side down.'

'Don't you think you're being a little hypersensitive, Aunt Becky?'

'You know nothing, sweetheart. Sometimes I think there's *gornisht mit gornisht* in that supposedly educated head of yours – nobody home. Anyway, I don't know what you have to be so smug about. You don't exactly possess a lifestyle certified kosher by the London Beth Din.'

'Thank goodness for that.'

Minna tsk-tsk-tsks.

Rainbow sticks her tongue out. (No one, herself included, seems to notice it's bright blue.)

'You do get off on being shocked, don't you, Auntie Min? Your cheeks have turned a fabulous shade of puce.'

Rainbow then grins, giggles, chuckles, guffaws, imitates the riotous woodpecker of vintage cartoons, fills the room with hiccuping laughter, shrieks and whinnies, mutates from hyena to horse and then winds up, before subsiding, with a few good wolfish howls.

'Period starting soon, dear?' asks Becky, solicitously.

Out of our heroine's unsuspecting mouth I hurl a belch of spectacular proportions, performed at operatic volume and lushly perfumed with unadulterated brimstone. Rainbow, mortified but not yet capable of speech, mimes an apology.

'Hah!' says Minna. 'That just proves you don't eat right.'

'I . . . eat . . . plenty,' Rainbow gasps in self-defence.

'Oh, no doubt about that, but all the wrong things. You and your oriental sweet-and-sour deep-fried *traif chazzerai* . . .'

Are we going to let the old bat get away with that? Of course not. I slip out for an instant, and set off her car alarm.

Down on the street, once my little cobbled-up crisis has got them there, Becky remembers one final bit of Rainbow business. She crosses the pavement again, puts her finger on the downstairs buzzer marked Rosenbloom and keeps it there, until Rainbow wrapped in her duvet, pulls up the window and leans out.

'What is it now?' Neither she nor her aunts seem to notice that her voice has somehow recovered. Not a croak mars its limpid tone, not a sniffle hinders her breathing.

'Before I forget, Aunt Goldie wants you to come and have tea with her next week.'

The old, original dybbuk-less Rainbow would have groaned at Goldie's invitation. Rustled up fifteen different polite and plausible excuses, and maybe even gone so far as a handwritten note to the poor old lady saying how terribly, terribly sorry she was, but driving schedules, *Outsider* editorial meetings, etcetera and so forth . . .

The new improved Kokos-driven version shouts back, 'Great. I'll see if I can juggle one of my driving shifts. Tell her I'll ring her soon.'

'Well, wonders never cease. Next thing I know you'll be telling me you're getting married and emigrating to Israel.'

'Pigs will have to fly first,' bellows Rainbow. 'On El-Al.'

'Crazy,' pronounces Minna, getting into the car. 'That girl is absolutely *meshuggeh*. Always was.'

As I've said before, this is a particularly tricky assignment. It is a long-held article of faith, among the sisters Rosenbloom, that their dear late brother's daughter is completely mad. And always has been. Makes me feel pretty redundant. What on earth is a dybbuk to do?

Just as well I'm not wedded to an orthodox approach.

A date is set for later in the week. Rainbow can hardly wait. Not because she longs for her aunt's company or famous marble cake. It's the prospect of gaining a foot in the door to Stamford Hill – nearer my goddess to thee.

And suddenly she's off and running on a campaign to rediscover her Jewish roots. Others might start with a refresher course in ancient history; Rosenbloom begins with a sandwich.

We start in a kosher salt-beef bar, in the ice-white heart of

London's diamond district. Through the plate-glass window, we look out upon a rialto of Chasidic gem-dealers: long black coats, a thicket of ear-locks and beards, whispered conversations, handshakes, small packets – no doubt containing Stars of India and other transmuted lumps of Palaeozoic coal – passed from one pocket to another.

As in Stamford Hill, it makes me feel quite skittish to see these remnants of my favourite client-group so close at hand. I am tempted to show off before such a potentially receptive audience by causing Rainbow to levitate above the pickle jars, fly out of the shop at hat-skimming height, and waft up into the yellow sky towards Clerkenwell with an entourage of starling outriders. But I restrain myself. I'm not that anxious to come to the notice of any passing Limnititzkers . . .

All right, all right, I admit. So I may have acted just a little rashly in the matter of Rainbow and the holy man's daughter. But you have to understand about demons. We are only supposed to have sex with our own kind (homo or hetero, depending on personal preference) but we really fancy humans. Indeed, some of the old occult scholars would tell you that our endless fascination with the mortal race comes down to nothing but unrequited passion.

What's done may not be undone. My hands are tied. Obsessions, especially those demonically induced, rapidly develop their own momentum. And, what with the ridiculous deadline they've slapped on me, I certainly don't have time to work out an alternative scenario.

Neither does Rainbow. She makes a beeline for the second-hand bookshops in the courts and alleyways off the Charing Cross Road. Ignores her customary fare of film books, feminist thrillers, or the memoirs of bohemian ladies with their hands up each other's blue stockings.

Instead, it's the J-word. Jewish history, folklore, customs, theology. Sociologists on Jewish identity; historians on the Diaspora; philosophers on the Holocaust; feminists on Jewish womanhood; revisionists debating Zionism; even a couple of mystically inclined WASP wannabees romancing the Kabbalah.

Her purchases would astonish her aunts, and probably alarm her friends. Religion – even when God wears a feminine suffix and a flounced Bronze Age Minoan skirt – has not previously been high on Rainbow's list of ways to spend a rainy lifetime.

You can't kid me, *chiquita*, I know what you're doing: trying to bluff your way into the heart of that ultra-orthodox sweetie from Stamford Hill. Drop the odd impressive remark – 'As Martin Buber says . . .', 'As I was reading, just the other day, in the Shulchan Aruch . . .' – Is that it?

Forget it, baby. The joke's on you. This is one reading list you'll never catch up on. If you spent a thousand years doing nothing but turning pages, you'd hardly make it past Chapter 1. (Maybe that's why all those teenaged yeshivah scholars look so pale and harried.)

She takes her purchases home, and reads far into the night. I notice, with mild amusement, that she lingers for some time over an encyclopaedia of Jewish folklore, giving special attention to the entry D for Dybbuk. The authors appear to have at least half their facts right: I've seen worse.

Apart from this little excursion, I'm bored silly – all that stuff's old hat to me. But we must see Rainbow's crash course as a touching gesture. Romance still lives. Greater love hath no woman, in the search for a suitably kosher chat-up line.

I hope Rainbow appreciates the sacrifice I'm making on her behalf: if it weren't for the need to stoke her flames of passion, we could both be out at the pictures, watching *Desert Hearts* or *Thelma and Louise*.

'Get off that backside, Rosenbloom,' says our heroine to her mirror-image at tooth-brushing time, 'and go out and earn some money.'

Apparitions, disembodied voices and assorted uncanninesses may make her nervous, but it's the spectre of the bank manager that really brings out the cold sweat on her brow. So this morning we're back on the road once more.

In a manner of speaking. For if there is one thing worse, for a taxi-driver, than being stuck in a two-mile jam inside the Blackwall Tunnel, it is being stuck there without a fare ticking cosily away on the meter. How we got here in the first place is irrelevant, but now that we've arrived I decide to take advantage of the situation.

Trapped along with Rainbow in the next-door lane is a Volvo packed with black-hatted Chasidim. This, of course, starts Rainbow's camera running for a brand new Riva movie:

Scene: Night. Int. Rainbow's flat, immaculately and unprecedentedly tidy, and stuffed to the gunwales with fresh flowers and ice-buckets full of champagne. Rainbow, thinner and six inches taller, with a perfect haircut and a soft silk shirt, poised elegantly at ease on a sofa, reading something mystical and profound. On the stereo, a honey-voiced alto sings lush, nineteenth-century Hungarian melodies that blend the wildness of the Romany with the passionate yearning of the Jew.

Suddenly, an urgent pounding on the door (no mundane electronic buzzers to break the spell), which opens to reveal a wild-eyed, weeping, windswept Riva, who flings herself at Rainbow's buttersoft-leather-booted feet and begs for shelter. That single, fleeting encounter between them has cast the scales from her eyes, and seared the image of Another Way into her brain, and now she wishes to be rescued forever from the blinkers of fundamentalism and the shackles of heterosexuality, and only the brave and beautiful Rainbow will be strong enough to protect her from those who wish to enslave her once again.

Rainbow lifts the maiden into her arms as if she is lighter than a rose petal, bends to press her own hungry mouth against the parted peach-blossom lips of the panting Riva, then suddenly hears a voice roaring through a megaphone:

'Cut!!!!'

The rose petals and peach blossoms whirl away into the wind, along with the room, the soft lighting, silk shirt, gypsy music and all . . .

'All right, luvvie, thanks a lot. Don't call us, we'll call you

. . . and better start your engine up, because the car ahead is about to move forward by about six feet, and if you don't close the gap sharpish there will be an almighty cacophony of angry horn-blowers behind you!'

She jumps as high as is feasible with her seat-belt to restrain her, then looks into her rear-view mirror.

'Don't be silly. There's nobody there. Skip the theatrical gestures. You know you can't see me.'

'I don't know who you are, or where you are. But get your voice out of my head, or – '

'Or what will you do? Try out your self-defence techniques? (you really should have kept up with those classes). Call the police? Wait till it's time to get the taxi serviced, and ask them to excise the ghost from your machine?'

She's a crafty one. Already she's working up some evasion tactics. Fills her head with noise:

the names of Shakespeare's plays

the multiplication tables

the quickest routes through rush-hour London

the stations on the Piccadilly line

the film reviewers on every British newspaper and magazine

the titles of every film she has seen in the past year with the names of its producers, director, and leading actors

the PIN number for her cash-card

the names of all her past lovers and the current or previous partners of everyone she knows

her favourite Chinese restaurants and their house specialities

the names of stage and screen stars who are openly lesbian or gay

names of ditto who have been forcibly dragged from the closet

lyrics to songs from way back when: By yon bonnie banks and by yon bonnie braes, the Old Dope Peddler with his powdered happiness, the king sat in Dunfermline toun a-drinkin' the bluid red wine saying where shal I find a guid Scotch sailor to sail this ship o' mine?, the answer my friends is blowing in the wind, the answer is blowin' in the wind, for any woman can be a lezzzz-bi-an when the saints, oh when the saints, oh when the saints go marching in like a bird on the wing, o-o-over the sea toooo Skyeeeee . . .

'Great stuff, Rainbow. Pity you can't carry a tune. I notice you didn't bother with those old Pesach favourites, "Dayenu" and "Chad-gad-ya". Never mind, they wouldn't have been any use either. I'm still here.'

Way, way down, underneath all that brave defensive barrage, I hear another soundtrack: 'I want to go home, I want my mother, I want to go home . . .'

'OK, OK. Just calm down. This bit isn't any easier for me than it is for you. Don't fight it. It'll be all right in the end, really it will, just stay with me . . .'

But then her fear is swept away by a scalding white tsunami of rage. 'How dare you!! This is a fucking mental rape!'

Now I'm the angry one. 'It is not. Damn it, no way is it anything remotely like that! Not, not, not, not, not!'

She's hit a vulnerable spot. Lil and I have had several heated and completely unresolved arguments about this very issue over the last thousand years or so in the staff canteen. But I pull myself up. This is no time to indulge in tantrums. The moment for introductions has arrived.

Once the initial gut reactions – the old fight-or-flight instincts, hard to quash – are over, she begins to stand her ground. But, to be honest, this comes as no surprise.

For centuries, the women of Rainbow's tribe have engaged in one-way conversations with their unseen God, sometimes pleading and praying, more often arguing to prove a point.

So why should it be so hard to do the same thing with a demon? Particularly for a celluloid-struck Gittelspawn at the fag-end of this bizarre and disrespectful century, nurtured on *The Wizard of Oz*, drugs/sex/rock'n' roll, and accustomed to boldly going where no man has gone before. And who, after all, has already been primed by my delicate little tricks and interventions.

She tries to take control. Offence the best defence, and so forth. 'Don't you bandy words with me, you faceless coward. What the hell are you playing at? It's an invasion, a violation, and a bloody power trip!'

Oooh, the language. 'Why don't you shut up for a minute and let me explain? Besides, you're making quite a spectable of yourself. Waving your arms about. Shaking your fist. Jabbing your finger at the empty air. People have noticed. You're providing the cabaret for half the traffic jam. Just look at them staring.'

Rainbow glances out the window. The occupants of surrounding cars quickly avert their gazes, busy themselves with pocket calculators, or pick their noses.

'Oh shit.' She gulps a deep breath of heavily polluted tunnel air, and falls silent.

Aha, I knew it. Underneath all the bluster and that bellicose haircut, she's just a well-brought-up, nice Jewish girl. Trained not to make a fuss, not to be conspicuous, so the goyim don't get the wrong idea. Stick your head above the parapet and sooner or later a Cossack will gallop by and lop it off.

'Come on, Rainbow, you've done a bit of yoga, haven't you? How about some of those breathing exercises to calm you down.'

'What?' she shrieks, and the voice keeps rising. Thank goodness for shatterproof windscreens. 'Whoever you are, you've colonised my mind, from Goddess knows where, some kind of extraterrestrial Outside Broadcast unit, you've scared the shit out of me and made me think I've fallen completely over the edge, and now you want me to calm down with a few breathing exercises?'

'That's better. At least you're not roaring any more. But if you insist on pursuing this argument, you might like to wait until we find someplace a little more discreet.'

'There's nothing to argue about . . . I want you to piss off out of here, you spirit of Christmas past, or spot of undigested beancurd, or whatever you think you are.'

'I'm Kokos . . .'

'And what's a kokos?'

'It's my name. More precisely, one of my names. And only moderately dangerous. I have a few others that, if you so much as whispered their syllables aloud, could make the sky split open.'

'Look, Cocoa, or whatever you call yourself, I want you out of my head. There's no room. I've already got the voices of my late parents, the Rosenbloom aunts, a couple of ex-lovers, my best friend Naomi, my bank manager, Radio Control, my old history teacher, and Rabbi Wasserstein.'

'You have a rabbi in here?' I have a good sniff and a scan. 'No, you don't.'

'Well, who else is it I hear chortling, "Aha! *Meshummad! Heretic!* That'll teach you," whenever disaster strikes?'

'Nothing to worry about. He's just an old voiceprint. Like a fading photograph with sound effects. So are the rest of them.'

'That's what you say.'

'Believe me, I would know if it were any different. Anyway, you can't scare me with your family album, or Rabbi Whatsis-name. There's all the room I need in here. I'm your dybbuk. You may think you're as modern as they come, with your liberal education and your posters of dead lesbian poets and even deader Minoan goddesses on the walls . . . But you do know what a dybbuk is, don't you? Good. That's a start. I'm glad you aren't entirely ignorant of your own cultural heritage. Because I like to be appreciated. Accepted for what I am. And you might as well get used to the fact. I'm here to stay.'

I give her a little while to assimilate this. The traffic jam begins to clear, and we emerge from the tunnel into a dull, wet excuse for daylight. Rain buckets down; she turns on the windscreen wipers and we both find their rhythm soothing.

Several soaked and desperate-looking people hail her, but she ignores them all, and switches off her FOR HIRE light.

95

'Hey, can you afford to do that? You took all yesterday off work, not to mention the weekend.'

'Great. A nagging dybbuk. You've been taking lessons from my aunts. That's all I need.'

'I'm only looking out for your best interests, *bubbeleh*.'

'Yeah, yeah. That's what you all say.'

'All who?'

'All you devils.'

'Are you telling me – sob – I'm not your . . . first?'

She snarls. 'Come on, pal, I've read, seen, heard and hummed along with every version of the Faustus legend; I've watched every piece of demonic celluloid from *The Devil with Hitler* to *Rosemary's Baby Meets Damien Seven at the Senior Prom*. Whatever else you lot are, nice isn't in it . . .'

'Well, you'll just have to get rid of some of your preconceptions, won't you?'

'What I really ought to do is get rid of you.'

'That's not so easy. And, besides, you told Naomi just the other day that you didn't feel entirely negative about my . . . attentions.'

'I didn't say I was exactly thrilled about them either.'

'Well, lighten up. I'm not going to kill you, or force you to drive off a cliff, or carry you off to some lesbian version of Hell full of out-of-town shopping malls and executive starter homes complete with husband and three-piece suite. A dybbuk isn't always bad news. You might even find it fun. Your great-great-etcetera-grandmother certainly did.'

'My what?'

'Oh yes, my dear one, I do have a tale to tell you. I am what you might in a manner of speaking call a little legacy, handed down to you by ancestors long forgotten.'

'Why me?'

So I tell her, in a highly abridged and edited 16-millimetre version, the tragic tale of Gittel and Anya the Apostate, that Slavo-Semitic opera of love, lost hopes, thwarted passion and botched revenge. Rainbow listens spellbound, slightly shocked to realise that her great-great-etcetera-grandma got up to some of the same tricks that she does.

Then she explodes, in a fit of pique. 'Very nice!' she bellows. 'Some long-dead trendy bisexual does a bit of toying with a dyke's affections, and I – me of all people, who has strong views about such things – gets landed with taking the rap for the cold-hearted little swinger, just because she happens to be my nine-zillionth-generation ancestor! What humiliation! Hardly fair, is it?'

'Life, my dear Rainbow, as I'm sure your elders have mentioned, rarely is. Anyway, let us contemplate an amusing Catch 22. If your great-great-etcetera-grandma Gittel hadn't gone off and Done It With a Man, you, in all your quirks and quiddities, would simply not exist at all. So perhaps you can find it in your heart to forgive her. Try to see the poor thing as a kind of martyr – not only to compulsory heterosexuality, but to the ultimate genesis of your own sweet self.'

Rainbow ponders this. 'Do all old Jewish curses have such a long shelf-life?' she asks. 'Is London full of dybbuks running around avenging ancient snits?'

'I don't think so. Ours is – well, a special case.'

'Why?'

'Suppose we save the rest for a rainy day.'

'It's raining now,' observes my subject, pointing to the windscreen wipers working to little effect as the rain pours down. 'How did Gittel – '

'No, my dear,' I tease her. 'To Be Continued. Always leave 'em wanting more. And if that isn't enough to keep you interested, I also have a little proposition to make. Regarding your new acquaintance between Seven Sisters and Manor House.'

I knew that would make her sit up and take notice. She pulls abruptly into the nearest empty parking space.

Heartbeat, respiration rate, body temperature and biorhythms are all giving me an eminently satisfactory read-out. I think we are about to do a deal.

'Forget it,' she glooms. 'I have a bad habit of lusting after lost causes.'

'What makes you think she's a lost cause?'

'Oh, come on . . . Do me a favour.'

'Rainbow, do you know how those people live? The sexes hardly talk to each other . . . She's more like a classic right-on radical separatist than you'll ever be.'

'Get lost . . . She's black-belt Jewish God Squad. Do you know what that gang calls people like me? Abominations, that's what.'

'Now you're the one making bigoted assumptions. What makes you think they're all 100 per cent heterosexual? After all, what about Gittel Number One and Anya?'

'And look how they ended up.'

'That was then. There they were in the middle of nowhere, and not a positive role model, a lesbian detective thriller or a labyris earring to call their own. But now, if you consider the contemporary situation in straightforward statistical terms, one in every ten, or whatever it is, then, if you have twenty fundamentalists in a room together, on average two of them will – '

'Well, nobody's letting me into that room to find out.' She taps an irritable little tattoo on her steering wheel.

'This could easily be arranged . . .'

Tapping stops.

'Oh yeah?'

'Yeah.'

'What do you want to bet you can't set it up?'

'Gambling with the Unknown, are we? I hear there's a great scene in Bergman's *The Seventh Seal* where Max von Sydow plays chess with Death . . .'

'If you say you want me to wager my soul, I'm driving straight to the nearest exorcist.'

'We don't deal in souls. Bang goes another one of your silly preconceptions. And as to exorcists . . . Piffle.'

She doesn't rise to this. She's pondering my offer.

'I don't need you to get me into that house, you know. My Aunt Goldie's a friend of the family.'

'I know, I know. But it's not just the house you want into, is it, now?'

You should see the train of thought now leaving from Platform One. I wave Rainbow off as it heads for her own particular Garden of Delights. And when she finally gets off, pink in the cheeks and probably elsewhere, our taxi windows have steamed up completely.

'All right, so what sort of deal did you have in mind?'

'You take me to as many movies as I want to see, I feed you all the right lines to attract the attention of a certain person.'

She considers this.

'It's too easy. There's a catch somewhere.'

'No catch. A straight business arrangement. You're a film critic, right? So you'll be doing your job, which is seeing films, and I'll be doing mine.'

'But what exactly is yours?'

'To be where I am, and do what I'm doing.'

'Which is . . . ?'

'To drive you mad.'

'Mad? Piss off.'

The flippancy's a pretence; inside she's quaking.

'Look, calm down. It's all right . . .'

What has become of me? If Nick or Lil could hear me now, all soft and soothing, they'd think that I was the one possessed. As if some disembodied human had taken up residency inside my demon brain.

'It does not mean,' I tell her, 'that you will wind up with electrodes wired into your head, or awash in a slurry of supposedly curative chemicals. Let me hasten to reassure you. You don't need us for that work any more. When our rulebooks were written, we had not quite realised how totally insane your species could be in carrying out what it claimed was business as usual. Maybe the spirit was always willing, but your technology was weak. Nowadays you lot are far more hellish than we are.

So my visit to you, in fulfilment of a veritable period piece of a curse, is something in the manner of a final fling.'

'What's that supposed to mean?'

'What do you want, a seminar in late-medieval Slavo-Semitic semantics? It means I get to play the game any way I want to. As long as I make you do a reasonable quota of strange and crazy things.'

'For that, my aunts would tell you, I don't need help from a dybbuk.'

'And who would argue with the verdict of five Jewish matrons, women of valour, their price above rubies? Too bad the evidence of the second sex doesn't count for anything among the patriarchal fuddy-duddies who run the cosmic courts. So I'll just have to turn you even more peculiar than you are.'

Mission accomplished. The panicky earthquake in her gut has subsided, but she's still suspicious.

'Hmmf. I've met your kind before. All talk and no action.'

'Let's go for a walk on the weird side. Look . . .'

The opaque mist coating the taxi windows instantly evaporates.

'What the f—?'

Even big-mouthed Rosenbloom is speechless. When she parked the taxi we were somewhere down by the river, in Limehouse. Now, with no help from her and nothing on the meter, we're a few miles to the north, parked outside a kosher bakery in Stamford Hill.

'I'll bet good old Aunt Goldie can't do that,' I jeer.

I knew she'd be impressed.

I send her inside for half a dozen bagels and some onion platzels. We're both starving.

As she heads in, who should come out but the fascinating Riva, accompanied by another young woman. Engaged in some mild, mundane squabble over a shopping list, our dream girl brushes against – but doesn't notice – Rainbow, who stands in the open doorway and stares after the pair until they vanish round a corner.

I then allow Rainbow to get back to work. We have to make a living. After all, even *Outsider*'s ace reviewer doesn't get into every film in London free. And, in any case, it's hardly in my interest to let her starve to death.

After her shift ends, I steer her towards the cinema. She does not resist. (Sometimes I think this lady likes movies better than sex.) Her choice of what to see is governed, I admit, by my own wish to complete my education and pursue my travels in this brave new world of movieland. Tonight's celluloid treat is a *grandes dames* revival, a triple bill of Garbo's *Queen Christina*, Dietrich's *Blue Angel*, and Katharine Hepburn in *Adam's Rib*. And maybe, instead of letting her go home to sleep, I'll make her take me to a late-night screening of that old lezzie boarding-school classic, *Mädchen in Uniform*.

I don't let her sleep more than the barest minimum. There are so many films to catch up on: new releases, classic revivals, every treat that this city of cinemas has to offer. What we cannot see on a proper giant screen, I demand to be shown on hired video.

But just as things seem nicely up and running, I am stymied by a second urgent summons back to base. If I wanted to be paranoid, I'd say it was industrial sabotage.

'I won't be away for long,' I whisper into Rainbow's whirling mind. 'Don't see any good pictures without me . . . And don't try any tricks. Because I'll know.'

9

'As usual, there's some good news and some bad news,' says Nick. I'm sitting in his office, furious. And a little nervous that I am about to be ticked off for my unorthodox and amiable occupation of the Rosenbloom.

'How about a new opener, for once, Nick?'

'That's the situation, petunia. Find me a more accurate analysis, and I'm yours.'

'Spill it.'

'The good news is that it is finally your turn to go to the Fair. The bad news is that your pass is for today and Friday, and Lil won't allow you to make up the lost time in the field. The deadline stays the same, kid. Sorry.'

Sod's law. I've been waiting for this chance since the days of the Witch of Endor. This particular event only happens once every 400 years, and up until now it's always been someone else's turn.

'I'm not stupid, Nick. It's a bribe. They're trying to buy me off in hopes I'll bow to their idiotic new arrangements without a bleat.'

'To be honest, Koke,' he says, leaning forward confidentially and letting out a few vapour jets from behind his ears, 'I think you overestimate your potential as a thorn in the corporate side.

'Lil says that if you don't want the ticket, she'll pass it on to someone else in the division. But she can't promise if or when your turn will come up again.'

Of course not. Everyone in the business wants to be seen to be there, but the places are limited. If you've been self-employed since five minutes after Lucifer's fall, and can fork out the massive outlay required, you might just find a way to bribe yourself on to the single-ticket waiting list; if you belong to a small, minor-league organisation, your company will probably club together with several others to rent a cheap and jerry-built booth in one of the minor outbuildings, and argue with its partners over a tiny allocation of entry passes, whose holders will be consigned to overpriced lodgings in distant and inconvenient suburbs.

If, however, you are Mephistco, you will do the Fair in style. You will send all your senior managers for the entire week of the event, and dole out shorter visits to deserving underlings, either those with long service records or those who might be able to learn something to the company's advantage. You will erect a handsome stand, tastefully decorated, and subdivided to accommodate both intimate meetings and larger entertainments. Attractive junior members of the delegation will be on duty daily, to pour champagne for visitors and serve canapés.

The most serious business, though, will not take place at your stand, despite its prestigious location in the most important of the fair's nine airport-sized exhibition halls. The most significant deals will be done, the most important hands shaken, and the most vulnerable backs stabbed, in your luxurious corporate suite in one of the tower-block hotels adjoining the fairground. A large balcony will give you a panoramic view not only of the exhibition centre, with its pavilions, marquees and satellites linked by walkways, but of the city beyond it, under a permanently crimson-clouded sky.

Normally, I'd like nothing better than this little visit to the big time. But right now I'm loath to leave Rainbow even for a minute. Still, I'm no fool; a chance like this doesn't come along every day, so I can hardly pass it up. I nip down to Engineering and borrow a remote (must keep tabs on things in London), then set off for the circus.

*

I've been at trade shows before, but this is the big one. Even I'm feeling overwhelmed. Thousands of spirits, demons, affrits, djinni, ghouls, familiars, kings of the winds and gates, princes of the stars, ancestors, shetani, rakhashas, angels of come-uppance, the lot, all milling about, sniffing the trends, eyeing up each other, watching the new-product demonstrations, gathering free samples. We all suffer from information overload. And the crowd noise is like the day the dinosaurs died; on top of the din, amplified announcements in the nine principal languages of the otherworld page the missing, declare the starting times of special events, invite attendance at lectures and reveal the winners of prize draws and promotional lotteries.

Inevitably, you run into old friends. I spend part of the afternoon in the refreshment tent, enjoying a few reminiscences with some mates I haven't seen since Moses's big match against Pharaoh's magicians. I am stopped mid-anecdote by an imperious tap on my shoulder. It's Lil, power-dressed to knock your socks off, with all eyes blazing.

'Kokos! Didn't you hear them paging? We've been looking for you everywhere for the past hour! You'd better hustle back to the stand, pronto! There's a crisis.'

My companions, subtly signalling commiserations, melt away. They wouldn't want their own bosses catching them, with gossip on tongue and glass in hand, during company time.

Lil means what she says. There's a crisis indeed. And it's got my name written all over it, in shiny gold letters.

On the Mephistco stand – created, at staggering expense, by this year's hottest design firm – the fixtures and fittings are swaying and rattling. The leaves of the giant rubber plants bounce up and down. Behind the elegant partitions, leading to our private conference rooms, something roars.

A hapless junior colleague, posted on the reception desk, tries simultaneously to flash a winsome welcome at browsing passers-by, and to pretend that nothing odd is happening behind her.

'Go in and say we've found her, dear,' orders Lil.

From behind the scenes, a scalding eruption sends the poor

receptionist scuttling out again. Something follows close behind him, and rushes at me. A furious face jams itself up against mine. Talons clutch my throat.

'Cheat!' it bellows.

I am nearly choked, and temporarily deafened. Nervous colleagues form a living barricade between us and potential onlookers. This is not the brand of publicity Mephistco courts.

Still clasped together, my attacker and I are frogmarched behind the scenes, into one of the little meeting-rooms. Nobody seems to think it necessary to separate us while this manoeuvre takes place. So I have to prise off the foe unassisted, which, believe me, takes some doing.

Meanwhile, Lil takes on a sort of coaching role, hissing admonitions from her seven sets of lips. 'This is your ball game now, Kokos. It's down to you. And I could think of better places, public imagewise, to negotiate with a dissatisfied customer.'

She turns to the visitor, who has now subsided on to a settee. 'All right, now?' she purrs. 'I'm sure Kokos will be very glad to clear things up with you. So we'll leave you both to it.' And takes her troops away, to distract any curious onlookers with free caviare canapés and an armful of promotional leaflets.

Now that she's off me, I can manage a better look. It's Anya the Apostate, irate and undead. I thought she might turn up.

From time to time, the ranks of dybbukry are augmented by new recruits from the mortal world – the spirits of those who died dissatisfied. (A grudge is the one thing that you can take with you.) I blush to admit it, but those of us who were born into the trade tend to disdain these crossovers as an inferior breed. For a start, they're too single-minded to do the job properly.

Anyway, now that I know what I'm dealing with, we can get down to business. I try a bit of banter. 'Long time no see.'

She's not amused. Demands to know what's happened to our contract on the Gittel job.

I tell her I'm hard at it. Perhaps she hasn't heard about the little delay in the proceedings, caused by the contretemps with ben Issachar, and the stint in the tree.

She knows all about it. (Who doesn't? It looks like I'll never live that fiasco down.)

Apparently, that's not the problem.

She's been monitoring my progress, since I've taken up the job again, and she is far from pleased. I am giving Gittel-plus-nine much too easy a time. All this mateyness not what she asked for. She wants to see some good old-fashioned special effects – wailings, writhings, ghastly visions and foamings at the mouth. She wants torture and unspeakabilities. In other words, the whole B-movie scenario.

'Isn't that a little dated?' I chide her. 'The profession's moved on.' (I hear myself say this and cringe. I sound just like Lil.)

Anya dismisses this notion with a well-aimed expectoration. I wipe it out of my eye.

These humano-demonoids are all alike. It's no accident that you won't find many of them working at Mephistco, despite our much vaunted equal opportunities policy. I know I shouldn't say so, but they're obsessive, reactionary and excruciatingly provincial. Stuck in a late-medieval rut.

She sits there, nearly crushing the spindly, modish bench some twee designer has deemed appropriate for business chit-chat. Implacable, with arms folded, and a mulish pout. Admittedly, 200 years of wandering the earth in search of vengeance does little for anyone's hairstyle or personal charm, but what on earth did that first Gittel see in her? All right, it was just a phase the girl was going through, a season of adolescent fumbling, but even so . . .

She says she doesn't like my softly-softly approach.

I say back that she doesn't understand it. How can she, when she doesn't have a clue what we're dealing with here? I try to explain that Rainbow Rosenbloom has almost nothing but a few genes in common with Anya's faithless Gittel. There's a lot of blood and water under the bridge since her day. The world has changed. Jews have changed. Women have changed. Sex has changed.

106

'Oh yeah?'

She wants to argue. This retired chicken strangler wants to quarrel with me – me, the great Kokos – over methodology. Wants me to – as she so delicately puts it – get off my behind and scare the loathsome Gittelspawn to death.

'I have to tell you, you don't know our present subject very well, if you think all the Gothic fripperies are going to impress her. This is a lady who giggled her way through *Nightmare on Elm Street*.'

'Nightmare on what?'

'Never mind. Look, it's early days yet. I've only been back on the case, in cosmic terms, about two-and-a-half minutes. So have a little patience. Trust me.'

'You? Trust you? Hoo-ha!'

She wants me off the case. Had been appalled to discover, through the industry grapevine, that I'd been allowed to continue with the assignment after taking such a beating from ben Issachar.

I can't bring myself to tell her that if she'd stayed dead her views might have carried more weight. A contract is a contract; a client's a client. But, as an unattached freelance (I can't think how she even scraped together the entry fee for this Fair), her opinion counts for very little with the company. We own this project now, not her, and whatever the history of the deal, we'll run it our way.

Using all the tact I can muster, I try to explain this. I think she's on the point of kicking up another fuss, when one of the Hospitality team slips in with cakes and glasses of lemon tea. Perfect timing.

She obviously doesn't get a lot to eat. You can tell by the way she falls upon these offerings. Poor old thing. I'll bet she hasn't had a decent meal since her own funeral.

But my little spasm of compassion doesn't last long. With her mouth full of blueberry muffin, she issues a warning.

'I've got my eye on you, Kokos. Now, you get back out there and give it to her but good. Or I'll come and finish the job myself.'

She scoops up the rest of the cakes, shoves them into some recess within her tatters, rushes out of the cubicle and disappears into the crowd.

I keep silent. At least she's off my back. Empty threats don't worry me. She's a second-rater, a mere amateur. But I could have done without this messy little scene in front of my fellow operatives, Lil, and some big guns from other departments.

The one thing I am not going to do is look remotely fazed or ruffled. Affecting a casual air, I linger at the reception desk, scanning the schedule of special events.

'Hmmm,' I muse aloud, 'should I go to the lecture on Binding Spells and How to Break Them, or try the Apparition Graphics Workshop in Hall Number One?'

'I really wouldn't know,' says the pert young thing behind the desk. 'Not my field. I'm from Central Admin, myself. But have you heard about the metamorphosis demonstration out on the main plaza? It's supposed to be brilliant. Everybody's talking about it. I'm going over when my shift ends, in about ten minutes. Want to come along?'

What cheek. I outrank the stripling by at least eighteen degrees.

'No thanks, dear. I know the group that's doing it. Seen them dozens of times before. But if you haven't, don't miss it. They're the best in the business. They'll show you a trick or two you never thought of.'

As I drift off into the aisle, I see Lil gliding back towards our stand, escorting a pair of avenging angels. They look camp as a row of tents, in their traditional uniform of gold lamé, but that's what they wear: nobody ever said their boss was high on fashion sense. For their benefit, Lil is doing the old PR dance, and giving it plenty, with an animated chat about Mephistco's new multi-dimensional surveillance technology.

I nod discreetly as I pass her, expecting no response. But a moment later I feel the prickle of seven steely glances boring into the nape of my neck. I smell trouble.

*

After several hours at the Fair I feel as if I have overdosed on new technology, professional seminars, leaflets and free samples. All I want to do now is stagger back to the hotel, steep in a hot bath filled with spices and unguents, order a snack from room service, and key in my remote to check up on Rainbow.

But, as Ms Topaz has reminded all fair-goers in her predeparture interdepartmental memo, this is not a frivolous junket. We have work to do. All staff are expected to help entertain key clients, socialise constructively with suppliers and trading partners, and carry out any on-the-spot research projects deemed necessary by our department heads. (Well, she may call it research; I call it industrial espionage.)

The day at the Fairground is only the beginning. Now, with half an hour's grace to freshen up, it's all hands on deck at the hotel, in Mephistco's corporate hospitality suite. A booming hearty from the higher reaches of Personnel fills our glasses and remembers nearly everyone's name.

I scan the room – colleagues, floral arrangements, sofas, inoffensive paintings of pastoral scenes, and a bravura display of bottles on the cocktail trolley. Plus the city spread out below us, beyond the wall of windows. No sign of Lil anywhere. Presumably her absence is itself a status display: you have to be really important to skip this little get-together.

Someone from Central Admin, with a sharkish smile, hands out the evening's assignments. Middle-ranking staff from Accounts go off to sample the city's famously steamy nightclubs in the company of a bevy of angelic recorders. Engineering seniors will be conveyed, by limousine, to a country mansion, where a major chemicals supplier has laid on fireworks and a champagne supper for favoured customers.

We field operatives are given a looser brief. As creative types, we're notoriously unpredictable, and thus liable to put our foot in it in front of touchy clients. So we are encouraged, instead, to go out on the town with our peers from other Mephistco departments, for the betterment of internal relations back at base. I groan inwardly at the prospect of a night playing

Happy Families with a bunch of desk-jockeys and number-crunchers. But, suddenly, the cavalry rides in.

'Now, Kokos,' says the pin-stripped hammerhead, 'as for you. There's a dinner meeting at eight in Suite 1607, and Lil particularly wants you to attend.'

No rest for the wicked. But if I'm going to let myself be bored to death, at least I can do it right here in the comfort of the hotel.

The door of Suite 1607 stands ajar. I am – deliberately – ten minutes late, both for the sake of a dramatic entrance and to show them that frankly, my dears, I don't give a damn. But within, all is silent. No susurrus of pre-dinner chat or rumble of businesspersons interacting. Did I get the room number right?

Of course I did. There's a table all set up and waiting for the dinner meeting. The agenda now becomes clear: champagne in an ice-bucket, a pair of crystal glasses, a platter bearing two cold lobsters, a little still life of perfect fruits in a silver bowl. Lil's out on her balcony, facing into the room, with the city lights for a backdrop. I'm pleased to see that she's reverted to something close to her original appearance for the evening, though the casual style now carries designer labels.

'What about your other six heads?' I ask. 'Did you give them the night off?'

'Oh, come on, you know they're just power-dressing. My badge of office. But we're off duty now, so let's relax.'

'If you say so.'

'Prickly as ever, Koke. How about some fizz?'

'I thought this was supposed to be a working dinner.'

'Oh, it's work, all right. Believe me.'

Well, if this is a meeting, she can bloody well chair it. I raise my glass and watch the bubbles dance.

'I see you still have your penchant for gaseous drinks,' I remark. 'But in the old Engineering days, it used to be beer.'

'And you still have a chip on your shoulder. Why? Surely you're too much of a maverick to be jealous of my latest promotion. Or have you suddenly discovered ambition?'

'Don't be stupid!' I snap, eyeing the lobsters, and observing a dozen fat oysters, discreetly arranged around them, which I hadn't noticed before. 'I'm an artist, remember. Not a climber of corporate totem poles. When do we eat?'

If I'm being buttered up, I want it lathered on lavishly. But at this point I can't decide if the evening's cabaret will consist of, 'Deep down, I'm just the same old Lil you knew before, so how about it?' or 'I'm a star now, baby, and I can make or break you, so let's do it my way.'

Lil should know me better after all these years.

Nevertheless, I eat more than my fair share of oysters, and filch one of her lobster claws after I've eaten my own. Then I let her warble on for a while about the trials of high office, and feign interest in titbits of gossip from the upper echelons.

Room service comes and goes, fresh champagne supplies arrive and the broken meats of our supper disappear. We lean over the balcony, marvelling over the way this industrial city, drab and dour by day, transforms itself at night.

'Listen to me, Kokos,' she says, almost pleadingly. 'I have a piece of advice for you. With your present bolshy attitude, you're riding for a fall. I'd hate to see your career cut short. If you're on the team, you have to change with it.'

'So it seems. The future lies before us. All production quotas and standardised spook pools. Flowcharts. Cost-effectiveness. Qualitative and quantitative research. More gobbledegook than a carnival conjuror. I can see the time coming when no one will be allowed to haunt a house without an MBA.'

She has the grace to crack a smile.

'I have access to a hefty training budget. I could send you anywhere you like to study for one.'

'And what course would you recommend, Madam? Postgraduate Diploma in Arse-Kissing? Looks like that's the one you did.'

She flings the dregs of her champagne over the balcony railing. I hope some lucky starling catches it before it evaporates. 'Blast you, Kokos, you really do know how to break a spell!'

'I make 'em and break 'em, pal. That's one of the things I was trained for. And, unlike some I could mention, I've stuck to my trade.'

She's really riled now. I hope she doesn't throw the empty glass out into the void to follow its contents; pity the hapless passer-by under that little bolt from the blue! And they'd find the guilty party: a giveaway print of designer lipstick mars the rim.

I drift back indoors, in case she decides to go all the way and tip me over the edge while she's at it. Only my pride would be hurt, of course, but that's more than enough.

She follows me into the room and plants herself square in the middle of one of the sofas, leaving me to pace back and forth across the thick carpet while I deliver my diatribe.

Which begins with a disclaimer, denying even a grain of professional jealousy. Management status at Mephistco, I inform her, isn't something I'd envy. As far as I'm concerned, she's merely copped out and joined the boys in suits. I liked her better when she wore a thick coating of machine oil.

Doesn't she know, I go on, that she used to be a role model? Not only was she the first female to break through the glass ceiling in Engineering, but to become a star throughout the company because she did the job with such panache? How could anyone forget some of the spectacular effects she designed, the likes of which have not been seen since the days when Hank Bosch was head of Graphics?

'You never said so at the time,' she mutters. 'And you have no idea how isolated I used to feel. I could have done with a bit of support from you once in a while. And I still could.'

'What about your little acolytes?' I ask. 'Don't they give you what you need?'

Thanks to Lil, Engineering is now mostly run by feisty little females who seem to have been born with spanners in their hands and quantum physics on the brain.

'I don't need groupies, Kokos, I need friends.'

'Very touching.'

112

She ignores the sarcasm. 'Besides, did it ever cross your mind that I might be jealous of you?'

This stops me.

'You know what I'd really like . . .' she breathes, leaning forward, her eyes shooting sparks. 'I'd like to go along with you. Just once.'

'Go out with me? Into the field?'

'Why not?'

'Impossible. It's never been done.'

'I never thought I'd hear such reactionary words from you!' She's getting into it now. Kicks off her obscenely expensive boots, sits up cross-legged on the sofa, just like the old days. 'We could really make waves! Imagine, senior management finally getting off its collective backside and finding out, at first hand, what the front line has to grapple with. Have a first-hand look at our technology in action. Redesign everything according to our operatives' true needs. It's what we've always dreamed of, Kokos: revolution from within.'

'I think our definitions of revolution differ.'

She ignores this. I haven't seen her so enthusiastic since she worked out the cybernetics for the Golem of Prague.

'Come on, Rainbow, let's do it!'

What's this? She's almost pleading. The wolf-woman turns puppy-dog. But not quite. It's half supplication, half a challenge.

'Well, I don't know,' I hedge, shaking my head. 'I'll have to think about it . . .'

It's not an outright denial. She bursts into triumphant laughter. Then pulls me down beside her, and gives me a sisterly squeeze. Well, possibly more than sisterly. And I confess I feel a little ripple of interest, in response. I cast a sidelong glance, to see if she's noticed. But what do I expect? She's an engineer. Trained to pick up even the faintest change in vibrations.

The light that fills the room curls like a wave and washes over us, signal for a quick change on Lil's part. Now she's back in her official regalia, in all its gleaming purple magnificence.

But for once I have the wit to realise that this is not an attempt to pull rank on me, or exercise a power-play. Those seven heads, with their seven mouths and seven tongues, have other things in mind.

What else to do but return the compliment? I always did admire the Eastern approach to these matters. So I come to meet her, equipped with three sets of sinuous arms and flashing hands.

We're well matched where it matters, Lil and I. And, if the earth doesn't move, so what? There's certainly a quake or two on Venus.

Another thing that Lil and I have in common: we have always conducted our – wildly different – love lives according to the premise that one should Leave Them Wanting More. So, in the morning, whatever our true inclinations, we practically trample each other in our race to be the first one up and doing. Lil in any case has a breakfast meeting with those Fox Ghosts I saw snooping around Mephistco on my last trip back. And I think it's time I slipped off to my own room for a while, to look in on Rainbow via the remote.

Sitting on my unused bed, swigging room service orange juice, I switch on the Rosenbloom show.

My, my, our Rainbow's been a busy girl.

One benefit from the Mephistco takeover has been a definite improvement in remote capability. While my attentions have been engaged elsewhere, the nifty little device has been quietly humming along. Every moment of Rainbow's existence during my time at the Fair has been tracked, recorded, docketed and programmed for easy-edit, so I am able to wipe, play-back, freeze-frame or skim fast over the boring bits.

Not bad, for a first directorial effort.

Even in my short career of moviegoing with Rainbow, I've seen worse.

Naomi has moved in, with all guns blazing. The cavalry, unaware it is unwanted, has finally arrived. She will, nice Jewish girl that she is, and aunt of the future, never take No for an answer. Rainbow's faint protests cut no ice. Her pal has hijacked her, complete with taxi, and gone in search of the Jewish Lesbian Agnostic version of Lourdes.

First stop: The Shrink.

It's someone well recommended, by Cousin Michael's lover Noah (also a workmate of Naomi's, as it happens, in this small world of yours). Said to be a right-on progressive, none of your phallicky Freudians here, no oral-aggressive-anal-retentive-come-and-see-me-five-times-a-week-for-years-at-vast-expense-or-how-do-I-know-you're-really-committed school of psycho-therapy.

While Naomi reads a fat paperback in the parked taxi outside, the psychotherapist (Mitteleuropean Earth Mother, in a book-lined Hampstead house that smells of the world's best coffee) poses questions on everything from Rainbow's grief at her parents' early deaths to how often she was scolded in primary school. She generates interesting theories, offers stimulating possibilities, makes her pitch for a long exploration, and all but does the dance of the seven veils to persuade Rainbow to join her on a journey of self-discovery.

What she does not do is believe for one moment that Rainbow has been possessed by some kind of demon. She doesn't say this, of course. But her silence, and her eyebrows, speak volumes.

'Well that's Frau Doktor struck off the list,' says Rainbow to Naomi a little later, as they wait in a traffic queue at Spaniards Corner. 'But I might just feign insanity some day and come back for another cup of that damned fine coffee.'

Second stop: The Rabbi.

'Oh God, no!' Rainbow cringes at the thought of some pompous sky-pilot in a three-piece suit, like the smarmy Rabbi Wasserstein, star enemy of her adolescence, who barred her from the Synagogue Youth Group for blasphemy and bad manners.

('Ha!' sneered Aunt Lila, at the time. 'That'll fix her. Where else does she think she'll find a nice Jewish boy to marry now?')

Rainbow and Naomi do, thanks to their colourful social network, know of a female – indeed feminist – indeed decidedly lavender rabbi. But the divine divine is out of the country at the moment, at some coven of inter-faith priestesses in California. So Naomi shepherds her elsewhere, to an earnest, ageing liberal, whose crisply greying beard speaks less of Torah scholarship than of Sitting Down against the Vietnam War in Grosvenor Square.

He goes only slightly pink at the sight of her Lesbian Switchboard T-shirt, speaks enthusiastically of his congregation's Social Action Committee and seminars on Issues of the Day. But she sees him suppress what could only be a smirk at her very mention of a dybbuk. He counsels against reading too much Isaac Bashevis Singer. She takes away some photocopies of his published articles – on green issues, gender, hunt sabotage and Jewish ethics – and promises to keep in touch.

'I wonder,' she muses to Naomi, getting back in the taxi, 'if my tongue will fall out because I lied to a rabbi?'

Third stop: The Seance.

Urged on (and accompanied) by a stoically-not-giggling Naomi, she joins hands with several strangers in a frantically floral sitting-room in Palmers Green. Other people's ghosts oblige with tappings and – via the medium – messages regarding insurance policies left in hat boxes on top of wardrobes, but those Rainbow might claim as her own spirit guides are – as usual – out for the evening, probably off somewhere playing a gig or eating dinner.

There is a hackle-raising moment when she hears a saxophone, but the hackles fall again when the Mistress of Ceremonies leaps up, marches outside, and bellows 'Not *now*, Christopher!!' to someone in a room upstairs.

'Maybe your dybbuk's gone,' says Naomi afterwards, as they pause for a takeaway kebab. 'You haven't done anything particularly strange all day.'

'No way. Sleeping maybe. But I know the feeling. So'd you if you'd seen as many horror and sci-fi movies as I have,' says Rainbow. She intones, in ominous transatlantic baritone: 'We licked them this time, but they'll be back again. So remember. Keep watching the skies. *Keep* watching the skies.'

'You do seem more . . . cheerful.'

'I guess so. Hard to explain this, but I think I'm beginning to like the wretched thing.'

'Since when?'

'Since I've decided I prefer the poison to the antidotes.'

Even on the remote, with its slight fuzziness, no one could miss that little twinkle in her eye.

Good, good, good. The old chemistry's still working.

Thus reassured, I head for the exhibition halls and spend the day collecting promotional leaflets and free samples of new products that I haven't the faintest intention of buying. Then it's back to Mephistco, to return the remote and sign out again. Before I leave, I stop by Contracts to sprinkle a little salt in the wounds of deskbound Nick Thumb by describing (almost) all the fun of the Fair.

10

'So where have you been?'
'This is where the power relationship comes in, I'm afraid. As your dybbuk, I just don't need to answer that.'

I will say this for Rosenbloom, she keeps her cool. But then again, so did Gittel Number One. That brazen little hussy. Wanted her cake, and the other stuff too.

As I see it, the difference between Gittel One and this year's model Gittel is one of attitude. Back in our first Gittel's day, everybody understood what was expected of them – humans, demons, angels, the lot – and knew what punishments would befall them if they stepped out of line. Heavenly defenestrations and hellish pratfalls, eternities spent in boiling cauldrons or with frogs and lizards applied to one's tenderest parts.

But all this cuts little ice with someone who's seen every celluloid shocker from *Nosferatu* to middle-period Ridley Scott. On the one hand, when it comes to matters of morality, theology and cosmic truth, Rainbow's a sceptic. On the other, she betrays a touching credulity towards such mumbo-jumbo as antibiotics and Dolby sound. She wouldn't acknowledge an Eternal Verity if one came up and smacked her in the chops.

'Do I take it you're not entirely disappointed to see me back?'
'I haven't decided yet.'
'Your unconscious tells me different.'
'You leave my unconscious alone! And what do you know about it, anyway? If you are what you claim to be, you're nothing but a dusty relic from some medieval ghetto . . .'

'So where else do you think Sigmund Freud got all his bestselling gimmicks?' I snap back. 'You want *The Interpretation of Dreams*, look at the Torah, Genesis, chapter 40, verse 8 . . . And penis envy? Don't get me started – '

'Shut up, I'm being hailed.'

And guess where our next customer wants to go. Rainbow's current favourite street in the entire galaxy.

Indeed, by sweet coincidence, the dream girl is glimpsed yet again, headscarfed and aproned, washing an upstairs window as we pass by. Rainbow gets so excited, she almost forgets to collect the fare.

'Can't keep away from this part of town, can we?' I needle her. 'A little homesick, for your roots, maybe?'

'For what? Are you joking? This place is nothing to do with me. These people don't live in the same century.'

'So you say. But already I'm beginning to feel like I belong.'

All very well for you,' says Rainbow. 'You're part of their scheme of things. They might fear you, hate you, and try to exorcise you back into the fifth dimension, but they accept you for what you are. Me they'd probably stone to death. A Jewish lesbian who breaks the Sabbath and most of the Commandments, eats forbidden food and hasn't put foot into a synagogue in twenty years . . .'

'Beloved,' I say, 'this may be news to you. To your Aunt Becky, you're Jewish. To your old Rabbi Whatsisface, you are – just possibly – still Jewish. To Hitler and his henchmen, may their memory be cursed in all the languages of all the worlds, you'd be Jewish. And, to me, of course, you are – or I wouldn't be here to begin with – Jewish. But, in the Jewishness stakes, sweetheart, the kosher ayatollahs who run this neighbourhood would place you somewhere between a Tibetan lama and the fairy on top of the Christmas tree. So break any rules you please. Because frankly, my dear, they don't give a damn.'

To her own surprise, Rainbow enjoys the most restful night she can remember. Perhaps because she now has a set of causes to attach to the peculiar incidents of the past several days, from her inexplicably word-perfect rendition of an Aramaic drinking song to the appearance of demonic names on the optician's chart. Perhaps because I have proven I am no mere parasite, and have helped her knock out one dazzling 1,500-word column for *Outsider* in record time. Or perhaps because I've lulled her with bedtime stories embroidering our favourite theme: once upon a time there was a girl named Gittel, who had a curse called down upon her . . .

'And what happened to her, in the end?' asks Rainbow sleepily.

I am not about to confess to Rosenbloom how and why I missed that part of the story.

'The archives,' I say, 'record no permanent ill-effects. As far as I know, she went on to live a long life, enjoyed the notoriety, and used it to advantage in the family business, exploiting rumours of her Evil Eye to scare off creditors, and to get the best out of every bargain.'

I browse among her dreams. Where, at the end of every crazily tilting corridor, halfway up every spatially impossible staircase, inside every pair of lilac satin sheets, we find the mysterious Flower of Stamford Hill. Wearing something dark and old-fashioned, puffed of sleeve, and high in the neck, with ever so many unbuttonable buttons. But just as the cameras start to roll for one particularly steamy scene in Rainbow's secret movie, the director remembers she is not quite alone.

'Blast you, Kokos!' she hisses, and we fade to black.

Needing less downtime than my subject, I have plenty of spare energy. I decide to improve the shining midnight hour, and make my mark upon her home life. Wreaking further havoc among the dirty socks, discarded takeaway containers, unwashed dishes and unanswered correspondence is – as we have already determined – impossible, so I do something even more earth-shattering: I clean up. When I am finished, everything is in its place, and there are places for everything. Dust motes discorporate, surfaces sparkle, windows gleam. Her late Grandma Gittel-plus-seven would have been proud.

But, does Rainbow notice? Not on your life. When she

staggers out of bed, at some ridiculous pre-dawn hour, I have to make her trip over an unaccountably uncluttered expanse of floor before she sees that something is missing: the usual mess.

I know my *modus operandi* doesn't find favour with everybody at Mephistco, not to mention with the unmentionable and unemployable Anya, but I prefer collaboration to outright conquest. Psychic imperialism is not my style. Deep down, I suppose I just want to be wanted. And usually, in some corner of the subject's soul, I am. Just ask Gittel Number One, that prototype of the Bored Housewife. It certainly jazzed up her domestic routine.

Anyway, enough of the footnotes. Let's go win some hearts and minds.

Halfway through the next working day, Rainbow pauses at a cash machine. It spits out four times the amount she asks for.

'Damn!' she mutters. 'I'll be overdrawn up to my eyeballs . . .' Then she sees a slip of paper coming out of the slot for statements.

'Relax,' reads the message. 'It was from somebody else's account. Rich git who'll never miss it. Right-wing racist sexist bastard, too. Hits his wife. Have A Nice Day. Love, Kokos.'

'Well, I'm glad to see you're on the side of the angels,' breezes Rainbow, getting back behind the wheel. Then catches herself. 'Oops, sorry. Was that a *faux pas*?'

'You really don't know much about me, if you have to ask that, do you?'

'No.'

'Do you want to?'

'Don't know . . .'

'Well, just so you don't die wondering, I'll tell you one titbit that should cheer you up. I am definitely and permanently female.'

She gasps, and jumps as if a weasel has bitten her backside. Until this very instant, no other possibility has occurred to her. What a sheltered life she leads, in her self-built lavender

121

ghetto. She shudders. Imagine the mortification – if the faceless whisperer camped in her brain turned out to be male! Out comes a stream of expletives foul enough to turn the ears of Beelzebub blue.

'Enough of this chitchat, Rosenbloom. Keep your mind on your driving. Look over that way; I think you're wanted.'

It's the fat doorman at a terribly grand hotel, dressed in the livery of an olde worlde flunkey to give foreign tourists a thrill, and blowing a little whistle, his cheeks puffed like Aeolus sending out the wind.

A lean and lovely couple, with small pieces of designer luggage. Two greyhounds, sleek and ready to race.

'First Fulham; then on to Roehampton. And sharpish, please.'

Born to boss the lower orders; you don't buy a bray like that off the peg at Marks and Spencer's.

By the time she hits Hyde Park Corner, they're entangled. Nothing too conspicuous: this is broad daylight, and one never knows who might be sitting in the next taxi, stuck in a queue along Knightsbridge. But her silky skirt's climbing high, and so's his respiration. Rainbow is glad the partition behind her is firmly shut.

The rear windows have steamed up by the time we decant her, and do not clear again until we are nearly over Putney Bridge. For the duration of the journey, our remaining passenger attends to his grooming – pocket mirror, spot-clean of cheek and mouth with moistened tissue, whisper of breath spray, and a quick blitz of masculine cologne.

He directs Rainbow into a side road, and on to a semicircular driveway before a handsome villa – probably late Regency, perfect of its kind. And perfect too is the reception committee that tumbles out of the door as our tyres rasp on the gravel: two golden-haired children, two golden retrievers, and one golden wife.

'Daddeee!! Hooray!!' The voices are crystal bells.

'So glad to be back! Brussels was dreary.' He flings us the

fare, with a slender tip, and brandishes an overnight bag. 'But I've brought back lots of chocolates . . .'

As we pull out of the drive, we catch a parting view of the king once more at his castle. He proceeds up the garden path, one arm round his wife, the other holding out a gaily wrapped parcel to his clamouring young. But the taxi suddenly brakes (easy, when you get the hang of it), and reverses. Four golden heads (six if you count the retrievers) turn towards us in mild surprise. The window rolls down; Rainbow's arm comes out.

'Excuse me, sir, I think you've forgotten something. Catch!'

It is a very pretty, if minimal, pair of black lace knickers. Before he can blink, we're off down the road, in a hot smear of rubber.

'Kokos!!' Rainbow snorts. 'I can't believe you made me do that!'

'Fun, wasn't it? Serves him right. He should learn to give better tips and keep his loins on a leash. Anyway, who said I made you . . . ?'

'Nonsense. Don't pass the buck to me. I might think he's a total shit, but I would never – '

'But you wanted to . . .'

We launch into a little Talmudic logic-chopping of our own on the question of free will and responsibility when a dybbuk is in residence. Squabble, squabble, squabble. A right little pedant she can be, when it comes to an intellectual argument. Of course, I have the advantage of several thousand years of experience and w'der reading, so, unsurprisingly, I win.

'I'm going to my aunt's for tea.'

'I know.'

'I suppose you're planning to make me foam at the mouth and gabble in obsolete tongues.'

'On the contrary. I'm planning to sit back and enjoy it. I like your Aunt Goldie. She's my kind of girl.'

11

Rainbow hasn't been to Goldie's house in years. So she is as interested as I am in our surroundings: china cabinets full of dishes and ornaments inherited from the households of several unknown and long-dead cousins, armchairs with bloated cushions, a piano that no one has played in forty years.

On top of this silent instrument sit photographs: toddlers perched in pony carts; young men in the uniforms of various armies, including one doomed corporal with a poet's face; skullcapped patriarchs; brides and grooms. One group portrait has been taken in a garden: three generations arranged on a Turkish rug. The most venerable sit at their stately ease in armchairs, with their adult offspring ranked behind them, and the grandchildren, in fat hair-ribbons or sailor suits, cross-legged at their feet.

'That's me.' Aunt Goldie points to a moon-faced infant in a perambulator as high as a royal coach. 'Minna's the tot with the sour expression at the end of the row – so what's changed, eh? The other girls, and your father, weren't born yet.'

'And that,' she points, 'is my favourite snap of you.'

Not bad. A minute Rainbow in a cowgirl's hat, fringed buckskin skirt and tiny spurred western boots. She sits on a little wooden bench, and seems to be engaged in animated conversation with the empty space beside her.

'I remember the day that was taken. In your parents' back garden. We were having a picnic tea for your third birthday.

And ten minutes later you threw a temper tantrum because nobody gave Zimberalda any cake – '

'Zimberalda?'

'Your invisible friend. That's what you called her. That's who you're talking to, on the seat beside you. You adored her. Never went anywhere without her . . . Don't you remember?'

Whether Rainbow remembers or not, history will never know, because she is too busy choking on a gulp of tea that has suddenly slipped down the wrong way.

'All right, darling? I'll just pop into the kitchen and get a cloth, so you can mop up that splash on your shirt before it stains.'

'And I thought I was your first.'

Rainbow can hardly speak for laughing. 'Zimberalda? . . . Zimberalda . . . you've come back to me at last!' she snorts, wiping the tears from her eyes.

'Don't you Zimberalda me, pal, or I'll start flinging the china around the room!'

'Better not. Or poor old Zimberalda will miss out yet again on her share of cake.'

That shuts me up. From the kitchen wafts the fragrance of fresh-baked minor miracles. And in comes Goldie, right on cue, driving a groaning tea-trolley.

'Taste this rugelach – it'll melt in your mouth. I'm the only one left in the family who knows how to make it right. It's a real lost art.'

'Delicious.'

'Eat some strudel.'

Rainbow demurs.

'Go on, treat yourself. Diets you can do tomorrow.'

Rainbow's been waiting for an opportunity to nudge the conversation round to Stamford Hill. She thinks she's found it.

'Do you do any baking,' she wonders, all innocent, 'for those friends of yours I met last week?'

Ha, subtle. Very subtle.

'Oh, yes. Baking, cooking, rocking the babies . . . whatever needs done. You never saw such a busy house. Children, grandchildren, lots of relatives visiting for weeks at a time, always the doorbell ringing, with people coming from all over the world to see the Maggid.'

Rainbow admits that she'd find it just a bit too cosy.

'The Maggid's wife, Gluckel-Sarah, says that if there's room in your heart, there's room in your home. And when I come to stay, that darling girl Riva – the one you met last week – always gives up her own bed and sleeps on a sofa in her father's study . . .'

Rainbow leans forward. We're getting warmer. No morsel of Goldie's virtuoso home-baking is half as delectable as this nugget about Riva's sleeping arrangements.

'I'm going down to them again tonight.'

'I thought you only went on weekends.'

'Ah, this is a special occasion. The Maggid's nephew's wedding reception.'

Inspiration strikes (i.e. I poke Rainbow in the mental ribs). 'Would you like me to drive you, Aunt Goldie?'

'What a nice offer. But only if you let me pay, dear.'

'I wouldn't hear of it.'

'I don't care what my sister Minna says. You're a good girl . . .' Suddenly Goldie's eyes light up. 'In fact, if you're not otherwise engaged, why not come along to the wedding with me? I'm sure you'd enjoy it. It's going to be some party.'

What? Is she serious? Rainbow Rosenbloom at a wedding? You'd sooner see a vegetarian at an abattoir.

But you might see a certain person . . .

The words rush out of her mouth without even passing through her brain: 'I'd love to . . . But wouldn't they mind an extra guest?'

'With 600 people there, who's going to worry about one more?'

Then the balloon deflates. 'Damn. I can't.'

'Why not?'

'Dressed like this?'

Goldie considers her niece. 'Mmmm, I see what you mean.

They do think girls ought to look like girls . . . And those boots – oy, vey!'

But she snaps her fingers. 'Got it! You're about the same size as your Aunt Molly . . .'

'Am I?' Incredulity. Rainbow doesn't even think she's the same species.

'And I just happen to have her long sky-blue evening skirt, that needed the seam stitched. Gets me to do all her tricky mending, my sister Malkele, always has done. Come on into the bedroom, we'll try it on.'

'I can't wear that!'

'Shush. She won't mind. And it's very tasteful. A classic. Anybody can wear that.'

Rainbow is hustled into it. Goldie stands back, considers. 'Well, you may be right . . . It doesn't look quite so elegant with a Wonderwoman T-shirt . . . Wait! I have just the thing.'

As some spiders trap their insect prey in silky webs, so Goldie ensnares Rainbow. With a little unsuspected help from me.

'Noooo!' What a squawk. 'I will not wear anything with sequins!'

'You will, too. There we are – it looks lovely. Very suitable – high neck and nice long sleeves. And it will be beautiful with this chiffon scarf. Now . . . underneath . . .'

On legs and feet, we have to compromise. Goldie takes one look at Rainbow's shaggy ankles and sighs; Rainbow says that if she has to wear tights or stockings, we might as well forget the whole damned thing. No contest on the teetery high-heeled shoes: mercifully for Rainbow, Goldie's spare golden slippers are much too small.

'Well, that skirt's nice and long, anyway. It should cover a multitude of sins.'

Like Rainbow's neon-striped socks and vintage Doc Martens? It had better.

After a small riot over a beaded evening bag ('But darling, it belonged to your lovely mother, rest her soul! She'd be thrilled to see you using it!'), a blast of Evening in Paris ('Aaargh!')

and a final skirmish over lipstick ('Just a dab! Hold still, you little bandit!' 'Mmmmmnnff!') we are finally on our way.

'Think of it as a romantic sacrifice!' I console her, as she struggles to disentangle her gearstick from her Cinderella gown.

'Balls!'

'What did you say, darling?' Goldie leans forward. 'You'll need to take the second right after those lights, dear. The hall's about half a mile up that road.'

We sweep out of the taxi, and towards the festivities, joining a troop of other arriving guests. Bearded men in massive fur hats, their wives clad in all the colours of a peacock's tail, and crowned with high-fashion wigs of rococo splendour.

Goldie is swept up into a whirlwind of greetings and kisses.

'Oh, shit!'

Rainbow attempts to hide behind a broad-shouldered patriarch in a kaftan.

'What's the matter now?' I growl.

'I know those two women.'

Strolling down the street, sports bag in tow, comes the circulation manager of *Outsider* magazine, arm in arm with her sweetie.

'Relax, you idiot. Wearing what you're wearing, and in this particular crowd, you're as invisible to that pair as I am.'

I'm right, of course. They amble straight past us, unawares.

Inside the hall – a catering palace of strict and impeccable kosher credentials, as Goldie reassures us, lest we fret – the two sexes part into separate rivers. The female guests and the bride will celebrate in one half of the enormous room, the males and the groom in the other, protected by a high white screen that bisects the dancefloor.

'See, I told you you'd enjoy yourself,' beams Goldie, nudging Rainbow companionably with a purple-satin elbow.

'I feel like I'm in drag,' says Rainbow.

'You look lovely, darling.'

So does Riva, in high-necked dress, long silky sleeves and some sort of fetching little headpiece, glimpsed at a far-off table. A bevy of women, old and young, wait their turn to

128

embrace her. I have a hard job preventing Rainbow from trampling several dozen old ladies, babes in arms, and colossally pregnant matrons, in her eagerness to join the queue.

'Popular, isn't she?' I tease my subject. 'I told you she had charisma.'

'Why are they mobbing her?' The crowd has thickened; Rainbow stands on tiptoe and cranes her neck to keep the object of our desire in her view.

'She's what you might call Limnititzker royalty, being the daughter of that great overblown patriarch, who is probably even now receiving homage from his own throng of mystical groupies on the other side of the sex-wall.'

'You don't sound too enthusiastic.'

'I've met his type before.' I don't elaborate. And Rainbow, fortunately, doesn't ask.

At the table where Goldie sits, surrounded by other elderly ladies, Rainbow attracts even more interest than the hors-d'oeuvre platters. Especially when eyes drift to her wedding-ringless finger.

Between mouthfuls, our neighbours take it in turns to interrogate Rainbow. But Goldie, quick on the draw, intervenes. She has her own Stamford Hill street credibility to think of. Before Rainbow can swallow and draw breath, Goldie supplies the appropriate responses.

I love it. 'Don't you dare blow her cover,' I warn, 'or I'll make you stand on your head and sing "We Wish You a Merry Christmas" in the middle of the dancefloor.'

'Relax,' says Rainbow. 'I wouldn't dream of it. This is Goldie's show, not mine.'

So we are both intrigued to learn that the only reason Rainbow remains single is because of some unspoken romantic tragedy, delicately hinted at by Goldie, in her youth. 'And she's not the first one in our family,' sighs Goldie, flushing a becoming pastel pink.

Sympathetic murmurs greet this delicate reference to her own spinsterhood, and the hunters then move in for the kill. From all directions, our heroine is discreetly sized up, assessed for age, health, economic status and Jewish upbringing. Her kinship with the respected Goldie apparently quells any nagging doubts. Unmarried nephews are spoken of, as if by chance, and the names of youthful widowers off-handedly mentioned.

Mrs Cohen implies, although not in so many words, that the Maggid himself, if appealed to, can produce a suitable stud-list of pious and scholarly stallions.

'I don't think I'd have much in common with them,' Rainbow demurs, through discreetly gritted teeth.

Mrs Cohen tanks straight over this protest. 'You know there are young people, even more *meshuggeh* than you – who used to be involved with drugs and being hippies in India and God knows what crazy stuff – until they met the Maggid and Returned to the Faith. Now they're better Jews than their own parents ever were – I know one chap from Willesden Green who won't even eat in his mother's kitchen any more. Not kosher enough.'

Her eyes light up. She gives Rainbow a speculative once-over. 'Come to think of it, he happens to be a very nice boy – not so young, really. And still single . . .'

Rainbow strives to ignore this red herring. This is not the moment to give Aunt Goldie's friends a seminar on sexual orientation. Restless, she scans the room, desperate for another glimpse of our little Limnititzker princess.

But we are saved by the bell. Or rather by the tootling and jingling of a good old-fashioned *kletzmer* band. Playing tunes that bring a smile to my face and a sentimental tear to my eye, for the last time that I heard them was the day of the first Gittel's wedding.

And no way will I let Gittel-plus-nine, or myself, miss the fun. To Aunt Goldie's surprise, her reticent niece needs no coaxing. In a flash, I have her up off her skirt-covered backside and steaming on to the dancefloor.

We join a wild circle-dance at the feet of the giggling teenaged bride, who – perched on a chair – is hoisted high on the shoulders of her guests and paraded through the crowd. Soon Rainbow's cheeks are flushed, her eyes are sparkling. As she whirls and spins, she grins ecstatically at everyone who meets her eye.

But never imagine for a moment that she has abandoned a lifetime of hard-won apostasy and now rejoices in the mating rituals of her long-lost tribe. If Rainbow seems high as a kite, half-delirious, with racing pulse and her heartbeat dancing the *hora*, it is only because the delicious hand of Riva now lies firmly clasped within her own.

'Finding your little cultural field-trip interesting?' asks Riva, when they pause for breath.

Rainbow feels caught out, blushes, nods a diffident assent, but says nothing. Probably because we are busy, inside her head, doing a little mental arm-wrestling.

'Go on, Rosenbloom! Make a pass!'

'Get off my back, Zimberalda . . .'

'I am not your imaginary playmate. Call me that once more and you'll be very, very sorry.'

'If I put a foot wrong now, I'll scare her off.'

'Take risks, be heroic!'

'Your timing's crap, Kokos. Don't you know the first thing about seduction?'

'How dare you! Remember what I am?'

'We don't all have demonic powers. Give me a bit of credit for knowing how to act on my own turf.'

'Your turf, Miss Would-Be Lesbian Heart-Throb, may include every dyke bar and women-only disco between here and Brixton, but it does not include a Chasidic wedding hall. If anything, this is my territory, not yours. So just behave yourself, and show a little respect, or you'll find yourself doing a striptease on top of the wedding cake in ten seconds flat!'

'OK, OK. I just don't think this is the moment to pounce on her . . .'

'Who said anything about pouncing, *schmendrick*? It's not her tit I want you to grab, it's her attention. Say something that will get her . . . interested.'

'Having a good time, Rainbow?' asks Riva, between dances. 'I suppose this all feels pretty foreign to you.'

Rainbow fumbles. 'Well yes . . . no . . . I mean . . . oh, I don't know. It does and it doesn't. It makes me wish I knew more. For a while now, I've . . . umm . . . sort of regretted not . . . ah . . . feeling more in touch with my . . . you know . . . cultural roots.'

Oh Rosenbloom, princess of hypocrites. By 'for a while' you mean since exactly 5.30 p.m. last Friday night. Have you no shame??

But it's a good try. A very good try.

Riva brightens. 'Maybe I could help you. If you're interested, that is. You know where I live. Come round some time soon, and we'll talk.'

Bull's-eye!

12

With visions of one particular Limnititzker sugarplum dancing in her head, Rainbow floats through the rest of the evening, returns Aunt Goldie to Ilford, then heads back to town. She has to deliver her disgracefully overdue copy to *Outsider*.

Not even the most dedicated *Outsider* hack works after midnight, except on deadline days. The office is dark: she rummages in her jacket pocket for her key, then realises the door's on the latch. When she pushes it open, and switches on the light, she finds the breeze blowing through broken windows. It riffles the torn papers on desks daubed with red, white and blue paint. VDUs lie smashed, with their electronic entrails ravaged, keyboards are smeared with something sticky, every drawer in the place is open and filled with pools of liquid, there is a coil of excrement on the floor.

The air is smoky, from fires in dustbins, and from the smouldering rags pushed through the letterbox as a valedictory gesture. Nevertheless, the hacked-out swastikas and spray-painted messages are still easily visible on every wall: KILL POOFS and NEXT TIME YOUR DEAD MEAT are the mildest of the lot. WE KNOW WEAR YOU LIVE is scribbled, in felt tip, on an overturned, and looted, filing cabinet.

The telephone wires have been cut, the sockets torn from the wall. Pausing only to pour buckets of water into the burning dustbins, and to be sick in the basin on the landing, Rainbow races for the nearest pay-phone, to ruin several people's evenings. She wants a phalanx of allies at her back before she climbs those stairs again.

After the collective clean-up, Rainbow goes home brooding. Casting glances over her shoulder. Hopeful that the glass panes are unbroken, that the key will turn smoothly in the lock. WE KNOW WEAR YOU LIVE.

The trouble with Rainbow is good old liberal guilt paralysis. Not something that's ever troubled me. Perhaps it's time to lend a hand.

It is never truly dark in London: a dome of pale orange light seals off the city from the stars. But, as a black taxi rolls through certain suburbs, the street-lamps fail.

Rainbow proceeds, according to my directions.

'Turn left. Cross the next junction. Slow down over there.'

At specific points on the journey, the taxi pauses, and a window is lowered, to allow for the spitting out of a hoarsely whispered phrase, in a guttural ghetto tongue: 'May tall buildings fall on them, when they walk down the street.'

On the spire of a disused church, the metal clamps that hold a weathercock begin to strain and weaken.

The taxi moves on.

'May their blood turn to whiskey so one hundred thousand fleas get drunk on it and dance mazurkas in their navels.'

In a bedroom, its walls lined with posters of death and blue-eyed warriors, a hand begins to scratch and flick and swat and scratch and scratch.

The taxi moves on.

'May their mouths never close, and their arses never open.'

The taxi moves on.

'May everything they wish on us happen instead to them.'

Thanks to me, speaking through her, these words have power.

WE KNOW WEAR YOU LIVE.

The next evening, after too many hours in London traffic, Rainbow takes us swimming, in an old Victorian bathhouse with cracked municipal tiles. Is this, I tease her, the shadow of a race memory? A ritual bath to purge the body, and purify the soul?

'Don't be ridiculous,' snaps Rainbow.

It seems our Rainbow's quite the athlete. Wherever does she find the energy? Backstroke, breast stroke, sidestroke, crawl. I lose count of the lengths; she's at it for almost an hour, with her mind as empty as she can make it.

(Except for my voice, restoring to her a fragment of her own inheritance. I tell her old aquatic stories. About the fishes who swallow human sins, and carry them away to the ocean. About the sea monster Leviathan. About the carp with a wishing-ring in its belly. About the first Gittel, splashing with Anya in a stream deep in the woods. And how the only strokes they knew were those they practised on each other's bodies.)

For some reason, this last little tale sends Rainbow up out of the water and into the showers. Then home, at speed, to pull several garments from her wardrobe and consider them with mounting irritation. I'm not sure, as she scowls at herself in the mirror, about the choice of films in which she contemplates a role. But when the fashion parade is finally over, we stride out in something that hints, simultaneously, at western cattle-drives, American baseball diamonds, a gypsy encampment and a medieval joust. Oh my, I think we're going hunting.

I don't see what the big fuss is all about. Women dancing with women. Men with men. Big deal. It's the same at any respectable Chasidic wedding.

Why did we bother coming? We could have lolled peaceably at home tonight, watching *All That Heaven Allows* on BBC2.

She has come with Naomi and Mary-Catherine, and sees several other friends, but makes few attempts at conversation. For a start, it would be drowned out by the music. She is not in the mood for gossip, unwilling to pass on her views of current films (let people buy *Outsider* if they want to know the Rosenbloom line), and uncharacteristically indifferent to news of cheap Thai restaurants in Crouch End.

Naomi sends questioning looks, keen for an update on the dybbuk saga. But Rainbow refuses to meet her eye.

The room fills up, it's hard to move; the air grows thick and smoky. Like a Mephistco office party, but even less entertaining.

But why does she keep looking towards the door? Whatever she's seeking here, she doesn't find. But then, for someone who trades in tricks of the eye, she can be pretty unobservant. (Case in point: has she even noticed the metamorphosis I've achieved in her flat? Not on your life.)

It's time to remind Rosenbloom who's in charge here. Let's dance.

All right, so she's no Ginger Rogers. You work with what you've got.

And those sturdy thighs of hers are just what you need for a good rumbustious *kazatzki*. Down she goes, arms folded across her chest, crouching low and punching out kicks from the knee. You'd think she'd been doing it all her life. Her pounding boots beat out the rhythm of a wild Slavonic stomp. Strobe lights dazzle her: if there are witnesses, she can't see, and I don't care.

I make her work hard. Dancing with a dybbuk isn't a passive thrill. Sometimes it goes on until dawn or death from exhaustion; sometimes it carries off the dancer to an unknown destination. Sometimes the waltzer whirls in a graveyard, sometimes in an empty house, encircled by a ring of shadows, who flap their wings to keep time. Sometimes there is a sudden change of partner – a lost parent, an abandoned lover, come back to bring a message or to settle an account. Sometimes, for those who don't quail, there is a happy finale – as there was for the hunchback of Belorussia (or was it Kovno Gubernia, or the far side of the Pale?) whose demon companions danced his hump off, and sent him home with his shoulders straight and strong. Sometimes those who start out dancing end up flying.

Which would be as good a way as any for me to get Rainbow off the premises, before those inhibitions of hers – which I've left bound and gagged at the back of her wardrobe – work their knots out and come riding to the rescue.

But wait, someone is shouldering their way through the crowd. Someone who sees the dance that Rainbow is doing, and wants to join her.

Hey, wait a minute, whoever you are. This is not in my script.

But there's nothing I can do about it, as the two of them, stomping and shouting 'Hey!', run through a repertoire of leaps, kicks and contortions. Face to face, in perfect synchronicity, they grin and swoop as the sweat drips off them. A ring of onlookers forms, taking up the beat with echoing handclaps while the glitterball shoots sparks and the whole room spins.

What do they think this is? Some kind of Busby Berkeley number? I'm not in the mood for co-stars: this is meant to be a solo. I speed the pace a little – Rainbow twirls so fast that the wind hisses through her shirtsleeves, and the wax on the well-sprung dancefloor melts and bubbles. But the interloper keeps right up with us, and even introduces a few new movements of her own.

Gradually, the merry-go-round winds down and the music stops. Up in her booth, a puzzled DJ stares at a machine with nothing on it, shrugs and puts on a current hit to get things moving once again.

Rainbow and the stranger, both panting, stand face to face. The other woman's eyes, like a cat's, flash with reflected light.

Bugger this for a lark. I've been hijacked.

With a peremptory jerk of her head, and a wordless signal of command, Rainbow's dancing partner orders me out of my subject and into the nearest dark corner.

I obey (I have no choice), but I'm not happy, and I make it plain. I hiss and spit: 'And to what do I owe this dubious honour?'

'We did discuss the possibility . . . In the hotel suite at Diabolexpo. Or have you forgotten – everything – so soon?' Lil shoots me one of her sultry, murderous glances.

'I said I'd think about bringing you out into the field with me. I didn't promise.'

'It's not your say-so. Remember, I outrank you. And, as it happens, I haven't come to watch you strut your stuff on this dubious little contract. I've been sent – by those even higher up than I am – to fetch you back to the office.'

'What, in the name of the Old Snake, do they want me for?'

'Emergency meeting of the Contracts Review Board.'

'You could have bleeped.'

'We didn't think you'd respond.'

'You were right. I'm just getting the bit between my teeth on this job. This is not the moment to go toddling back to the office to fart about over some fine print in sub-clause seventy-nine with a bunch of anal-retentives from Accounts.'

'We're not talking sub-clause seventy-nine, sunshine. We're talking about rescinding the entire brief.'

Having lobbed this nauseating gobbet of news, her mouth opens wider and wider. If I don't go quietly, she'll probably swallow me.

Don't let anybody tell you demons have no feelings. I think I'm going to be sick.

She stands back, folds her arms, waits for the message to sink in. Enjoys the sight of me wrestling with shock, rage, and panic. She sniffs rebellion coming; the prospect tickles her. She'll break me anyway she can.

I find my voice again.

'You wouldn't dare! I was promised I could see the project through as far as Gittel-plus-nine.'

'Not my decision. The Review Board's waiting for you. You can take it up with them.'

'We're just getting started, here. It's going well. But I need a little more time.' A lie and she knows it. What I really need is for ever.

'Not authorised.'

Just look at her. Loving every minute of it. Devastated I may be, but I'm damned if I'll give her the satisfaction of hearing me beg for mercy.

'Afraid your lords and masters will fire you if you allow me a few minutes to put the subject on hold?'

'What's the point? You're not coming back here. The game's over.'

'Not necessarily. I might just be able to win over the Review Board. I've done it before.'

'Oh, really?'

'Yes, really. Two days before the sack of Rome, I was doing a job on a Jewish fortune-teller working the Appian Way, and – '

'Spare me the ancient history. I can read it all on your file when we get back. And if I were you, I wouldn't bother resting on your very dusty laurels.'

She sure knows how to hurt a girl.

But then again, so do I.

'If I go down, so do you. Once you became head of the department, you could have pulled me off this job at any time. I can't see that little managerial fumble looking too good to that bunch of number-crunchers Upstairs. Especially when the usual Boys' Club up there can hardly wait to see the highest-ranking female in the industry's history come a cropper.'

This is true and she knows it.

'So if I buy more time on this job, you stand to benefit.'

She mulls it over.

'It would be highly unorthodox.'

'Neither of us, sister, got where we are today by toeing the line.'

'OK, you have forty-two seconds. Then we're off.'

During this little confab I have left Rainbow standing on the edge of the dancefloor, adrift in a daydream, with her hands in her pockets, and that nice chunky backside of hers bouncing in time to the music. I look at her. And, for the slenderest sliver of a human second, wish I were just any other ordinary short-life mortal lesbian on that dancefloor . . .

But Lil's breathing brimstone, and checking her watch. Wrapped in smoke and shadow, I stroke the back of Rainbow's neck, and whisper in her ear: 'You're on your own now, for a little while. But I promise, I'll be back . . .'

'What?'

'No time to explain . . . See you soon . . .'

My last glimpse, from a mirrored square of the ceiling glitterball, shows a female looking lost. She's not the only one.

All that rush, rush, rush from Lil, hustling me back to base, and then what?

Nothing.

They stick me in some kind of waiting-room Upstairs, in a wing of the complex I've never seen before. They apologise for the delay. Everything's running late. An earlier item on the Review Board agenda has taken longer than expected.

But they refuse to let me leave the room. I could be called in at any moment. And we wouldn't like to keep the Board members waiting, would we? These important folk are busy, busy, busy.

I remind them that my time is also money. That they are sabotaging the deadline they have themselves imposed. I refuse to be mollified with coffee. I announce that I plan to throw one honey of a tantrum, complete with sound effects and meteorological events, if I am not instantly issued with a remote to keep tabs on my subject.

It's all bluster. My heart, or what passes for one in demonic physiology, is in my mouth, for fear that I am about to be exiled from Rainbow Rosenbloom, and from Chinese food, movies and other earthly delights, for evermore.

But, though I may be nothing but a clapped-out old-time field operative, whose career – indeed, whole existence and identity – seems on the point of swirling down a drain, I still know how to scare the stuffings out of your average desk-jockey.

Heels clack, wings flap, doors are rapped upon, confabulators buzz and murmur. I win a small victory. A remote is on its way. A good omen. I can keep Rainbow in my sights for a little while longer.

*

What I see is a Soho pâtisserie, where Rainbow, awaiting Naomi, stares into her coffee. An oily film on top of her *café au lait* resolves itself into the faint image of a face. Rainbow, unaware that she has succeeded in reviving an old Babylonian technique for the conjuration of spirits, blinks at something which is certainly not her own reflection. In a swirl of pink-blue-purple scum, the eyes stare up at her, unwinking.

'Kokos?' she whispers into the cup.

The tiny bubbles, stirred by her breath, foam up briefly and dissolve. A hand strokes the back of her neck.

'Boo!'

Rainbow jumps, spilling coffee all over the table and herself. 'What the hell did you do that for? Bloody stupid . . .'

'Oooh, edgy are we?' says Naomi, snatching up a fistful of napkins and mopping enthusiastically. She orders a passion fruit tart, a puff-pastry butterfly, and a slice of death by chocolate.

'Sorry,' says Rainbow, 'I'm just not hungry.'

'So who said I was sharing? Now, what's with you then?'

Rainbow offers up the horror story of the trashing at *Outsider*. Naomi is furious. 'And not an effing word in the papers, was there? I'll bet if the offices of *The Times* got vandalised, we'd hear about it, all right.'

But she's shrewd, is little Naomi. She squints at Rainbow, purses her lips and shakes her head. 'Bad stuff. But that's not all I want to hear about. What's new on the – you know – demonological front . . .'

Rainbow ignores this, launches instead into a soliloquy about workday stress, and the loneliness of the London taxi-driver. Gives a highly edited account (you bet – not a mention of irresistible you-know-who) of Aunt Goldie and the Limnititzker wedding. But Naomi raises a palm to stem the flow.

'Stop holding out on me. Now spill it. Or I'll never eat dim-sum with you again.'

Rainbow shrugs. 'Too bad. I can always eat dim-sum with my dybbuk.'

More coffee arrives. Rainbow peers, with some wariness, into her cup, seems relieved to find no faces in the froth, then scalds her mouth in an attempt to down it before any more visions appear.

Naomi persists.

'Is it here now?'

'Not it, she.'

'Well, there's a mercy. Heaven knows what would happen to your street credibility if . . .'

'And I don't know where she is right now. Sometimes she goes . . . quiet.'

'Quiet?'

'I don't know quite how to explain it. But I can feel the difference.'

(Not that it's anybody's business, but even a dybbuk needs to have some downtime. It so happens I spent most of mine at the cinema. Where else?)

'And last night,' Rainbow continues, 'at the disco, she told me she had to go off somewhere in a hurry, and disappeared.'

'You mean she was there with us, and you never said?'

'What did you want me to do, Naomi, tell you to look deep into my eyes so I could make a formal introduction?'

'If I'd known, I might have asked her to dance . . .'

'Find a dybbuk of your own, dear.'

'I've been doing a bit of reading,' ventures Naomi. 'Yours doesn't sound exactly typical . . .'

(What does this woman want? Make-up effects and melodrama straight out of the 1920s Yiddish theatre? Do me a favour.)

'And what kind of dybbuk informs their victim that they're slipping out for a little coffee-break or whatever?'

(Coffee-break? I'll give her coffee-break. What a cheek! Just as well I'm not actually present, or little Naomi might find herself picked up, spun three times round the café ceiling, and hauled off screaming to some horrendous netherworld. How dare she? Just because she's read some trashy paperback she thinks she's some kind of expert on the *modus operandi*. But, watching this at a distance, there's nothing I can do but spit and hiss.)

142

'It's . . . strange. And don't you dare tell anybody this, not anybody, even Mary-Catherine,' commands Rainbow, 'but I kind of like having her around. Some . . . interesting things are happening.'

'Like what?'

But Rainbow will not be drawn on this. Good for her. There have to be a few secrets between a woman and her dybbuk.

'Rainbow . . . come on!'

Rainbow looks past Naomi, suddenly interested in some pigeon-politics on the window-ledge.

Naomi looks her straight in the eye, and demands, in a stage-whisper, 'Is it anything . . . to do with . . . sex?'

(What chutzpah! Even for a lifelong friend this is skating on thin ice!)

'No! Absolutely not.'

'Rosenbloom, I always know when you're being economical with the truth.'

Rainbow throws Naomi a different bone. 'She sends me messages.'

'Messages?'

'Over the radio in the cab, on bank machines, street signs, all sorts of places. And we have conversations inside my head.'

'Arguments?' asks Naomi.

'Yes.'

'Well, that tells us something. She's obviously Jewish.'

'I don't think they have any religion.'

'If not them, who?' (Quite the little metaphysician is our Naomi, so it seems. I suppose you have to be if you sleep with an erstwhile nun.) 'Anyway, I still think you should see someone. Maybe we can find a proper exorcist.'

'Sure thing. I'll check the Yellow Pages. Harrods probably has one they send out in a little green van. Forget it, darling. I've seen the movie, plus all the rip-offs and sequels. Spare me the victim shit. What she and I have seems more like a partnership. So for the moment I think I'll just stay possessed.'

Good for you, Rainbow, baby. Music to my ears.

13

But the next episode of this little soap opera will have to wait a while. My turn has come. As I hear the summons, I feel almost human, thinking of dentists' offices, tumbrils, guillotines.

A secretary whips away the remote.

'Keep that handy,' I warn him, 'or I'll have your head for a hat-rack.'

Expressionless underlings hold open double doors, forty feet high and bronzed with sculpted reliefs of our corporate symbols. The five Board members sit along one side of a long table. The central figure points me to a single chair, placed opposite.

Any handbook on assertiveness techniques will tell you that the first rule is to make eye contact with your interviewers. Not so easy. I find myself confronting:

a skull made of Mexican sugarwork;
a tragical grimace from the old Greek theatres;
an orange jack o'lantern;
a scarlet-lipped Himalayan demon;
the coffin-cover of a bearded Egyptian queen.

They all have eye-holes in the appropriate places, but little good this does me. The sockets hold nothing.

So charm won't wash with this crew.

As I take my seat, Lil rushes in, with an apologetic nod. The doors clang shut. Someone points her to an unimportant stool in a far corner.

'Your divisional head is here purely as an observer. She will not be called upon to contribute at this time.'

She's in her full official regalia, all swishing pomp and scaly grandeur. All seven of her faces wear a blank expression. She may look like a fire-breathing dragon, but butter wouldn't melt in her mouth.

Perhaps I have been a litle obtuse. Because it suddenly occurs to me that I might have been left alone to get on with this assignment if my divisional head hadn't beamed in on my activities and seen something she didn't like in my relationship with Rainbow.

Something I have until now neglected to say aloud to myself.

But trust a trained engineer to get to the root of the problem at a glance. That this particular dybbuk has fallen in love – not with Lil, the magnificent, many-talented, shape-shifting demon queen who has lusted after her for millenia – but with one ordinary, down-to-earth, mortal dyke.

My attention is drawn back to the unpleasant here and now by a banging gavel: thunder shakes the firmament. They get right down to business.

I am informed that the contract originally made between our organisation and one Anya the Apostate for demonic occupation and torment of the souls of thirty-three Gittels is now null and void. Terminated. File closed. I am to report immediately to Personnel for redeployment.

I plummet to the bottom of a deep, deep well. But there is no sky at the top; defying folklore, I can see no stars. All I can see is the face of Rainbow Rosenbloom, receding backwards in time and space and vanishing in a little pinpoint of light.

'Thank you,' I reply, in a voice so matter-of-fact that I see Lil pulsate in a seven-headed double-take. 'May I go now?'

Permission granted.

In the absence of any finer and more private place, I retreat to a stairwell, and crouch on the floor, studying the grime in the corners, while I mull over what to do next.

For a quiet life, I should now head straight to the welcoming arms and biscuit tin of Ms Topaz, to be lectured on the error of my ways and dispatched to the new homogenised spook pool for retraining.

But I had enough of quiet in that filthy tree.

In nearly 3,000 years with this company, I have never been known as a quitter. I've played it fast and loose before, and on the rare occasions when I've disobeyed orders (in the Rhineland during the First Crusade, in a little whorehouse in the back-streets of Byzantium, and on a cargo ship bearing perfumes from Punt) I have come up smelling of roses. Maybe getting the corporate equivalent of a little slap on the wrist, but always followed by a handshake and praise for my lateral thinking.

I remind myself that this entire industry began with a single act of rebellion against the management Upstairs. So I ignore the directive I have just been given, and head straight back to London.

14

It takes me a while to get there. By Rainbow's reckoning, days and days. Because, given the circumstances of my unauthorised departure, I have had to make the transit by very antique and cumbersome methods, without the assistance of Engineering.

I find Rainbow in her taxi, on the prowl. For obvious reasons she has chosen Stamford Hill as her starting point. Not the richest of pickings, usually left to the fly-by-night minicabs. But if business is slow, she can always cheer herself up by detouring down our favourite street in search of a glimpse of Ms Unattainable. I decide to keep silent for awhile, while I scrutinise her aura and retune myself into her wavelength. Let us wait for some more opportune moment to give her the news that Kokos is back in town.

Over the radio comes the call for a pick-up in the next street over. But before Rainbow can reply, a star goes nova on her near-side window, courtesy of a broken brick.

Nothing personal, as it happens. The missile has been thrown from the top of a cemetery wall. The men it was meant for now rush into the road in front of her, one of them vaulting straight over the taxi bonnet as Rainbow bangs on the brakes. They thunder into the wasteground opposite, then stop and wait, itching for a fight with their pursuers.

The graveyard wall itself has just been spray-painted – the colour is barely dry on a five-foot-high blue swastika, and the artists have not taken time to dot the i's on the words DEAD YIDS INSIDE.

Now, over this wall, come the graveyard's defenders.

Rainbow sees a band of teenaged yeshivah boys, skullcaps askew and earlocks swinging, armed with cricket bats, bricks and lumps of rock. They dash across the road and prepare for battle. But I see more than Rainbow does: I see something else coming over the wall. Row after row of ragged shadows. Their sleep disturbed, their murmured resentment rises into a wind, stirring up the packed clay of the wasteground as if it were desert sand. When the dirt storm subsides, seconds later, the vandals have vanished, and the defaced wall has been scoured almost clean.

The young men mill around in the wasteground, their fury and their hormones surging. Rainbow, who has pulled off the road for a closer look at her broken window, can almost smell the bloodlust underneath the righteous wrath.

But, as in so many old tales, the warriors get a fresh chance to strut their stuff. A second gang of skullcapped boys emerges from an alleyway, and fists start flying. Rainbow can't tell the two groups apart. Shame on her for her ignorance. We have here another skirmish in the kabbalistic truth wars. One team studies in a school established according to the tenets of the pious eighteenth-century mystic, Rabbi X; the other follows the interpretive theories of his contemporary rival, the Sainted Rabbi Y.

But their battlefield, between a supermarket loading bay and a playground sprinkled with used syringes, is also a civilian shortcut. A young woman with a shopping trolley finds herself caught in the crossfire.

The holy warriors don't notice the non-combatant. First of all, they have been so accustomed to avert their eyes piously from unknown members of the female sex that they no longer see them. Secondly, their eyes are on eternal truth, of which each party deems itself the sole defender.

Although I have not yet announced my presence, this

148

doesn't stop me giving Rainbow a little treat. To wit, the chance to be Ms Galahad, the Amazon on the white horse (or, in this case, the dyke in the black taxi), who rescues the fair damozel in distress. Because the innocent bystander wandering into frame is, predictably, the delicious Riva herself. Such a credulity-straining coincidence is only possible when a dybbuk pulls the strings.

Rainbow sees who the woman is, and jumps back into the taxi. With a scream of rubber worthy of the car chase in *The French Connection*, she brakes, swerves, jumps the pavement and steers straight at one set of combatants. She really doesn't care which cowboys are wearing the white skullcaps in this particular showdown.

They scatter at her approach. The opposition cheers. Until Rainbow spins her wheel and hurtles towards towards them. They drop their bricks and sticks, and run as if the hounds of hell are at their heels.

And so they may be. Woof. Woof. Down, girls!

As the battlefield clears, Rainbow pulls up in front of the transfixed Riva, rolls down the window, and roars, 'Get in!'

Never mind the crater in the window, never mind the tyres with several thousand miles scraped off their lives, never mind some brand new little glitch that had better be sorted out a.s.a.p. in the cab's suspension.

Consider instead the delicate beading of perspiration on a downy lip. The flush of the olive cheek. The bosom rising and falling underneath who knows how many decorous layers of cloth.

'Are you all right?'

'Yes, yes. Fine. Thanks.'

A brief silence, while Riva catches her breath. Then, 'Don't I know you?'

Wha-a-at? What ever does the woman mean? Is the little dark-eyed doe implying that she hasn't been haunted, since the moment of their first encounter, with images of our fascinating, leather-jacketed heroine? Has she not throbbed at the memory of their dances hand in hand?

'I'm Rainbow. Goldie Rosenbloom's niece. Remember? The other night? The wedding?'

'That's right. How could I forget? I'm sorry . . . All the upset back there . . . and I'm useless on names and faces.'

Even Rainbow's? You mean this ingrate hasn't been yearning, dreaming, fantasising, slavering ever since that magical, lyrical, blossom-scented night when first they met? You mean she's actually washed the hand that lay palm to palm with Rainbow's as they danced?

No to the first, yes to the last.

Well, that puts you in your place, Ms Galahad. Throw the heedless jade back to the dragons.

'Could you please take me home now?'

'Wouldn't you like some tea first? Sugar's supposed to help calm people down after a shock . . . I could take you to a really good tea-room, just up the road . . . They do a brilliant chocolate fudge cake – '

'Thanks. But I never eat out.'

'Oh, right. Silly of me. I guess you're black-belt kosher . . .'

Oops. A little flippant . . .

Mercifully, the goddess laughs. 'Yes, you could say . . . Anyway, I have to get back. My kids will be driving their aunts and their *bubbeh* round the bend . . .'

Your what???

Dull flop of human-heart-shaped stone into very cold, damp pool of water. Sinking down, down, down.

'Your kids?'

'Didn't Goldie tell you? I have six.'

'*Six???*' Rainbow almost runs us off the road.

'Maybe you're the one needs the sugary cake,' observes Riva.

'I didn't even know you were married. Aunt Goldie never said.'

'Well, my husband's been away for a while. He's in New York. Studying. With a very great scholar. Too good a chance to miss. He won't be back until next summer. So I'm living with my parents. It's easier. Lots of women I know do it. Nothing strange about that.'

150

'You . . . you just seem so . . . young, that's all.'

'That's the nicest thing anybody's said all week. My birthday's next Wednesday, the dreaded three-o. I had my first baby just after my eighteenth. So what about you?'

'I'm thirty-five.'

'Husband? Children?'

'No way.'

'That's terrible. How can you stand it?'

'I might ask the same thing of you . . .'

A little scandalised gasp from the passenger seat. 'But what else is more important? Don't you even want children? Don't you want to get married? How can anybody live like that?'

'What about my Aunt Goldie? She's not married. Do you say that to her?'

'Poor old Goldie. I think maybe there was someone who died in the war or something. She never talks about it. But you – for you, you're still young. You could find a nice Jewish man . . . maybe a youngish widower, in his late thirties or forties. You will have a chance.'

'I like the way I live, thanks.' Rainbow says this coolly, but grits her teeth and takes her feelings out on the gearbox. If she's not careful, her poor old taxi is going to find itself off the road for a week. But she has something else on her mind, and blurts it out.

'But I'd really like it if we could get together some time,' she bumbles, 'and talk about . . . mmm . . . Jewish stuff?'

'Of course, why not? Is Thursday night, say 7.30, all right for you?'

Rainbow would prefer right now this minute, but plays it cool. Then blows the gaff on herself by driving straight past Riva's house.

'Hold on . . . Mine was that one with the red gate.'

'Oh, sorry.' She bangs on the brakes, still incredulous at this gift from the goddess.

'Well, thanks for the rescue.' Riva hauls out the shopping trolley, which, as Rainbow now sees, is crammed to the gunwales with disposable nappies. 'How much do I owe you?'

'Are you serious? You don't think I'd charge you?' Rainbow is appalled.

And rightly so. Did the Handsome Prince send Rapunzel a bill for a cut and blow dry? Did Fair Una receive an invoice for travelling expenses from the Redcrosse Knight?

'I didn't mean to insult you. I just thought I'd better ask . . .'

'On the house,' says Rainbow, smiling wanly. 'What else are friends for?'

15

Like Rainbow, I too need time to recover my equilibrium. So I decide to hold my peace for a little while longer. When her shift is over, I propel us straight to a Vintage Horror All-Nighter in an old cinema near King's Cross for some spiritual refreshment.

The audience is as weird as anything on the screen. It looks like one of Mephistco's junior-staff training sessions.

The programme provides us with a quaint selection of Sons, Brides and other relations of Frankenstein, all based on some English lady's knock-off of Rabbi Judah Loewe and the golem of Prague.

I announce my presence, and speak my mind. 'They call that botched up bit of hand-sewing a golem? If you ask me, the good Rabbi Loewe should come back from the dead and sue – '

'Well, look who's here! Seems like somebody else has come back from somewhere too. Where in hell have you been?'

There's no answer to that one.

'I could have done with you around, you know. Pissing off like that . . . You really left me in the shit . . .'

So all of a sudden my supposed victim's berating me for my absence. Whoever heard of such a thing? I'd never live it down if Lil got wind of this.

'I knew you'd be all right. I checked up on you when I could.'

'How?'

'Trade secret.'

'All the time?'

'Not quite, alas. But I enjoyed your tête-à-tête with Naomi in that choochy little pâtisserie, although I'd like to smack her for one or two of her remarks.'

'I thought I saw you there . . .'

'When? What are you talking about?'

'In the foam on top of the coffee.'

Blast, I'd forgotten all about that little oddity, although it did give me pause at the time. Too distracted by the wretched Review Board.

'Impossible. It doesn't work that way.'

'Well it did. I saw something. A face . . . staring out of the froth.'

'It wasn't mine.' I wish it had been.

The Eighty-ninth Law of Dybbukry: Never, ever let your subject know you've been thrown off balance. So I abandon this problematical topic, and pursue her earlier point.

'So why did you say you needed me around?'

'Because I'm starting to do some really strange things.'

'Sorry, mate. It comes with the territory . . . Just shows the treatment's working, even when I'm not on the spot.'

'I somehow don't think you'd manipulate me into discussing religion with a real-live rabbi. That doesn't strike me as quite your style.'

'A rabbi?? You bet your boots it's not my style. What rabbi? Not that syrupy old Whatsisname you told me about at the beginning . . . When did you see him?'

'Not Wasserstein. He's long gone to the great Hadassah fund-raising dinner-dance in the sky. No, this one's a woman. In fact, she's a dyke.'

'Liar.'

'Honest.'

'Impossible.'

'It's true. She is. Naomi once did a motorcycle maintenance class with her and her lover.'

Gobsmacked again. Things really did happen while I was in the tree.

154

'Naomi fixed it up, in fact. She's been trying to fix it up since . . . since you turned up, but the rabbi was off in America. She thought I might find it . . . helpful. Bullied me into it. If you'd been around, I'm sure I would have been able to say no.'

'So did you ask this sapphic rabbinette to do an exorcism? I don't think they teach those tricks at the seminaries any more.'

'No, I did not.'

'So why not?'

'Well, for a start, I felt like a twit. I don't think she's into all this mumbo-jumbo.'

'*What did you say?* Mumbo-jumbo? How dare you . . .'

Just to show her who's boss, I compel her to let out a shriek. At this moment, there is no movie on the screen. We've reached a break in the programme: she seems to be over-reacting to an advert for the hot dogs and popcorn on sale in the foyer. The rest of the audience cranes its collective neck to spot the guilty party.

Rainbow slumps in her seat. Mercifully, the lights go down.

'Sadist! Anyway, you know what I mean . . .'

'I don't, actually. But that puts you in your place, dear. So cut the nonsense, tell me more.'

'She's an intellectual. Her shtick is dissertations on the epistemology of Martin Buber, or the influence of *Gematria* on Spinoza's mathematical thought . . . Not exactly bell, book and candle. Anyway, what makes you think I suddenly want to get rid of you? I've got a date with Riva tomorrow night. The fun's just beginning.'

I should be appalled by her attitude. It suggests I'm falling down on the job. But, of course, I am sneakily flattered. We settle down to watch the next film. It's *Rosemary's Baby*. I simply can't contain myself. Halfway through, Rainbow is ejected from the cinema, after complaints about too much raucous laughter.

Time to go home.

I let myself unwind at last – how good it feels to be back in the field, especially in this cinnamon-scented corner of the mortal sphere.

Just for once, I give Rainbow a little holiday from dreams of Riva. Instead, I let her discover the advantages of a demon lover: no sharp elbows, no ragged fingernails, no limits to the reach of hand or tongue. Everything seamless, inexhaustible, and all at once. But whatever I do (and I do plenty) I cannot change Rainbow's belief that it is as blessed to give as to receive.

Even swinging from the hypothetical chandelier, her sense of irony does not desert her: 'OK, Kokos . . . now it's your turn.'

Chance would be a fine thing.

Then I let her sleep. She'll need all the rest she can get for the task now facing her. For today is the day Rainbow must honour a special all-day booking, made weeks in advance. She has been hired – 'And we'll pay the full fare. We don't want any special discounts. Treat us just like any other passenger' – by three members of the auntly mafia. The occasion is a state visit, by Minna, Rebecca and Goldie, to their sister Molly in her south coast retreat.

'I must have been crazy to say yes,' mutters Rainbow in her morning shower. 'Why, why, why did I do it?'

'Not guilty. I wasn't even here then. If I had been, you know I'd have helped you out.'

'If you really want to help me out, Kokos, the best thing you can do today is lie low and keep your mouth shut.'

'Hmmmm. We'll see,' is the best I'll give her.

I find it an interesting drive. Some of the scenery between the city and the seaside reminds me of the industrial landscape around Mephistco Plant Number Three, but the light's even duller.

'The radio says we're in for heavy showers,' Aunt Becky glooms.

'I told you from the start when we arranged all this that

today wouldn't be a good day, Rebecca. Didn't I tell her that, Goldie?' demands Minna. 'I said, that's not a good day. But did she listen?'

Rainbow would dearly love to shut the window between herself and her passengers. They have, after all, insisted on being treated like any other fare. But she has tried this once before, after nineteen helpful interventions (eight from Becky, the rest from Minna) on her speed, her gear changes, her posture, clothes and haircut, and – most often – on the roads she has taken to get out of London.

'I didn't know you'd sat the Knowledge Exam, Aunt Minna,' she snaps, after this lady has sighed, not for the first time: 'So many traffic lights if you go this way . . . so many . . . If you'd only taken my advice and gone over the other bridge – '

'Well, I didn't and I'm the one driving this hack, and that's that.' And bangs the sliding window shut.

Rap-tap, rap, rap, rap, rap, rap, rap, rap.

'Come on, Rainbow darling, don't be like that.' It's Aunt Becky, who wants to be rescued from an undiluted dose of Minna. Goldie's no help; she's dozed off, as usual, before the taxi left Ilford. 'I've got a message from your cousin Michael.'

Rainbow relents. 'Great. How is he?'

'Fine. He sends his love.'

'Is that the whole message?'

'He's your favourite cousin. He adores you. What more do you want?'

'You made me open this window under false pretences, Aunt Becky.'

'Come on, *bubbeleh*, this is supposed to be a pleasant family outing.'

You bet.

'I can't tell you how nostalgic this outing makes me,' I inform Rainbow as we get under way. 'A bunch of Jewish women laden down with bundles. Reminds me of at least ten different migrations, forced and voluntary. Did I ever tell you about the time in the Persian Empire when – '

'Just shut up, Kokos,' mutters Rainbow, hunched over the steering wheel.

'Did you say something, darling?' pipes up Aunt Goldie.

The aunts have brought more baggage than the passengers Rainbow takes to long-haul flights at Heathrow. Most of it contains the lunch.

'You'll stop somewhere with a nice, scenic view around eleven o'clock,' came the order from the back of the taxi, 'and we'll have our little picnic.'

'Isn't that a bit early?' asks Rainbow. 'Don't you want to wait until we get to the seaside? We should be there by noon.'

'If I leave it too long between breakfast and lunch,' says Minna, 'I get terrible acid bile coming up.'

'Besides,' Becky adds, 'if we waited until we got to Bourne-mouth, Molly would be insulted if we didn't go and eat at her hotel. And I don't care what she says about the wonderful home-style kosher cooking. The food in that dump is a disgrace. I tried it once and it nearly killed me. No wonder her Saul has all that trouble with his gall bladder.'

'Bowel!'

'Eh? What?'

'Bowel! Bowel!' It's Goldie. The mention of food has awakened her. 'The trouble's not with his gall bladder. It's with his lower gut.'

'Molly said – '

'I know for a fact that . . .'

'You're both wrong. She told me he had tests taken and – '

'WILL EVERYBODY BACK THERE PLEASE SHUT UP???!!!!'

Rainbow freezes them all into silence with a daredevil lane-crossing manoeuvre, and pulls up with an intentional lurch in a crowded lay-by. 'Right. It's ten past eleven. Here's your precious lunch-stop.'

'This you call a pretty place? It's two inches from the traffic. We'll get asphyxiated from the diesel fumes.'

'Aunt Minna,' says Rainbow, softly, gently, sweetly, patiently, 'it is pissing with rain. The weather is not going to lift between here and the coast. I realise that a parking space next to an overflowing litter bin, in between a lorry full of cattle carcasses and a carload of adolescents playing heavy metal with their windows open on a sound system loud enough for Wembley Stadium, is not exactly the quintessential southern English landscape that would inspire a Constable painting, a Betjeman poem or an Elgar concerto – but it is the best you are going to get.'

Minna looks at her, surprised and offended. 'So who's complaining?'

'Are we going to eat or not?' demands Goldie. 'I didn't have a mouthful this morning, I was so afraid of not getting myself ready in plenty of time for Rainbow.'

'Poor Goldie,' murmurs Becky, 'and you needn't have worried, what with her turning up half an hour late. But never mind. Just pass us back that wicker hamper, Rainbow, like a good girl, and the cool-bag, and the Marks and Spencer shopper – no, not that one, that's the poppyseed cake and the mandelbrot for Molly . . . It's the big blue one. Yes, that . . . And the Tesco's bag has serviettes, paper plates and the cutlery, and plastic cups.'

'And the striped holdall,' adds Minna. 'Don't forget the striped holdall. I was up 'til midnight making the *gekhakte* chicken liver and roasting the turkey for the sandwiches and doing the potato salad, so you'd better not give me any nonsense about your latest low-fat diet, Rebecca, or you either, Rainbow, though a little slimming routine might not be such a bad thing for you, except today's a special occasion, so just tuck in. I'm not about to wrap all that stuff up and take it home again, and God knows it's a sin to waste it.'

Goldie, meanwhile, busily unwraps her own lunch. A single hard-boiled egg. Minna glowers. 'Not eating Becky's food I can understand, Goldie, but really – I should think my kitchen at least is kosher enough for you!'

But Goldie ignores this. 'Are you going to sit up in front there, all by yourself, Rainbow, darling?' she asks. 'Come back here and join the party.'

'I never ate looking at the back of somebody's head before,' Goldie muses. 'Except when I had lunch on the train going up to Leeds for Sissie Steinfeld's son's wedding . . .'

'Only a mug would pay those prices for a meal,' declares Minna. 'And not even kosher. You of all people, Goldie . . . tsk, tsk.'

Goldie smiles ruefully. 'Sixty-seven years old,' she confides to Becky, shaking her head, 'and my sister Minna still forgets she shouldn't speak with her mouth full.'

Becky, the pacifist, refuses to participate in this little sideswipe and returns to the main attack. 'Rainbow, sweetheart, there's plenty of room for you back here,' she says. 'If I just move over to the jump seat – '

'She's too good for us,' Minna huffs. 'That's what. And you think your poor Aunt Becky should maybe ruin her back twisting around to hand you things every two minutes?'

'Oh, leave her in peace, if that's what she wants, Minna. There's nothing wrong with my back. You stay right there, Rainbow, if that's what you really want, and I'll make you up a nice plate and we'll pass it over to you.'

If Rainbow were left to her own devices, she would undoubtedly now choose to remove herself from the taxi altogether, and pace back and forth in the lay-by, enjoying the comparative peace of the rain and the fumes and the roar of the juggernauts until she could get the show back on the road once more.

But I feel the need to make at least one more small intervention, so a little friendly torment is called for. The aunts are too busy criticising each other's cooking to notice the small skirmish taking place up front: Jacob wrestling with the angel has nothing on several stone of reluctant Rosenbloom wrestling with an invisible me.

'All right,' she concedes, slightly breathless, dealing with a shirt that has unaccountably unbuttoned itself, before letting herself out of one door and into the other. 'If you're sure there's enough room back there . . . And for goodness sake, let's try not to spill anything on the seat. I just had the bloody thing valeted.'

160

'Language, language,' clucks Minna, and plugs the offending mouth with a home-made pickled cucumber.

If I hadn't chucked away the rulebook shortly after Johannes Gutenburg invented printing, this would be the proper time for me to rise and shine.

Here we are, dyke and dybbuk, penned up knee to knee with a gallery of blood relations. All eyes, assisted by lenses ground to various prescriptions and set into a range of tasteful frames, rest upon us. The gallery is avid for entertainment to sauce its lunch. Plus fresh fodder for their next summit conference on Rainbow's appearance, attitudes and ultimate destiny. I suppose I should warm up the audience with a few Hound of the Baskerville howls, send Rainbow's eyes swirling round like Roman candles, and cause fruity Yiddish curses to croak and gibber from her mouth. Then eject her from the taxi, propel her on to its bonnet, and let her do the business from *Singin' in the Rain*. Then bring her back inside, complete with Groucho Marx cigar, to run through a repertoire of hoary Borscht-belt gags.

Did you hear the one about the rabbi who sneaks out of the synagogue on Shabbos to play a secret game of golf when he should have been praying? He's only a so-so golfer, but today of all days he gets a hole in one! Hoo-ha! That's his punishment, because he can never, never say a word about it!

And did you hear the one about the rabbi caught out, on the most solemn fast-day of the year, slurping down a dozen oysters. 'So what's wrong with that?' he asks his scandalised congregation. 'Isn't there an R in Yom Kippur?'

And speaking of forbidden food, there's the one about the Catholic priest who says to his pal the rabbi, 'Come on, don't kid me on, haven't you ever even sneaked a taste of ham?'

'Well,' says the rabbi, 'I must confess, just once, when I was a student . . .' And then he looks at the priest, and adds, 'Now you tell me the truth . . . I know you chaps take a vow of perpetual celibacy, and all, but didn't you ever . . .?'

161

'Well,' says the Father, blushing, 'once, when I was still a young man in the seminary, I . . .'

The rabbi smiles, and nudges him. 'Better than ham, isn't it?'

But seriously, folks, we can't sit around here all day entertaining the troops, there's a war to be won. Right now I should be putting the frighteners on the lot of them – by flinging Rainbow back behind the wheel, and sending the taxi southwards down the northbound carriageway at a speed so fast that all the aunties' lives flash in a whizzing 360-degree pan before their eyes, or by rendering the whole equipage airborne while the driver uses the remnants of her chopped-chicken-liver-on-rye to strafe the unsuspecting Anglicans of Wherwell, Winchester and Nether Wallop.

So do I do these things? No. I have other plans. I can't resist it. If Rainbow won't entertain these dear girls, then maybe I should. Out of Rainbow's lips comes my rendition of a little amorous ditty from a shtetl on the banks of the River Vistula.

Rainbow herself only becomes aware of her own performance when she finishes singing, and is greeted by a scandalised silence.

'Since when do you know any obscene Yiddish folk songs?' asks Minna.

'I don't.'

'Then what do you call that little number?'

'What little number?'

'The one you were just singing.'

'Was I singing something?'

The aunts look at each other. Aunt Goldie has turned puce. Becky leans over her, fanning with a lacy handkerchief, until Goldie catches her breath.

'What's wrong with Aunt Goldie? Do you want me to get some water?'

'She's in shock,' announces Minna severely. 'From those disgusting lyrics.'

But Goldie herself erupts in a fit of giggles. 'Who would have

162

ever thought it!' she whoops. 'Heh-heh-he – Imagine that! And she did all that with a – he-he-he – rolling-pin!'

'Kokos!' demands Rainbow in a *sotto voce* hiss, 'just what exactly were you singing about?'

'Ask your aunties,' I reply. 'But I bet they won't tell you. And I also bet none of them will ever bake a pie again without going pink from top to toe!'

'Are we going to hang about all day?' demands Minna. 'By the time we get there we'll have to turn around and come straight back.'

There is a flurry of crumb-collection and general house-cleaning, under Minna's supervision. This is one art at which she's undisputed family champion. Sister Becky might once have shown promise, but she turned out too left-wing.

Rainbow gets the show back on the road, and tries to give herself a little holiday from aunty interventions by searching the radio bands for a local traffic report. Goldie, replete, snaps her eyes shut and is soon snoring. Rebecca and Minna, too full to bicker, chat placidly about the people they know. In a moment of radio silence, Rainbow's attention snags on something in their conversation. She turns the sound down.

'. . . and won't even eat a mouthful in his own mother's house any more. Because she doesn't keep a kosher kitchen. I ask you. And this is a boy who used to smoke marijuana and lived in a squat with a girlfriend who had a tattoo on her backside and two kids by somebody else, if you please . . .'

'Did you ever?'

'Dropped out of Oxford, term before last. Within months of finishing his PhD. Started growing his hair long . . .'

'Like a hippie?'

'Hippie-schmippie. Darling are you ever out of date. No, like a Chasid. Earlocks, beard, the lot. Wears a long black coat, and a hat, and a skullcap under it, would you believe?'

'What kind of *meshuggas* is that?'

'It must have nearly killed his father. Him being a Labour councillor, and all.'

163

'But they'll do anything to shock their parents, these little *momzers*. And not every mother is as . . . tolerant . . . as you are.'

'Minna . . .' A warning shot across the bows. This is an old no-go area. Rebecca may be proud mother of the flawless Michael, and well-adjusted mother-out-law of delightful Noah, but some conversational terrain still needs mineswept. Minna, preferring the smell of Chanel Number 5 to cordite, changes tack.

'Oh, you know these kids, Becky. As soon as he gets bored, he'll be back on his motorcycle, having sex with shikses.'

'I don't know about that. He's got himself tied up with one of these groups – you know – ' with lowered voice, and a cock of the head – 'like that crowd of fanatics Goldie runs around with. And, apparently, they're going to set him up in some kind of arranged marriage.'

'Oh, my God. Back to the Middle Ages . . .'

'He's living in a whole houseful of them. All children from nice normal Jewish homes, who've turned into religious maniacs.'

'Penitents!'

'What?'

Not a snore, but a snort, from the Goldie corner. She's awake. 'You two know nothing. That's what they call themselves. They're trying to return to their roots. To tradition. So what's so wrong with that?'

'So what's so great about tradition?' demands Rebecca. 'Tradition also means getting massacred every time the Cossacks get restless, and catching cholera and girls married and pregnant from the time they're fifteen, and a whole bundle of medieval superstitions, and no plumbing, and women doing all the dirty work as usual. You can leave me out of it.'

This is going to be one of those arguments. Rainbow would love to listen in, but there is a little problem with roadworks, a contraflow, a multiple collision initiated by someone impatient with his brains in his backside, and a queue of drivers tortoising past the mess for a spot of ghoulish sightseeing. By the time she's cleared the jam, they're in the outskirts of Bournemouth. She interrupts the shouting match behind her to seek directions to Aunt Molly's hotel.

Molly and Saul await their guests in the television lounge. Saul is wearing a set of bright orange oilskins, and a hood of the same colour. Affixed to the top of it, swaying as he moves, is a bunch of feathery artificial leaves. Aunt Molly is dressed in an overstuffed pouch of white feathers, with yellow leggings, plastic claws tied around each high-heeled slipper, and a red coxcomb wobbling on her head.

'Surprise, surprise, everybody!' she beams and bellows.

Minna purses her lips. 'This, Molly,' she declares, 'is the absolute limit. You look like nothing on God's earth.'

'Haah?' Goldie blinks, thinks she's still dozing in the taxi, dreaming.

'Oh God, Rainbow, let's just get back in that taxi and scarper straight home to London,' mutters Becky to her niece.

'This afternoon,' announces Molly, 'is the Over-Sixties Fancy Dress Competition. So I've put us all in together as a group entry – sorry, Rainbow, not you, *bubbeleh*, you're under the age limit – and I have costumes for you three girls upstairs.'

'What . . . kind . . . of . . . costumes?' Rebecca stiffens.

'I'm too fat anyway,' says Goldie with a complacent grin. 'You'll never get anything in my size.'

'It's all been taken care of,' Molly replies. 'Size doesn't matter in your case, Goldeleh. You're going as a pot.'

'A what?'

'Pot. A big pot.'

'What kind of a pot?'

'Stainless steel. Aluminum's no good. It gives people Alzheimer's.'

'Very nice.' Goldie, ususally bland and amiable as a kosher Buddha, shakes her head and frowns. 'A big pot. Some people might consider that insulting.'

'It's the most important part of the whole ensemble, dear.'

'What ensemble?' Minna stiffens.

'Our collective costume, silly girl. Can't you guess?'

'No.'

'Well, what do you think I look like?'

'Like a great big fool, if you want the truth. And Saul too, poor man.' Minna turns to her brother-in-law. 'It's none of your doing, I'll bet. Is it, Solly?'

Molly overrides his murmured answer. 'He's very happy with it. He thinks it's a very clever idea.'

'So what is it, already?' Rebecca demands. 'Give us the good news.'

'I,' declares Molly, fluffing out her feathery embonpoint, 'am the chicken. As any child of five – ' she glares at Minna – 'could plainly see. And Saul is the carrot. You must admit, I did a really nice job on the leafy top. Strips of green PVC – '

'What carrot?' Minna demands. 'What on earth do you mean – *the* carrot. Which carrot is he, for goodness sake?'

'You were always supposed to be the intelligent one,' sighs Molly, 'but I think Mama – God rest her soul – was maybe a little prejudiced in your favour. Now look, what have we here?'

'I'd love to know, God knows,' says Becky drily.

Molly ignores this. 'Chicken – me. Carrot – Saul. Big pot – Goldie . . . Come on, you'd be useless on those telly quiz shows.'

'I give up,' snaps Minna.

'I don't give a damn,' Becky adds.

'You girls have no imagination. We're *chicken soup*! Becky's costume is all green and frilly – she's the bunch of parsley. And Minna's suits her personality to a T – '

'I don't want to know.'

'You're going to be – '

Minna puts her hands to her ears and shouts: 'I SAID, MOLLY, I DO NOT WANT TO KNOW.'

Molly grabs her sister's hands away and roars – 'THE ONIONS! Nice, sharp, nippy ONIONS! And there's nothing to the costume – I've got a string of them from the greengrocer round the corner, for you to hang around your neck . . .'

'Leave me out. I'm not participating,' says Minna.

166

'Nor am I.'

'Oh, come on, Rebecca. You, at least, I'd expect to be a bit of a sport!'

'Wait a minute,' says Goldie. 'Am I a pot with water?'

'It doesn't matter. The way the costume is, you only see the outside. And you wear the lid as your hat.'

'Because my balance isn't good . . . I can't walk around with a costume full of water and not spill it all over the carpeting . . .'

'It's all right, Goldie. We'll just say the water is still to go in.'

'At least you can be sure she's a kosher pot!' Saul, loyally, tries to jolly things along.

'That's why I chose her. And she also has a sense of humour. Not like some snotty sisters I could name . . .'

'Molly, I am not humiliating myself in this manner.'

'Minna . . .' Molly's eyes fill. 'So instead, you'll humiliate me. In front of everybody else in the hotel.'

If we don't get out of here, I whisper inside Rainbow's ear, I will not be responsible for my actions. Or yours either.

'Well, since I'm not needed,' she pipes up, 'I'll just slip away for a walk on the beach.'

'In the pouring rain?' asks her uncle. 'Aren't you going to stay and watch us win the prize?'

Minna's head rises above the fray. 'Go,' she commands. 'The fewer witnesses to this débâcle, the better.'

'They serve tea at four, darling. You don't want to miss it,' sniffs Molly, dabbing at her cheeks with a scrap of peach-coloured lace . . .

'Don't forget,' says Goldie, 'we want to leave by five.'

Rebecca makes the last contribution. 'And get that grin off your face, young lady. You're not too old for a good smack.'

The hotel is very near to the beach; indeed, its marine view, as far as Rainbow can tell, is its only conceivable virtue. But I find the walk from its door to the water almost unbearable.

167

Even the worms on the pavement, flooded out of their homes in the municipal flowerbeds, exude a slithery gentility.

Aaaah, the smell of the sea. Salt, seaweed, ozone, iodine and women. What a tempting brew. I've not enjoyed a dip in the briny since a little moonlighting I did, some time in the 1500s, when I helped a Greek pal of mine sing some mariners to their doom.

'Hey! Stop that! What do you think you're doing?'

'Getting your clothes off. We're going for a swim!'

'We are bloody not! It's raining.'

'Come on, come on. Rain or not rain. It's warmer in there than on the beach today, I promise you.'

A zip comes down.

She tugs it up.

'People are looking! You want to get me arrested?'

'Nobody's looking. The promenade's deserted. Even the floral displays have their heads down.'

Buttons are loosed from their moorings.

'What about that damp dog over there? Where's its owner?'

She tries to prise them from my invisible grasp. Three fall off.

'It's a stray. And look what you've done. Your shirt's gaping. Don't blame me.'

Her T-shirt rises.

'Cars! People in cars will see!'

Down it comes.

'They're all in a hurry. Their windows are fogged. And who even wants to see the beach on a miserable day like this?'

What this one-sided wrestling match would look like to any of these non-existent passers-by, I can't imagine. But I've lied to Rainbow. We are not entirely unobserved.

The witness is perched on a bench on the promenade, just behind us. She wears a denim jacket faded almost to grey, jeans equally sun-bleached, with some sort of striped poncho slung over one shoulder. She seems oblivious to the weather, although her only shelter from the rain is the broad brim of a

168

black sombrero. I have never been to this town before, but I do not think she is a typical resident of Bournemouth.

I do not mention the onlooker to Rainbow. Her senses are, of course, less acute than mine: if she feels even the slightest admonitory prickle on her nape, she misinterprets it as a spattering of raindrops, instead of a stranger's gaze.

But she senses my momentary abstraction, thinks she's won the fight and lets her guard slip. Pow! The peeled-off clothes lie in a tumbled pile, and – at a velocity far greater than the usual speed of a naked mortal's shy and shivering run – I convey her into the water, and out of the shallows. Just as well the tide's in. We swim, with strong kicks and powerful strokes, far enough out for discretion, deep enough for fun.

We're not alone there. Even so close to shore, the sea is full of the souls of the drowned. The fish have eaten their bodies; they have nowhere to go for burial. As usual, they are lost and confused, having floated a long way from home.

Like the rest of the water-borne world, they can see parts of the spectrum invisible to the eyes of land creatures. So, inevitably, I am spotted, and recognised for what I am. We are besieged by shoals of them, all demanding help or directions.

Rainbow knows only that the waves break around us, rough and discoloured, and that things below the surface are brushing, nuzzling or jostling against her. She doesn't like it.

'Rags of seaweed,' I tell her. 'And curious fish. All harmless, harmless.'

I'm making her kick, trying to get her to shake or swat them off, and the last thing I need at this point is for her to panic, in which case I can certainly kiss the whole blessed contract bye-bye.

I don't think she screams. Or maybe I'm just too busy dealing with the importunate mob to notice. But the watcher on the promenade has seen that something is wrong. By the time I realise this, she's doffed hat and denims, and is swimming out to us. I propel Rainbow towards her, but hang back myself, struggling to remember the proper formula for deflecting these desperate wanderers. It takes some time, and a few false tries (you may well ask why a solitary hoopoe bird is even now patrolling the Solent with the sacred shamir-stone in its beak) but, eventually, the proper chapter and verse comes back to me.

'Sorry, but I really, truly cannot help you now,' I say, just before I dispatch them on a current running down towards St Malo.

I follow after the rescuer and the rescued. The mystery woman has clearly passed her life-saving exam with flying colours; her first act, on reaching frightened Rainbow, is to dodge the thrashing limbs and knock her cold. On shore, she rubs her down with the exotically striped blanket, waits until she stirs again, and helps her back into the clothes. Just as our heroine turns away to dress herself, I rejoin Rainbow, whose brain has stopped reeling even if mine hasn't, and is now murmuring her thanks.

'All right now?' the saviour-of-the-day adjusts her mirror-lensed sunglasses, yanks down her hat brim, shrugs off the gratitude laconically. 'Well, I'll be off.'

In silence, we study the prints of her richly tooled cowboy boots, recording her strides across the rain-sodden strand. They lead, not as we are somehow both expecting, to a tethered horse, but to a battered orange 2CV standing in a no-parking zone alongside the promenade. On its bonnet, someone has – rather badly – painted a pattern of green leaves and fat flowers.

We watch it splutter off around the nearest corner.

'Something familiar about that one,' I remark.

'Yep. Last seen riding into town in *A Fistful of Dollars*. But I guess Clint Eastwood's had a sex change. When I reached for her, I got a fistful of something much more interesting.'

'No wonder she had to knock you out.'

Needless to say, she's a bit slap-happy after the narrow escape. She laughs, great horse-laughs that turn the heads of the walkers on the beach (all venturing out again, now the rain's gone off) and set their dogs to howling.

'What time is it? The aunts will be going spare.'

'Relax. All that has passed has, in the pattern of the old grandmother-tales, taken but a twinkling. It isn't even three o'clock.'

Then she remembers. She's supposed to be, and quite rightly, very angry.

'Don't you tell me to relax, you wretch. That whole episode was your fault. Were you trying to kill me? Is that what all this is leading up to?'

'Absolutely not. Nothing could be further from my mind. I want you alive and well, sweetie. You're my bread and butter. And I'd swear to that on a stack of any books you consider sufficiently sacred, even if they burn my hypothetical fingers.'

'You could at least say you're sorry.'

'Impossible. The Nineteenth Law of Dybbukry: Never apologise, never explain.'

A brandy would do her a power of good, but she refuses. 'I'll be driving.'

'You should have something to steady your nerves.'

'Pity you dybbuks don't do massage.'

'Who says we don't?'

Which is why any passing busybodies who choose to peer into the rear seat of a parked London taxi are rewarded with a sight that may give them pause for thought.

Much refreshed, and afloat in the deep tranquillity of calm after storm, Rainbow returns to her aunt's hotel. She expects to find Minna and Becky sitting in a huff in the coffee lounge, keeping as great a distance as they can manage from their ridiculously costumed sisters and brother-in-law. Instead, the whole party is gathered round a table, toasting each other noisily in champagne. The loudest voice belongs to Aunt Minna.

'I told you that pair in the Roman togas didn't have a chance!' she cackled. 'Any idiot could stick a few leaves from a houseplant on their heads, and wrap themselves in a bedsheet. You could see right away how impressed the judges were!'

'That was the Lord Mayor's nephew chairing the panel, you

know . . .' Molly announces, holding out her glass for what is obviously not the first refill. 'Well, hello, stranger,' she giggles, catching sight of Rainbow. 'Pull up a chair.'

'We won first prize. Two bottles of kosher champa—oops, pardon – champagne,' announces Minna, delicately suppressing a belch. 'Have some.'

'Just give her half a glass, Saul,' Becky orders, putting her hand on her brother-in-law's carrot-coloured sleeve. 'Remember, she's driving . . .'

'She can't even have half a glass,' sighs Goldie. 'There's only one swallow left. We've polished off both bottles.'

'To the victors go the spoils,' intones Minna, with an outrageous wink.

'And here's to Sister Lila, in her fancy-schmancy time-share flat,' proclaims Molly, holding up her glass. 'Long may she stay there . . . heh-heh-heh. To absent friends!'

'L'*chaim*! To absent friends!'

'I see you all solved your little difference of opinion,' remarks Rainbow, unnecessarily.

'What difference of opinion?' Becky bridles. 'Girls, did we have a difference of opinion?'

'Of course not!' snap Minna and Molly in unison. They look to Goldie to support them, but her head droops, and she adds no comment but a snore.

They pile back into the taxi.

'Did you see that friend of Molly and Saul's giving you the once-over, Minna?' says Becky, digging her sister in the ribs.

'Who? The one with the cigar?'

'He really fancied you.'

'Do me a favour.'

'You should have given him your London address.'

'No thanks. And have that lecherous old goat hanging round my door?'

'I think you'd be safe enough, Sis. At that age, it's all in their minds, not in their pants.'

For the next hour of the homeward journey, we are regaled with a medley of the aunts' favourite songs and family stories.

172

'Raisins and Almonds'; hits from *Fiddler on the Roof*; the oft-told tale of Rainbow's father shocking the congregation at his own bar mitzvah by singing his Haftorah portion to a be-bop melody; Goldie's slightly off-key rendition of that old family favourite 'How Does the Tsar Eat Potatoes? How Does the Tsar Drink Tea?'; the chilling story, from the old days in the shtetl, of the night Great-Grandpa Rosenbloom heard the robbers climbing through the window; two cracked choruses of 'The People's Flag is Deepest Red'. . .

After a quick rest-stop ('You'll see, darling,' comes the warning, 'there will come a time in your life when the bladder just won't take No for an answer . . .'), the performance continues. We hear the saga of Lila, Molly and the so-called Charity Collector; Second-Cousin Sadie denting her best new soup-ladle on the head of a Fascist in the blackshirts' march down Cable Street; the one about the optician who gave Mama free spectacles in exchange for a bottle of her home-made slivovitz; What Minna told the Would-be Matchmaker; Lila and the Driving Instructor: and, finally, The Day We Moved from Whitechapel and Baby Becky Was Almost Left Behind.

Then silence until London. All three aunts are fast asleep, snoring and dreaming in unison. Rainbow wonders if, in fifty years, she and her cousin Michael will be part of anybody's family stories.

'You'll be part of mine, my love,' I whisper to her, below the hissing of the windscreen wipers. The rain is on again.

16

Such a good niece. She's tried so hard to refuse payment from her aunties for the day's outing, but has succeeded only in deflecting each one's departing offer of a clandestine, crumpled tip. You'd think she'd deserve to sleep the sleep of the virtuous, but forget it. I'm in the saddle and we have work to do.

Once more, she tries to lull herself into dreamland via a salacious scenario starring herself and Riva. The news about the lady's quiverful of kiddies does not seem to have been any more than a very temporary dose of saltpetre, and it's worn off. Life, as someone who's barely escaped drowning (no thanks to me, I blush), will tell you, is too short to give up hunting unicorns.

So there we are, real and imagined bosoms heaving, locked in one of those anatomically impossible embraces that seem so feasible in dreams, when I edit the film a little. The shot widens to take in another head, on the double bed's second pillow. It has a black fur hat, thick dark-framed spectacles, fuzzy earlocks and a rusty beard of patriarchal length that fails to disguise an anaemic adolescent complexion. The owner of these attributes seems not to notice the business going on beside him, being absorbed in a heavily footnoted Hebrew text.

Rainbow recoils.

'Yuk! Kokos – you slime-bag!'

And bolts from her own reverie. We spend the rest of the night in mutual recrimination.

*

Rainbow wakes, already counting the hours. Tonight's the night for her rendezvous with Riva.

'Rehearsing some good opening lines, I hope?' I chivvy her.

'Piss off.'

'Don't say that. If I do, you'll be up the River Jordan without a paddle. You need me for this one.'

'Oh yeah?'

Oh yeah.

Today we are a film critic. As a special mark of favour, Rainbow has brought Naomi to see the acting début of a lesbian country-and-western heart-throb who's branching out and sidling towards the big time. Naomi's quite excited; Rainbow's expectations are not high.

'Well?' asks Naomi tentatively, as they leave the cinema.

'Well, what?'

'Well, did you like it?'

'The film?' Rainbow stops, looks at Naomi. 'You know, I don't think I saw a single frame.'

'That boring, was it?'

'I don't know. I haven't a clue. I was – off somewhere.'

'Where?'

But Rainbow won't say.

'What about your review, then?'

'You write it.'

'What?'

'You can do it for me. You can even have the money. Don't get excited: *Outsider* pays a pretty paltry fee.'

'But it's your column.'

'I'll sort it out with Philip. Anyway, I've already cobbled together a thousand words on horror classics. He'll set up your bit as a separate item. Just do a paragraph. You can sign it. How about it? Fame at last. Your name in print.'

'I don't know . . .'

'You're just afraid to stick your neck out, aren't you?'

'Not everybody has your chutzpah, Rainbow.'

'I know,' she sighs. 'It's a lonely life, out here on the cultural front line.'

They reach Naomi's parked motorbike.

'Going back to Tottenham?' asks Rainbow. She asks for a lift as far as Stamford Hill.

'Where are you headed?' That nosey-parker Naomi.

'Oh just a boring errand, to pick up something from a friend of my aunt's.' Good girl. John Wayne himself could not be more laconic.

Naomi hands Rainbow her passenger helmet. Rainbow spins it round a few times, and whistles. 'Is this the one your grandmother wouldn't wear when you took her home from the seder? No wonder . . .'

'A little silver glitter never bothered Grandma.'

'What about the words on the back?'

'So what's wrong with Bike Dyke? It's snappy and it rhymes.' Naomi pulls her gloves on. 'By the by, what's with your dybbuk lately? You haven't said.'

'She went quiet for a bit. But she's back.'

Naomi squints at her. 'You don't look possessed.'

'I thought you believed me.'

'I do, I do. But it never seems to strut its stuff in front of me.'

What does this woman want? A free demonstration? Tell her to find her own dybbuk, I snarl into Rainbow's ear.

'Sod off,' is all the thanks I get.

'What? Did you say something?' Naomi's ears prick up. The little bunches of plastic bananas that hang from them begin to quiver. 'Is it here now?'

Why does she keep saying 'it'? How dare she! I'll fix her.

'Damn it! I hate those things!' Naomi suddenly shrieks. 'Get away! Owwwww! SHIT!!!'

They say the wildlife's coming back to London. Foxes on the railway lines, salmon in the Thames. But you don't get many wasps in Wardour Street.

'That'll learn you,' chuckles Rainbow, but not aloud.

*

176

Here we are in Stamford Hill, right on the appointed dot. And if anybody at Mephistco thinks I lack courage, they should see me now. This is what I call a sacrifice for the sake of the beloved. For I have walked her through the gate and along the path, led her up the steps and caused her to ring the doorbell. It has been answered, we have been admitted. We are in the Limnititzkers' lair.

Rainbow may smell furniture polish, baby powder, simmering borscht. I smell the spoor of the ben Issachars.

'Get her out of here,' I urge my subject. 'Propose a drive up to Trent Park to smell the blossoms. Or a walk along the River Lea.'

But the dove refuses all such offers. She prefers to remain in her nest. Hers is an indoor life. She marks the seasons' changes by the need to utter particular blessings, prepare ritual foods, explain the reasons for so doing in simple language to an infant audience.

'We can talk in here. Everyone else is out, or down in the kitchen; the children are in bed. There's nobody to bother us.'

Nobody you can see, Rainbow. But to me, this book-lined chamber is full of sneering, bearded ghosts.

But it's worth the gamble.

I look forward to watching Rainbow attempt to get religion in hopes of winning fair lady. Let her study every syllable of Talmud, pour her heart out to some kindly old *bubbeh* in a headscarf, learn to kosher a boiling fowl, or do a Esther Williams swan-dive into a ritual bath. All in hopes that it will bring her closer to the lovely Riva.

The next thing you know, she'll be asking her Auntie Goldie to hire a *shadchan* – a matchmaker – and find us a nice, undemanding yeshivah scholar for a husband. Who may make a few inconvenient sexual overtures on the ritually appropriate nights of the week, and will want his strictly kosher dinner cooked on time. But who will otherwise leave her undisturbed to play footsie with sweet Riva under the very nose of the current ben Issachar.

It's all fine and dandy with me. For nobody, back at base, can now argue that I am failing to complete the contract with panache and style. Because if this isn't a crazy way for a resolutely secular not to say heathenish lefty Jewish lesbian to behave, then nothing is. So let the Review Board eat its words, when I win the annual all-industry award for originality.

Rainbow opens with a bit of ill-rehearsed and now forgotten waffle about a hunger to renew her connection with the lore and wisdom of her ancestors. This may be her idea of juicy bait, but the tasty fish hardly nibbles it.

'If you're looking for some kind of . . . counselling,' says Riva, 'I'll ask my father if he knows of anyone who . . .'

Rainbow didn't come crawling across the Sinai desert to be shunted into a siding.

'Couldn't I talk to you?'

'I know so little.' Lowered eyes. What becoming modesty. 'If you're serious,' she says, 'you should have a proper teacher.'

'What about your father, then?' That's Rosenbloom's own inspiration, not mine. She'll do anything to keep her foot in this door, the lovestruck loon. I kick her in the mental shins. But she hardly notices. The smack in the gob comes from elsewhere.

'He doesn't usually talk to women outside the family,' replies Riva with a smile that carries the unspoken endearment – 'you ignorant git'.

'But my Aunt Goldie says – '

'Goldie's never spoken to him.'

'You're joking . . . But she spends Shabbos here, and stays over, and . . .'

'So?' Riva shrugs. 'This is a big house. Plenty of room for everybody, so we don't get in each other's way.'

'So she goes on about how wise he is, and what a brilliant speaker and . . . Well, how does she know?'

'Because she comes to his lectures. The women sit on the other side of the partition, but they can hear every word.'

Well, there's a mercy. Even if Rainbow has entered the jaws

of the enemy, the house rules regarding gender are crystal clear. I will be spared the perils of a close encounter with the current Limnititzker sage.

My friend Rosenbloom feels much less sanguine about these pleasant arrangements.

'That's outrageous. Don't you feel like a second-class citizen?'

Riva reddens and bridles in her turn. 'Listen, we like it the way it is. We don't need an *apikoros* like you to tell us how oppressed we are. We just live mostly separate lives, that's all.'

'What's an *apikoros*?'

'Look in the mirror.'

'Is that Yiddish for dyke, or something?'

'It means heretic. What's a dyke?'

!!!!!!!!!!!!!!!!!!!!!!

What's a dyke? What's a dyke? she says . . .

There will be a short pause while I restore Rosenbloom, who has temporarily mislaid her powers of speech.

We find ourselves once again in another time and country. Very other, and very alien. Virgin territory.

But, Rainbow, whatever you do, travel carefully across it. Here be seven deadly dragons: Shock, Disbelief, Distaste, Outrage, Nausea, Contempt and Pity. But, also, here's your only launch window into Riva's galaxy. Miss the moment, and your orbits spin apart again. Don't say you weren't warned.

Rainbow searches for the first step on the yellow brick road, the gate to the Emerald City.

(Would it help if she mentioned those nice Jewish *maydels*, Gertrude and Alice?

'Who?' Riva will enquire politely. The books she reads are different.

Perhaps a scriptural reference – Ruth and Naomi?

Perilous, that one. Scandalise this sheltered creature, and she'll kick you out, and bolt the gates to paradise behind you.)

Rosenbloom takes a breath. Where to start?

'A dyke . . .' she ventures. 'What's a dyke? Well . . . (one, two, three, take a deep breath . . .) I'm one, for a start. And our lives, like yours, are sort of separate too . . .'

As the lesson is taught, the lips of our listener part. The eyes widen, the breathing accelerates. Riva says nothing; Rainbow's words come slowly. But the room is nonetheless full of voices.

Some voices ban, threaten, list the rules for trials by ordeal. Reminding Riva, as if she needed it, of how certain laws ordain that a woman put to shame must be dragged to the temple mount and forced by priests to drink the bitter waters that will either poison her or prove her innocence. (Easy to adjust the dose, for the desired outcome.)

But Rainbow has just introduced her audience to one crime that even those expert excavators of the human heart did not choose to mention. Was this omission by accident, or design? Because those old boys knew their business. The tastiest forbidden fruit should be concealed, ignored, left to rot on the branch – not offered to the customers on a plate.

Nevertheless, though she may not recognise the name it goes by from any catalogue of thou-shalt-nots, our Riva knows an abomination when she sees one.

But a second phantom chorus sings louder than the first.

Rainbow, borne on wings of her own desperation, has summoned up a battalion of supporters: the odd, the wild, the hopeful, the visionary, the smarter-than-is-good-for-them, the reckless, the excommunicated, the ignored. Riva would not hear them, were it not for the fact they speak in the same language, use the same gestures, and wear the same scars or armbands as her saints.

But this time, once in a millenium, they do not simply stand outside a lighted window, looking in at what they've lost. They float right through the glass and make themselves at home.

Rainbow finds that she has finished speaking.

Riva, catlike, studies invisible eddies in the air.

*

Suddenly, the door bursts in, a small girl in candy-striped nightdress rushes in.

'We can't sleep without our stories,' she cries. 'We need them now!'

Riva smiles (is that in gratitude for the timely break, or a mark of motherly resignation?), and says, 'All right, all right, we're coming.'

The child notices Rainbow, sucks a finger and stares her down.

'You can come and listen, too,' says Riva to her visitor. 'But first I'll get us both some tea.'

Rainbow waits in a room full of children drinking juice from plastic cups, who study her in silence. Rainbow hardly notices. She has her own thoughts to think. Whatever did she say? Did she declare her passion? For the life of her, she can't remember, but she's throbbing like a drum.

Riva returns, and hands her a steaming mug. Rainbow blows, stirs and sniffs it. Then sips circumspectly. Darjeeling: not bitter waters. She has almost stopped shaking when the stories begin.

We hear of the wise fools of Chelm, of clever Khashinke and silly Bashinke, of David and his slingshot, of the fox and the fishes. Soon all the junior members of the audience are fast asleep.

But Riva still spins her tales, for Rainbow's ears alone. She brings us to a town where the sky is full of burning, the old synagogue about to be engulfed; white doves wheel round the rooftops, beat their wings, drive off the flames. Then deep into the countryside: midnight in a blacksmith's cottage, we hear the strangers' urgent knock, the peremptory demands to shoe four horses. The forge, gone cold, is stoked again, and in the firelight we see that the beasts do not have hooves, but human hands.

We fly backwards, retracing old tribal routes – dreamed up, or remembered – and into a city walled with honey-coloured stones, where the sage Hanina sends demons home to Hell with their putative tails between their legs, and where King

Solomon outwits mighty Ashmodai, Duke of the Underworld, and makes him do the royal bidding like any human flunkey.

Rainbow drinks it in, wants more and more. I'm not quite so enthralled. Indeed, I've had it up to here. Forced to listen to all those hoary chestnuts that cast me and my kind as the bad guys, and the butt of all the jokes. What arrogance, what cheek, what chutzpah! Has our charming storyteller forgotten that, once upon a time, the Christian world made no distinction between Jews and demons – knowing both had horns?

All things considered, I show admirable restraint. But enough's enough for one night.

So I jerk a reluctant Rainbow to her feet, cause her to blurt appropriate remarks about the lateness of the hour, and steer her out of this snakes' nest of baby ben Issachars.

'Well, you've given me something new to think about tonight,' whispers Riva, unlatching the outside door.

'There's more to talk about,' says Rainbow. 'Can we do that? Soon?'

The voice is mild, but the eyes, troubled, make no promises: 'Maybe. Maybe not. I just don't know.'

17

We head home in silence. Until Rainbow, fishing for the key of her downstairs door, sees the orange 2CV, with its childishly drawn botanical decorations, parked outside the Cypriot bakery, which stays open late.

'Look at that car,' she says. 'Doesn't it belong to our heroine from the beach?'

I dispute this. North London has at least one of those ridiculous-looking vehicles parked in every street.

'Not with those leaves and things. It's hers, all right.'

She seems surprised. And why not? For I have not bothered to tell her that I spotted the blasted thing on our drive back from Bournemouth to London, lurking in a lay-by. Nor have I mentioned several subsequent sightings during Rainbow's taxi runs, when the little beast prowled two or three cars behind us with all the tenacity of a television detective or a thirsty midge. Because this encounter, unlike those with luscious little Riva-leh, has no rightful place in my script.

Sunglasses and cheekbones still in place, Clint herself ambles out of the shop, chewing on an olive-bread. She pauses, to spit a stray stone on to the pavement with socially irresponsible panache, and meets the gaze of Rainbow, stock-still with key in hand . . .

'Disgusting,' I bridle. 'Litter-lout.'

Rainbow ignores me. I'll make her pay for that later.

'Hello again.'

'Hi-ya.' A studied, casual flick of the quiff; only a sap like Ms Rosenbloom could mistake it for a gesture of surprise.

'What a coincidence.'

'Yep.'

'You went off before I had a chance to thank you the other day . . .'

'Anyone would have done the same, under the circs. No need to go on about it.'

Rainbow doesn't. The first thing she learned in Baby-Dyke school, after fingernail-trimming, was Never Gush.

'Do you live around here?'

'No. Not yet, anyway. I might start looking.'

Rainbow holds up her key. 'My flat's above the bakery. Do you have time for coffee or something?'

'Could do.'

Coffee or what? I want to know. What chutzpah. Don't consult me, or anything. You'd think I didn't live here, too.

Mmmmm. Isn't this cosy. Whoever she is, her standard of housekeeping must be even lower than Rainbow's. Not only doesn't she blink at the mess, she doesn't sneak into the kitchen to give her mug an extra wash before the coffee's poured into it.

But everything is warm and gilded with the last glow of the sunset, through the room's west-facing windows. The glass glows scarlet. Anyone outside looking up would think the room was all on fire. Perhaps that's why this lanky poser has not yet removed her shades.

Rainbow and Clint (OK, her name now appears to be Annie; that's all we know so far) are getting on a treat. They have established, to their mutual relief, that they know absolutely nobody in common. Clint also turns out to be a film buff, and an occasional member of Rainbow's reading public ('but that damned magazine of yours is a bitch to find outside London').

'So is that why you're moving into town?'

For some reason, this strikes them both as hilarious. Snorts and guffaws bounce off the walls (nothing so trillingly femme as a girlish giggle). I don't quite see the joke, but then, I'm

184

busy sulking. Trying to think up some new and outrageous form of creative puppetry that will blow Rainbow's gaff, and send this interloper sloping off. I just don't like the feel of her.

Nosey-parkering round the piles of recently acquired books while her hostess goes off for a pee, she announces on Rainbow's return – 'I was right. You're Jewish, too . . .'

There follows the usual discussion on oppressed-minority self-detecting radar – Jewish, lesbian or otherwise – and some sniffing delicately around the problematical area of Israel, policies of and attitudes toward: Then Clint refers back to the books. 'You really seem to be into it. Are you – religious or anything like that?'

'No, nothing like that. I just decided it was time I . . . knew more. What about you?'

'Oh, yes. I'm the founder of a very strict order of kosher nuns. We're into the mortification of the flesh, and doing penance – we only ever eat bacon sandwiches and then make each other feel guilty at set hours every day.'

'Another *apikoros*.'

'What?'

'New word of the week. I learned it from a – sort of friend of mine a couple of hours ago. It means heretic. Good, isn't it?'

Snooping around the clutter on the mantelpiece, Clint fingers a photograph. 'My, my. Who are all these lovely ladies with corsages?'

'My aunts. At Aunt Lila's seventieth birthday party. She's the rich one.'

Clint spins on her heel to face her.

'What aunts?' Accusingly: 'You didn't mention any aunts.'

'It isn't usually the first thing I tell people about myself, although the old dollies do have their ways of claiming my attention.'

'Which side are they on?' She's insistent.

'What do you mean? Labour or Tory? Well, they range from steadfast old-style socialist to – '

With an impatient wave of the hand, Clint interrupts her.

185

'Not politics. What I mean is, are they your mother's sisters or your father's?'

Rainbow looks at her. 'What do you care?'

Clint defends herself by going on the attack. 'Why won't you tell me? What is there, some big secret about who they are? Something shady in your maternal family tree?'

Rainbow laughs, puzzled by the obsessive questioning, but happy to oblige.

'Of course not. They're not my mother's sisters anyway: she was an only child. These are all Rosenblooms, on my father's side. Very ordinary ladies, but worshipped their brother as if he was the Messiah. He was the family hero, almost famous in his day. The late, great Cy 'Silvertones' Rosenbloom. Star of jazz clubs, the better class of fifties holiday camps, and a thousand barmitzvah bandstands. I have not inherited his talents.'

Her visitor, much relieved, suddenly loses interest and drops the photograph. It flutters into the unused grate. 'Oh, that's all right, then. Is there any more coffee?'

Rainbow leaps to rescue the picture, then scuttles into the kitchen. Now that we're alone at last, I tell Rainbow what a fool she is.

'Are you sure you should leave her alone out there? She's probably nicking your cash-card this very minute.'

'There's not much in my account. As you might have noticed, you've slightly cramped my earning power. You seem to take up an awful lot of energy and time. Anyway, what's making you so paranoid?'

'The vibrations. Something not right. Trust me.'

'Oh, but I do. I've never felt so well protected. Unless you've been calling my bluff since day one, you should be able to see off any mere mortal who rubs us up the wrong way.'

'Hey, Rainbow, what's keeping you? Are you actually having to go out and grow those blasted coffee beans?'

Clint lounges in the doorway. The sitting-room's grown dark behind her. She has finally taken off that pretentious pair of shades. I look her straight in the naked eye. And look again. And yet again.

Mere mortals, dear Rainbow, as you so rightly say, would present no threat. But here we have something very, very different.

Out of Rainbow's parted lips, and from my molten core, I send a roar of fear and fury:

G-O-O-O AWAYYYYYYYY!

Through hell and high water, Anya the Apostate has tracked us down.

Blood runs in the firmament. You should hear the howls. And more than half of them, I hate to say, are mine.

When the thunder and smoke of combat clears (one wonders what they made of it, in the bakery below), this is how we find ourselves. Rainbow crouches in the corner behind an overturned armchair. The invader, panting, leans against the wall between the two improbably unbroken windows, nursing an arm hanging at an illogical angle, then slides straight down to sit, legs asprawl in a wide-open V-for-vengeance, on the floor. The skirting boards are slightly charred; a singed smell comes off the rug and curtains.

And I, as the walls stop whirling, realise I am not where I was before. If you think someone with no body can feel no pain, then think again. And never mind the wounds of battle – the weight of my own panic all but suffocates me. With whatever strength is left, and there isn't much of it, I wrestle with the cold, thick snakes of terror. For nothing I do, no emergency procedure I try, frees me from wherever I'm pinned down, or gets me back inside her.

'Hsst! Rainbow!'

At least she can still hear me. Whey-faced and wobbling, she slowly rises to a kneeling position behind the chair and peers out over a rampart of faded chintz, searching the room for the source of my voice.

'You don't have to listen to her any more, Gittel-plus-nine,' comes the breathless word from below the windows. 'She's off the case; she's history.'

'Says who?' I bellow.

'The person who signed you up for the job in the first place, remember.'

'I told you at the fair – it's out of your hands. You have no authority.'

'Oh, but I do.' She twists painfully, trying to move her injured arm. 'And if I could only reach inside the back pocket of my jeans, I'd show you the paperwork to prove it.'

'Liar.'

Rainbow looks back and forth, from the stranger on the floor to – to where? I'm not quite sure myself. It feels smooth, flat, cold – or maybe that's just the sudden lack of Rainbow's now-familiar body warmth . . .

The direction of my opponent's gaze, and Rainbow's puzzlement, gives me the answer. I'm in the narrow mirror that hangs beside the kitchen door.

'Rainbow, can you see me?' I hope not. If I can't control which of my forms she sees – and, at the moment, I'm definitely having trouble manoeuvring – the psychological effects could be disastrous.

(Imagine – 'What? That's Kokos?. . . *That* was living inside me – Aaeeeyurrgghaaaaaaaaaaaaahhhhhhh.........')

'Of course she can't.' A snarl from our guest. 'All she sees are several greasy smears across the glass.'

Thank goodness for Rainbow's lousy housekeeping. If she were a good spit-and-polish *balabosteh* like her Aunt Minna, where would I be now?

But how did that punch-drunk amateur do it? And how did she get here? Whoever let her across the divide?

She's on her feet now. The arm still hangs limp, but she ignores it. She seems to have acquired a second wind.

Rainbow rises shakily from her corner, rights the chair, and collapses into it. She slumps, exhausted, moving only her eyes from side to side as she follows our next exchange.

'Caught you napping, didn't I, Koke?'

I am so angry it takes me a long time to find the words.

'I don't know how you got here, lady, but watch out. You're out of your depth on this one.'

'It took you long enough to recognise me . . .'

'What do you expect? Those clothes . . . And the smell's gone. Not to mention half a ton of bloat, several wagonloads of smuts, and a sackful of matted hair. What did you do? Steal some other poor *gilgul*'s cast-off body?'

'No. This one's mine.'

'Never.'

'It's amazing what a sensible diet and some good workouts in the company gym can do to get a woman into shape.'

'The company gym?'

'Surely even a degenerate like yourself knows that Mephistco has a health club?'

'Of course I do. But who let you in?'

'Freelancers are now entitled to membership. It was in the last Staff Association agreement. Don't you ever read your memos?'

'If they're hiring your sort of freelance now, we must really be going downhill fast.'

'Ms Topaz told me you were always too big for your boots.'

'When it comes to someone getting ideas above her station, Anya . . .'

She makes a rude gesture, involving several hypothetical orifices, then strides over to plant herself on the arm of Rainbow's chair.

'An operative with your penchant for letting herself get trapped inside things should not attempt to pull rank. Look where you are, and then,' she reaches out the undamaged arm to drape it cosily over Rainbow's hunched-up shoulders, 'look where I am. *Quod erat demonstratum.*'

I strive to keep my temper in check. There's no way of knowing which containment code she's used. If my anger breaks the glass, I could be smashed to smithereens. In sarcasm, I find solace.

'Hmmm, the former chicken-flicker's taking evening classes in Latin, is she? Now there's ambitious . . . Well you must have skipped a page in the textbook, honey – it's *quod erat demonstrandum*, not *demonstratum*.'

This gets her goat. A freckle on one of those angular cheekbones pulses in a tiny tic; a cowboy-booted foot starts tapping against the base of the chair. There is a deep, ominous silence. If she has indeed acquired sufficient skill to send me howling into some black hole, now's the moment she'll try it.

'Shut up, Kokos.' She makes an obscene gesture. 'Ow!. . . Oy . . . vey-is-mir!' She's forgotten herself; has used her injured arm.

'I hope that hurt like hell, Apostate. Serves you right . . .'

She winces, and rubs the elbow hard.

My gamble has paid off. I've got her measure. She is still on the human side of the Great Divide. What she's done to me so far is – probably – the worst she can do.

She turns away and lays a gentle finger on Rainbow's still trembling cheek. The sight of that simple act splashes acid into my eyes.

'You, my friend,' this viper coos to Rainbow, 'are probably in shock. Hot sweet tea's the answer. It may take a couple of minutes, since one arm is temporarily out of order. But I'll be quick as I can.'

And presses her face close to the glass as she passes me.

'Ha-ha-ha!'

The exhalation blots out my vision altogether.

When the steam clears again, Rainbow stands before the glass. She peers into it, but sees only herself, looking shell-shocked, and the room behind her, resembling a Wild West saloon just after Jack Palance has thrown Elisha Cook Jr through the plate-glass window.

'Kokos, who is she?'

'Do you remember what I told you, about the woman who called down the curse on your many-times great-grandmother.'

'The rejected lover?'

'That's her.'

I can't see Rainbow, but I can almost hear the blood drain from her face. 'Is she a dybbuk too?'

'In only the broadest and I may say sloppiest usage of the term would this obsessive little undeadnik be counted as a dybbuk. And not in a million quintillion millenia is she anything like me.'

'For a start,' whispers Anya into Rainbow's ear, making her shriek and jump, 'I don't let myself get caught with my trousers down and get banged up in trees and looking-glasses.' She has sidled out of the kitchen.

'Izzat so?' I jeer. 'Well, how's your itch? Or did the Company Health Club take care of that, too?'

She ignores this, turns to Rainbow with a conspiratorial smile. 'Leave the poor old thing to sulk. Your tea's on the table.'

Rainbow, looking towards my mirror as if hoping for some kind of guidance, is pulled backwards through the kitchen door.

What on earth are they talking about? All I hear is low murmuring, words too faint, a radio band clogged with interference.

I too could use the equivalent of a cup of hot, sweet tea. Talk about shocks to the system.

First, the original client shows up on a plane of existence to which she would never normally have access. (Despite the claims of some sixteenth-century kabbalistic masters, most people get just one bite at the cherry of human life.)

Second, she has not only cleaned up her act, she seems to have adopted a remarkably apt late twentieth-century camouflage: from Baltic peasant to stereotypical dyke's delight is a transition not normally catered for in those women's magazines that offer readers new looks for new lifestyles.

Third, she claims to have authorisation from Mephistco to boot me off the assignment.

The first two of these little surprises, just possibly, have credible explanations. But the last? It all smells fishier than a barrel of stale salt-herring. If Mephistco really is determined to punish me for defying the Review Board, they have far more efficient methods at their disposal than sending some freelance vagabond who still has boneyard dust behind her ears to do their dirty work.

More efficient methods, maybe – but more expensive. I should have remembered: our new management likes nothing better than doing things on the cheap.

The realisation rips through me: my little act of derring-do has truly landed me in the shit. This is one time when the Powers that Be are not going to pat my head and say all is forgiven.

Once again, I'm stuck, as trapped as I was in that tree – and I don't think a well-timed lightning bolt from Lil will spring me this time.

I can hear Anya's voice – a low secret murmur – in the kitchen, along with the hiss of steam, the tintinnabulation of a teaspoon, the scream of a biscuit packet being torn apart.

'Don't believe a word she tells you, Rainbow,' I shout, but receive no response.

I am desperate to know what's going on in there. I strain every fibre of my transparent being, shove in all dimensions and directions. The glass does not yield. I doubt she has the technical skill to keep me static for very long, but she certainly has acquired just enough understanding of particle physics and the footnotes to the hard-to-find tenth-century Babylonian edition of *The Sword of Moses* to slow me down just long enough to cramp my style.

Who does she think she is?

Certainly not one of us. We dybbuks have our ethics; we do not do these things to one another. It just shows what happens when you let amateurs dabble in the trade. This is the sort of trick you'd expect some tinpot holy man to play, trying to impress the credulous.

Oy! I smack my hypothetical forehead as the mention of holy men reminds me – what about the delicious plum now ripening on the ben Issachar family tree. I'd made some plans for Rainbow's next tête-à-tête, scripted some frank revelations, an impassioned plea . . .

Anya will not take kindly to these developments. Not after she's been waiting 200 years to get her hands on the last of the Gittels.

And, I have no doubt, that's exactly where those hands are heading right now.

In the kitchen, actions speak louder than words. Those soft sighs and low moans can only mean one thing: the Apostate has offered to soothe away stressed Rainbow's jangles by massaging her neck and shoulders. Apparently her various self-improvement ploys have included a short course in relaxation therapy. She's certainly had some time to kill, while awaiting her big moment.

I don't think even Rainbow is so obtuse that she can be in any doubt as to her visitor's ultimate intentions. So what does she have to say about it? Not very much.

Is that Anya's doing, I wonder, as the clatter of kitchen chairs announces an imminent scene shift, or is it mine? Has my presence been bad for Rainbow? Made her too passive? Blunted her wits?

Enough of this introspection. It's not my style. Probably one of the chemical side-effects of Anya's fixative hoo-doo.

Anyway, here they come. Anya permits herself a triumphant smirk as she passes the mirror; Rainbow seems to have forgotten my existence. Did hypnosis figure in Anya's bag of tricks, as well? With my direct pipeline into Rainbow's thoughts blocked off, I must stoop to guesswork. How grating.

'Just a minute,' says Anya. 'Do you have a tablecloth?'

A what? She must be joking. Gracious living at maison Rosenbloom means eating from a plate instead of straight from the takeaway container. What's she planning? A seduction picnic, with champagne and grapes and naked French ladies, on the sitting-room floor?

'A spare sheet?'

What's she after? Rainbow points to the bedroom, where the pile of dirty washing lurks just behind the door. (The heap stands almost ceiling-high now; demonic possession leaves little time for trips to the laundrette.)

Anya drapes it carefully over the mirror. There goes my view of the proceedings.

'I can't stand being spied on,' she explains.

Rainbow protests. 'Do we have to do that? It's so depressing. Reminds me of when my parents died, and my aunts covered all the mirrors in the house.'

'A prudent custom,' Anya replies. 'And for the same good reason. It prevents the intrusion of unwelcome spirits.'

'You're a fine one to talk, *gilgul*,' I jeer, from behind the barrier of blue-striped no-iron 60–40 cotton-polyester.

'Shut up, Kokos.'

That's from Rainbow. Can I believe my ears? What a betrayal! Is this the Rainbow for whose sake I have risked my whole career? The only possible excuse for her behaviour is that my temporary excision has gone to her head.

'Rainbow,' I stage-whisper, 'whose side are you on out there?'

Then, would you believe it, she twists the knife. 'I'm sorry, Kokos, but I think I ought to hear what Anya has to say.'

Is there no loyalty among these mortals? I never asked her for total commitment (after all, if I were into monogamy would I have done such a good job of dangling that little Limnititzker *tsatskeleh* in front of her nose?), but I would have hoped the woman would stand by me in a crisis.

Now I am truly crushed; the wind's smacked out of me. If I were a free agent, I'd rattle her faithless bones like the bars of a cage.

'I take it,' says Anya, 'from your apparently cosy relationship with that . . . that creature in there, that you know something of how all this began.'

Rainbow admits that I have told her the tale of the Gittel affair, and why Anya called down the curse in the first place.

'I suppose she made me out to be a right little idiot,' says Anya.

'She didn't, actually.'

Good for you, Rosenbloom. Take the wind out of her sails.

194

'Well, I was.'

I don't need to see through the sheet to know that Anya's flushed brick red, and that her eyes are fixed on somewhere quite far to the east of the Walthamstow marshes.

'I did most of my thinking below the neck in those days. And being with Gittel was like – oh, I don't know the right words – like the first day when the sun turns warm enough to start the ice melting off the eaves. I think it was her smell that got me started . . . like the braided loaves fresh from the baker's oven. And she was the one with all the big ideas and plans for the future – not me. I just lived for the minute; if my tongue and lips and fingers travelled freely over her, that was good enough for forever.

'When I think back, knowing what I know now – and I have been so many places, and looked into the windows of other people's lives, and I have seen so much – I still can't say for sure what Gittel really wanted. We weren't brought up to want things – the issue didn't arise: you got what you got. So Gittel, who had well-intentioned parents and a place in the world, got a husband thought capable of putting food in her mouth and babies in her belly. I, who had neither place nor parents, got the prints of everybody's boots on my backside – Christian boots and Jewish boots both, everybody was quite impartial. But nobody ever came into the woods to shake their finger in my face and lay down the law, the way they did with Gittel in the dorf.

'It was only much later, when it was too late to change anything, that I glimpsed the possibility that this may have been one small way in which I had a slight advantage over Gittel. But that was long after the moment when my pathetic attempt to enlist the so-called forces of darkness on my behalf had backfired.'

I'm getting vexed. 'You watch your mouth out there, Apostate!'

'Why don't you just climb back into your tree?'

Rainbow speaks up. 'Could you both stop squabbling?'

'That . . . ghoul out there has no right to impugn my professional abilities.'

'Get off your high horse, Kokos. Who was it crumbled like a piece of stale matzo under the onslaught from ben Issachar? You really left me in the shit.'

Rainbow whisks the cloth off the mirror with an exasperated whoosh. 'Look, why don't you two slug this thing out on your own time? I am just a very confused mortal who has to get up and go to work driving a taxi in the morning. I do not know how to arbitrate industrial disputes between a disappointed ghost and a dybbuk on the defensive.'

We roar, as one:

'I am not a ghost!'

'I am not defensive!'

She covers her hands with her ears. 'Please . . .'

'Anyway,' I remind her, 'are you sure you want to go to work tomorrow? Just when you've begun to get Riva so nicely softened up. She'll have been awake all night, thinking and thinking and thinking. The seeds you've planted are sprouting the tenderest of young green shoots. Shouldn't you be there with the dawn chorus, knocking on the door, to strike while the iron's hot?'

Anya's ears point up. 'Who's Riva?'

'Oh, Anyushkeleh,' I chortle, 'do you have a surprise coming . . .!'

I may be heading for the infernal scrap-heap, but I still have my professional pride. Whatever else happens, I am not about to let Rainbow back out of this encounter. I worked too hard to set it up. And I won't have the Apostate scupper all my efforts by giving Rainbow the glad eye. After all, in the final analysis, I've choreographed this far-fetched fixation in the service of Anya's original curse. So does the Apostate want her contract carried out, or doesn't she? What else is she still hanging around for?

'I can't think straight,' says Rainbow, on the verge of tears. 'Even if it's only for a couple of hours, I have to go to bed.'

She pauses in the doorway and turns, to detach Anya's hand

from the small of her back. 'Alone, that is. Tonight of all nights.' She gives her an energetic push, backwards, into the sitting-room.

For this alone, I may find it in my heart to forgive her.

Perhaps hope is not dead.

Then she leaves us to each other.

Anya gazes after Rainbow. I know that loose-lipped look of old. Clint, it seems, has turned into a mooncalf.

'Stop slavering,' I snap. 'Someone else is starring in her bedtime story.'

'And what makes you think – '

'Hate to Love takes just one vowel-change and a shift of two consonants. Besides, you're an open book to me. You think you've somehow got your long-lost Gittel back. Wake up from your daydreams, *gilgul*. This is not the same person. She's nothing like her . . .'

'Wrong. There's a definite look about the eyes, and the cheekbones, and the pitch of her voice, and . . . certain other things . . .'

'Which you confidently expect to prove for yourself once you slip between her sheets. Well, forget it.'

She stands before the mirror, looking straight through her own reflection, scowls at the glass and blows a decidedly twentieth-century raspberry straight at me.

'I told you, it's nothing to do with you any more, Kokos. You're off the case.'

'You'll find out soon enough. The Gittel genes are well-diluted. You should see the most recent input from the paternal side, for one thing – those Rosenbloom aunts are one formidable band of Ashkenazic amazons.'

'So what?' Anya surreptitiously scratches a small reddish patch on her wrist. I must admit I'm mildly pleased to see that the ben Issachar rash still plagues her. 'She's still in the direct line of firstborn daughters.'

'But think of all the mating generations that have long since poured their different bloodlines into her. From the far side of the Carpathians, and the valley of the Rhine, and a drop or two from Constantinople that came westward along the Danube behind the invading Turks. And all those city-dwellers, disappearing into the courtyards of Kazimierz, arguing politics over the tea-glasses in Petersburg. Places as mysterious to your first Gittel as the back of the moon.'

She shams indifference, takes out a small pocket knife and begins to trim those meticulously tended sapphic fingernails. 'That's what you say. You've been wrong before.'

But I won't be shaken off. 'Not one of Rainbow's cells,' I persist, 'remembers the cold slap of the water in the stream where you and Gittel swam, or the taste of the berries from the bush near your hut, or the names of the birds in the woods where you screamed to the old native gods. And there's nothing you can do to change that.'

'We'll see,' she replies. And begins rummaging through Rainbow's desk drawers and chaotic cupboards, with a cat-burglar's speed and skill.

'So, is that how you earned your living, once they drove you out of the dorf? A *goniff*! What are you after?'

'Can't you guess?'

As the dawn breaks, she drags out a battered cardboard box-file with a rusty clasp, from behind a stack of unread texts on the deconstruction – or do I mean demolition? – of cinematic narrative. She dumps the contents on to the floor. A dusty photo album in an old-fashioned padded binding, a few studio portraits in crumbling cardboard frames, heaps of loose prints and curling snapshots, a few shiny leaflets. She reaches for one of these, holds it up: 'Aha! The last Gittel in her maiden days. And that, I presume, is the most recent male input into the lines.'

It is a promotional leaflet from some early tour – Gittel-plus-eight as the singer with Cy 'Silvertones' and the band, before she paused for motherhood and he decided that wedding and bar mitzvah bookings put more bread on the family table than life on the road.

'Now look at this one – redistribute the weight slightly, and change the hair colour and remove that ridiculous paint from the face, and there's my Gittel underneath.' She rummages further.

'Aha! And what about this one?' She holds up a sepia portrait of a turn of the century belle in a high-necked Russian blouse, standing before the backdrop of a painted Arcadia, with balustrades and beckoning groves. 'Even closer to the prototype. This could be the first Gittel's twin!'

'Sorry, friend, but I've seen that one before. At Aunt Goldie's house. The damsel in question comes from the other side of the family – it's Great-Grandma Rosenbloom, at age eighteen.'

'So what does that prove?' Anya scoffs. 'You know how inbred these people were. They only mated with each other – the old ones went into mourning if a child dared to marry out. (And believe me, with my parentage I know whereof I speak, except in my mother's case marriage didn't come into it.) So I'd say the probability is pretty high that there's Gittel blood on both sides.'

'The Rosenblooms came from the opposite end of Eastern Europe. They ran away from the Habsburg emperors, not the Czars.'

She shrugs. 'So what? Love knows no borders. You never heard of railways? River barges? Horse and cart? I say she's close enough to Gittel to satisfy me.'

'Satisfy-schmatisfy? Do you seriously believe you can pick up with this tenth Gittel where you left off with Number One before? What makes you think she'll play ball?'

'For a start, unlike the first one, she's not likely to get her head turned by some man.'

'No, I'll grant you that. Although,' I point out with a wicked twinkle, which shows up as a flash of prismatic light on the edges of the glass, 'Rainbow has – recently – been entertaining the flicker of a wild fantasy about returning to religion. With a little bit of orchestration, and the application of a few time-tested psychic tricks, I will soon be ready to steer her into a shocking spur-of-the-moment theological and sexual conversion. It will dawn on her that an arranged marriage with some elderly (and hopefully impotent) Limnititzker may be the only key to the door of this lost and tantalising world.'

'What's so tantalising about it? Bloody medieval ghetto,' scowls Anya, who should know.

'The attraction,' I announce, 'is her new and so far unrequited passion. Who happens to be a young wife and mother of impeccable ultra-orthodox credentials. Imagine her delight when a lost soul returns, through her good offices, to the fold. They can dance together at all the weddings.'

Anya doesn't like this piece of news. She grunts her displeasure. The old girl may have updated her image and cleaned up her act, but those eyebrows still crash together when she frowns.

'Is this the person she was supposed to visit in the morning?'

I don't like the sound of that. 'What do you mean – was supposed to? She's going. I'll make sure of that.'

'You seem to have forgotten, Kokos, you're no longer in a position to make sure of anything.'

'And what position do you think you're in, *gilgul*?' I suddenly remember a nifty trick I know, and turn my mirror – and her reflection in it – a ghoulish purple. 'What makes you think Rainbow would entertain a love affair with the likes of you?'

'Stop that!' She turns her head away.

'Don't forget your altered status. Your so-called Gittel's not the only one who isn't quite the girl she was in that far-off summertime.'

Point to Kokos. Anya sulks.

'Anyway,' I continue (while we have it, let's press the advantage home), 'you know as well as I do that these couplings between the separate spheres always come to grief in the end.' (I'm a fine one to talk. Some day I'll learn to practise what I preach.)

'Not true!' she retorts. 'What about the Posen affair?'

I should have known she'd bring up that old chestnut. It turns up as a footnote in every textbook and training manual. It happened a long, long time back in the town of Posen. A Christian family moves into an old stone house in the main street. When they start to unpack, they find they can't get the cellar door open. So they send one of their servants down to force it open, but he never comes back. They tiptoe down and see that he's got it open, all right, but he's lying there dead.

Next thing they know, all hell breaks loose upstairs: they find their best brass candlesticks snapped in half as if they were toothpicks, and the pot where their dinner is cooking on the hearth fills up with ashes. So they call out the local Jesuit priest, he takes a good sniff and says it's haunted. Three times he tries to exorcise the place, but no luck.

Then a Jewish magician, one Joel from Zamosc, arrives in town, and the family calls him in. He announces that there are invisible demons in the cellar, and that they claim that the house is legally theirs.

It turns out that the place used to belong to a Jewish tradesman – a cobbler, I think, or maybe a carpenter – who married a female demon. They lived together for a long time; she bore him children – who took after their mother and turned out to be demons too. When their father died, he did what any good parent would do and left them his property. They weren't very pleased when a bunch of mortals moved in.

'So that proves it!' announces Anya. 'That couple crossed the line and lived together – why shouldn't Gittel and I?'

'I wish you'd stop calling her Gittel. And anyway, you've forgotten the rest of the story. Joel the Magician agrees to act as a trial judge, and lets the demons bring a lawsuit to get their house back. Nobody in court can see them, but everyone hears their voices when they come to testify.

'So who wins? Surprise, surprise. Demons, says this wonderfully unbiased judge, only have right of residence in wildernesses and desert places. He evicts the children from the house, and gives it to the goyim. Very nice. I told you this kind of mingling always ends in tears.'

'I'm not trying to have babies with her, blast it!' bellows the exasperated Apostate, rattling my glass.

This roar brings a ravaged-looking Rainbow, in rumpled

London Lesbian & Gay Filmfest T-shirt, to put her head round the bedroom door.

'You look terrible,' I tell her. 'Those dark circles . . . Your eyes remind me of archery targets.'

'What do you expect? Sleep deprivation. Not to mention haunted twice over.'

'You poor thing,' croons Anya, placing a hand on Rainbow's cheek and letting it linger there.

'See what you've done, Apostate!' I scold. 'Deprived the poor woman of her rest!'

Anya bridles, unhands Rainbow to demand, 'So why's it my fault?'

'She only sleeps well when I'm in there with her. She needs my naughty lullabies to soothe her spirit.'

The *gilgul* snorts. I fail to see how Rainbow can find her repertoire of barnyard sounds attractive.

'It would have helped,' says Rainbow, 'if you two hadn't gabbled at each other all night long.'

'She needs coffee,' I announce. 'Make the girl some coffee.'

'So who do you think you are, dybbuk?' mutters Anya, 'Mission Control?'

But she heads for the kitchen, just the same.

18

' I still can't figure out why you need to see this person anyway.'

Drip, drip, drip. Anya's attempts at dissuasion, like an unsubtle variant on the old water torture, persist through Rainbow's three cups of black coffee, hasty shower, and struggles with the overstressed zip in her jeans.

'I just do.'

I can't follow every step of the action, but the flat is so small that I can hear the whole voiceover, even with the water running. And I am pleased, though unsurprised, that my programming remains effective, even if I can't get right in there to nurse it along.

'I'm coming with you.'

'I don't need a shadow.'

'A shadow?' Anya forces a bitter smile. 'Where I've been for the past 200 years or so, we count ourselves lucky if we still have one.'

The Apostate's no fool. She's found Rainbow's vital Jewish G-spot, the button in her mind marked Guilt. She has succeeded in convincing Rainbow that she alone must somehow atone for the misdeeds of the ancestress who caused poor Anya to wander forever in a twilight world.

Moral blackmail does it every time. But I'll give Rainbow this: she has the gumption to sound ungracious. 'Oh, all right, come with me – if you must.'

I snipe from the sidelines. 'Hey, Rosenbloom, remember,

the sins of the great-great-etcetera-grandmothers shall not be visited on future generations.'

But she doesn't hear this. She's switched on the radio for the traffic update.

'Oh yes, they shall,' whispers Anya into my mirror. 'The fathers have eaten sour grapes, and the children's teeth shall be set on edge.'

'You've been stuck in too many cheap hotel rooms, Anya, with nothing better to read than that overrated family saga. Anyway, I thought you'd given up the notion of revenge.'

'Oh, but I have. Compensation will be paid voluntarily. Rainbow is going to want to make it up to me, ever so nicely.'

Where did this women learn such arrogance? Surely not by selling chickens?

They are just about ready to go out. A final check in the mirror – Anya, ever so Clint-like, flicks out her comb.

'Well, look at the pair of you,' I sneer. 'A right brace of identikit old-fashioned dykes if ever I saw one. Creaking leather jackets, well-rubbed denim rustling between those confident thighs. Just the thing, Rainbow, to make sweet old-fashioned Riva feel really at her ease . . .'

Anya scoffs; Rainbow takes a worried look into my depths.

'OK, hang on a minute, Anya.' And zips out for a quick change into a respectable blazer (one of Aunt Rebecca's unused presents, a recent salvo in the family campaign to smarten up the recalcitrant niece) and an unrumpled pair of cords.

Anya fumes and fidgets.

'And how are you going to explain this creature to your little ladyfriend?' I ask Rainbow.

'That's my problem,' she tosses over her shoulder, and heads for the door, with Anya – spaniel or Rottweiler? – at her heels.

Left behind! I can't believe it! I blaze with impotent rage. Then I force myself to stand back and assess the situation. Undistracted by Rainbow's presence, or by the white noise that pulses continuously around Anya's troubled soul, I perform a little self-examination, to sound out the position of the binding points, and decipher the formulae that pin me down.

Now that I have peace to do all this, I realise what I had previously suspected: the *gilgul* has used a fairly primitive spell. I can't neutralise the treatment completely: she has pulled a fast one on the prince of my particular star (yes, it isn't only humans who possess them: we demons have our guardian angels, too). Until I can persuade her to unbind me – or make contact with Mephistco and convince someone back at base to forgive me my trespasses just long enough to do an override – I am confined inside the plane of reflected light.

But – hoo-ha! – this does not mean I have to stay in one particular mirror. Any sufficiently glazed or silvered surface will do. And the city's full of them. So enough time's been wasted. Let's get moving.

It's easy to see how often, of late, our Rainbow has covered the ground between her flat and Stamford Hill. I can find the way with my eyes closed. No North London native could navigate the route with more speed and certainty than I do – although my journey takes me, of necessity, from one plate-glass shop window to another, and then via the rear-view mirrors of thirty-nine different cars, vans and buses. In desperation, once we hit the less-trafficked back roads south-east of Manor House, I cover the last leg on the well-polished bodywork of someone's brand new Volvo.

19

I'm not all that far behind them, in the end. Anger makes a fine accelerator. When I arrive, I find Rainbow's taxi parked just outside the house. Anya sits in the passenger seat, arms folded across her chest, making a pretty poor job of concealing her impatience. She stares straight ahead, but she has opened the window just enough to eavesdrop on the interview taking place on the pavement outside, between Rainbow and the little dove.

If Anya weren't so busy pretending to study the licence number on the car in front of us, she might have noticed the momentary ripple of light across the glass. For I have come to rest in Rainbow's wing-mirror, where I can keep all three players in this drama within my sights.

Rainbow sings the praises of the weather and the day, offers a quick run to Alexandra Palace so they might continue last night's interesting conversation under the morning sky.

Riva responds with a recitative of all the pressures on her time, makes a counter-offer of a quick cup of tea in the family kitchen.

Rainbow confesses to a need to talk of private, painful things, outside the intrusive proximity of small children and sisters-in-law.

'Well, who's she then?' challenges Riva, thrusting her chin towards Anya, glowering in the cab.

'Oh, just a friend. I'm giving her a lift to . . . ah . . . Hornsey High Street. It's on the way . . .'

Only I see the *gilgul*'s nostrils flare, and the jawline sharpen.

'Just give me an hour,' pleads Rainbow.

'Well, just this once . . . Give me a minute. I'll just tell them inside that I'm going.'

Ingrate. On a glorious day like this, who could wish for anything more delightful than a walk in the park and a chance to share the secrets of Rainbow's heart?

To avoid missing any action, I've moved inside, from the wing to the rear-view mirror. In the back of the taxi, our two temporary travelling companions sit as far apart as possible.

With a nod, the Apostate takes the initiative. 'Hi, I'm Anya.'

Riva surveys her neighbour's clothes and haircut, then, fingering her own ornate wedding ring, gathers her dignity about her. 'Good morning. I'm Mrs Riva ben Issachar Cohen.'

That Apostate is an odd fish. I monitor her face for reactions to that familiar and, for us, unlucky surname. Not a flicker. The ensuing silence is broken only by the quick rustle of Anya surrepitiously scratching her knee through a layer of denim.

At a parade of shops, Rainbow suddenly pulls over. 'Right, Anya,' she announces, cool as anything. 'This is your stop, isn't it? See you around.'

Ha! That'll teach you, *gilgul*, trying to tag along where you're not wanted. But Anya makes no comeback, apart from a quick, razor-sharp glance at the back of Rainbow's head. 'Thanks for the lift, Rainbow. Cheers for now.' She hops out, bangs the door shut only slightly too energetically, and strolls off towards the shops without a backward glance.

'Look,' pleads Riva, while Rainbow eases the taxi into a parking space. 'I'm not some kind of rabbi. I know you're having some sort of big spiritual crisis or something, but I don't really see how I can help.'

Rainbow takes a very deep breath. 'What if I wanted to – get back to where you are?'

'To where I am? What are you talking about?'

'To being really Jewish.'

I can almost hear Riva chewing on the inside of her own

cheek to keep back the laughter. I don't have to be in my usual internal listening-post to know what she's thinking.

'Well, you could just try observing the commandments, for a start. You don't need me for that.'

'I need more. What if I wanted to . . . get involved with your community?'

'The Limnititzkers?' she squeaks. Then she does laugh. 'You? Pull the other one . . .'

The rest of this dialogue is lost to me.

Rainbow locks the taxi, and the pair of them head round the back of the Palace towards the pond. To keep them in my sights, I would have to hitch a lift on something shiny – Riva's wedding ring is the only thing I can think of that might work. But that feels just a little too close for comfort to the flesh of a ben Issachar, and anyway, I'm not sure that the Hebrew inscription engraved upon it would be terribly good for my already wobbly morale.

Also, there are far too many trees out there.

They're gone for ages. So much for Rainbow's promise to have Riva home in an hour. I deduce from this delay that Rainbow has kept her cool and not confessed her hopeless passion: if she did, the little dove would be out of the park like a shot, and finding her own way home.

I use the interlude to consider my own predicament. I'm cut off from any means of communication with home base. Just as well: this fresh humiliation and the subsequent return with tail between my legs would be the final nail in my professional coffin. Being treed by the great wonder-rabbi Shmuel ben Issachar might be written off as an occupational hazard; being trapped – on an assignment officially aborted – by an undead amateur is unforgivable.

By now I have a fairly clear idea about the binding formula Anya used. It should wear off eventually – in a week, a month or a year – depending on the astrological and meteorological conditions that prevailed at the time she launched it. If I can only think back to that precise moment, and recover all the necessary ambient data, I'll be able to figure it out for myself. But before I can begin the calculations, a shadow blocks the light. It's Anya.

She circles the taxi, trying the doors. Then she produces a key from her own jacket pocket, and lets herself in, to crouch down behind the driver's seat.

'That was crafty,' I remark.

She jumps up, banging her head on the partition.

'Kokos! You bitch! How did you get here?'

'Oh, sorry. I must have forgotten to say hello when I arrived. I caught up with you all at Riva's house. I think perhaps you should have paid more attention to Chapter 85 in your instruction manual. I'm not quite as rigidly confined by this spell as you may have hoped.'

She ignores this. Has bigger worries. 'Where are they?'

'I don't know. Walking round the pond, I suppose. Feeding the ducklings. Breaking down the barriers. Pouring out their hearts. Eyes meeting. Tentatively touching . . . Hand in hand . . .'

A bright red rash comes out on the Apostate's cheek.

'Stop! Don't scratch – you know it will only make it worse!'

'You're talking a load of dreck. That little holier-than-thou fanatic would sooner drown herself than let – '

'You'll soon find out. I think they're coming.'

Anya drops down out of sight.

Because of the angle of the mirror, I can't quite see them, but I can hear their voices as they approach.

'Riva, I'm so, so sorry.'

It's Rainbow. Oh dear, has she blown it?

But no, they both seem remarkably cheerful. And here am I, none the wiser.

'Shush! I told you, it's all right. And anyway, it was entirely my fault.'

They come into view. Riva seems to have undergone a total physical transformation – her hair is cropped short, and her long, full skirt is wrapped round her legs like a strange pair of baggy breeches. How bizarre. Is this what an hour's proximity to an out Jewish lesbian can do? Where's her *sheitel*, the wig of the pious married woman? Then I see it, limp and waterlogged in her hand. And the rest of her is pretty sodden, too.

'If I hadn't leaned out of the rowboat so far . . .' Riva continues.

'There's a blanket on the back seat. But get in first, before you freeze. Damn, I thought I'd locked this.'

Anya springs up at them as the door swings wide. That slyboots. She points a gun.

'Get in here. Both of you.'

After a hair-raising careen out of the park, through the backstreets of Muswell Hill, Bounds Green, and on to the North Circular Road (only in the broadest interpretation of the term could the Apostate be described as knowing how to drive), Rainbow persuades Anya to untie her hands and feet, and let her get back behind the wheel.

'Sorry, but the way you're handling this taxi, the police are bound to notice . . .'

'Wouldn't you just love that, Ms Rosenbloom?' scoffs Anya. 'Rescue of distressed damsel by those big strong WASP boys in blue?'

'Up yours. I'm the one who stands to lose the licence, pal. Or pay the repair bills when you've crushed us up against a wall.'

Rainbow promises that, if Anya lets her back behind the wheel, she will try no tricks, and will keep her two-way radio switched off.

'Better still,' Anya orders, 'call in and tell them you're on an all-day job out of town. Now.'

But, once the swap of places is made, the *gilgul* presses the gun into Riva's ribs by way of a guarantee. The little dove huddles in her blanket, and, though Rainbow puts the heat on full, does not stop shivering until we're somewhere in the depths of Essex, in the fast lane of the M25. But she's smart enough to keep her mouth shut.

210

For the moment, I also hold my peace. As far as Rainbow knows, I'm still stuck inside her mirror, back at the flat. Anya hasn't told her that I'm here. Perhaps she's forgotten – or simply doesn't care.

20

We go on for hours. I think we're riding this taxi to the edge of the world. The only breach in the silence comes when Anya raps out the occasional direction – turn here, take the first left off the roundabout, and so forth. Until, deep in the countryside, when we pass fields smeared lurid yellow by the oilseed rape, and Riva begins to sneeze and sneeze.

'Bless you,' says Rainbow, automatically.

Anya spits. 'Benedictions already. So who do you think you are, Rosenbloom, the new chief rabbi? Blessings from you are the last thing this pious little *tsatskeleh* needs.'

'What this woman needs,' ventures Rainbow, 'is to get home to her kids, and to change her clothes before she gets pneumonia.'

'Too bad. Let her shiver. And let someone else look after her little brats for a change. That house of hers is crammed to the rafters with mothers and sisters-in-law and groupies like your dear Aunt Goldie.'

'How do you know?' Riva pipes up. 'You don't know anything about me.'

'Oh, but you're wrong. I've made a special study of the ben Issachar clan. And I've known you a lot longer than has your so-called friend Rainbow here, thanks to whom you now find yourself in this lousy fix.'

'She's not my friend!' spits Riva, through clenched jaws.

'What a disappointment. I thought you two were just

beginning to get on swimmingly – sorry about that – up at the Ally Pally pond.'

Then, from Riva, 'You're either going to have to get a tissue out of my skirt pocket and wipe my nose for me, or untie me so I can do it myself.' She sneezes again.

Without losing her grip on the gun, Anya forages as directed. 'Here, but it's pretty sodden. Blow. You know, your skirt's still damp. You'd better get out of it.'

'If you think I'm going to take my clothes off in a car full of . . . of female sex-perverts, you can forget it.'

'Did you hear that, Rainbow?' jeers Anya. 'Your little kosher friend here is a dyed-in-the-wool homophobe.'

'You're doing your best to confirm her prejudices, Anya. She's never met any dykes before. We'd just started talking about all that when the rowboat tipped over. Then we get back to the taxi, and there you are waving your weaponry, and kidnapping us. Thanks a lot.'

'I think everybody in this taxi should start trying to be a little nicer to me. Remember, I'm the one with the gun. And slow down, Rosenbloom. You're going to take the second right, just after that pub.'

It's a narrow, rutted track – a ribbon of mud across a reedy marshland.

'Down this? Are you serious? Do you know how much new taxi tyres cost?'

'If that's the biggest worry on your mind right now,. Rosenbloom, you really do have no imagination. Just keep going.'

We've left the radiant spring weather miles behind us, or entered into some especially unfavoured zone. There's no horizon. The sky can only be distinguished from the land by the metallic glare behind its greyness. Nothing breaches the flatness except some kind of smokestack or cooling tower a couple of miles to the north.

Where the track ends, mud gives way to sand. We're very near the land's edge. There is nowhere else to go. Rainbow parks the taxi, next to a small cottage of salt-scarred brick.

'This is it. Everybody out.' Anya produces a rusty mortice-key, struggles with a lock and gives the door a kick that finally opens it. With a sardonic flourish, she ushers the other two inside.

Once again, I'm barred from the action. And, from wing-mirror or rear-view alike, the prospects are pretty depressing. There's a smell of salt and mud and dead fish, which I find unpleasantly reminiscent of somewhere else. Lacking only her native forest (now probably half chewed away by acid rain), and the dorf (whose last inhabitants' bones still lie jumbled in a secret pit) our Anya has found herself a little home from home.

But, within the hour, my mood has lightened. The rain begins to fall.

Old Shmuel ben Issachar was not the only Jewish sage who knew how to walk between the raindrops. Like them or not, those boys were smart. But, as I've always said, never be too snobbish to learn from the Opposition. So, given the current limitations on my mobility, I apply a variation of the same technique, and convey myself, travelling from one silvery globule to another, and thus on to the nearest windowpane.

The glass is so smeared that it hardly counts as a reflective surface. But never mind the niceties: it gets me in. I see an old, mottled mirror above the fireplace, wherein I make myself comfortable. With a speed smacking more of the arsonist than the Girl Guide, Anya's got a fire going.

Anya, possibly by waving her gun again, has finally persuaded Riva to change into drier clothes. The wet skirt and jumper, and the black, curly wig now hang across two chairbacks, before the hearth; their owner, I think, looks rather fetching – if completely out of character – in one of Anya's flannel shirts and a pair of faded denims with the cuffs rolled up.

Secure on her own ground (she's locked the door from the inside and pocketed the key), Anya cuts the cords binding Riva's wrists and ankles, and slips the gun back into a gangsterish shoulder-holster straight out of a B-movie props department.

Then Jimmy Cagney dissolves into Mrs Miniver. 'What we all need,' she announces, 'is a nice, hot cup of tea. Does anyone take sugar?'

She turns away to bustle domestically with mugs and kettle, pausing only to warn: 'Don't try anything cute, sisters; I don't have eyes in the back of my head because I don't need them.'

Rainbow and Riva keep still and say nothing. When the mugs of tea – from the smell, I'd say Lapsang Souchong – are handed round, they sip in silence. I suppose they're dumbfounded by their surroundings; I know I am.

We're in a room that occupies the whole ground floor of the cottage; in one corner, a steep staircase – more like a ladder – climbs to some sort of loft or upper room. Two walls are broken by windows, a third is occupied by the fireplace; a battered electric cooker and an old sink, which looks as if it were last used to dip sheep, stand on either side of another locked and bolted door. The furniture, scanty as it is, wouldn't fill the back of an Okie pick-up fleeing the dustbowl in *The Grapes of Wrath*: a stained wooden table, a couple of shelves and half a dozen kitchen chairs, an armchair with the padding leaking out of it, and an old car seat that has been dragged in, probably some years ago, to serve in place of a settee. The lamps look, to say the least, unreliable.

The décor expresses an uneasy marriage between *Cold Comfort Farm*, the house behind the garage in *The Big Sleep*, and the Hole-in-the-Wall gang's hideaway on the morning after the shoot-out.

Except for the pictures. They cover every available flat surface, of wall, shelf, door and ceiling; they have been cut out and pasted down without apparent plan or pattern, into a crazy-paving of paintings, posters, diagrams, photographs, cards, calendars and illustrations vandalised – though neatly scalpeled, rather than ripped – from books. Most, but not all, bear the images of women's faces.

A folding screen in the alcove under the stairs seems the handiwork of a Victorian nurserymaid gone mad, with coloured transfers of art nouveau sprites, screaming Medusa heads and crinolined paper dolls. Flanking the front door are the intricate cosmic diagrams of Hispanic kabbalists, respectfully mapping the mysteries of the godhead's feminine side. On the wall that passes for a kitchen, Gertrude Stein and Alice B. Toklas stare down in fastidious disapproval at Anya's *batterie de cuisine*, unfit for whipping up their favourite hashish fudge.

Above one window, Sarah Bernhardt plays a boyish Hamlet, next to a postcard of the painter Gluck, all Semitic profile, slouch hat and cool androgyny. Nearby, nicked from a book of Sunday School Bible tales, an incongruously pink-skinned Ruth kneels to swear devotion to a snub-nosed, Anglo-Saxon Naomi. Above it, an old woman in a white headscarf raises her hands above the Sabbath candles, to praise the hidden Queen who dances for her inside the flames.

Elsewhere are posters of dead Hollywood sirens and live lesbian rock stars, alongside colour prints of ghetto crones and Jewish brides from the workshop – if not the brush – of Rembrandt. In a medieval woodcut, a wistful Eve averts her eyes from the scene.

'Hey, what's that doing there? Where did you get this? And those?! My God!!' Rainbow's voice raises, in surprise or indignation. But not loud enough to waken Riva, who has temporarily escaped captivity by falling asleep in her chair.

I can't see what has agitated Rainbow: it's something right below the the mirror where I now lodge. But, from her barrage of questions to Anya, I can guess.

Outside my line of vision lies a picture gallery of all her dead female relations of the Gittel line. School photographs of Rainbow in every age from perky to petulant, pictures of her with Naomi, Mary-Catherine and various unknowns, and – I'll bet anything – at least one of Rainbow with the unsound sound woman, yesterday's love. Plenty of publicity shots of her mother singing, I suppose, plus holiday snaps and studio poses of all the clan, backtracking as far along the time-lines as the parvenu art of photography can carry us. Of the earlier Gittels we find nothing; none ever rose high enough in life to get their portrait painted.

216

Anya flops down next to Rainbow, on the car-seat settee. 'So you like my collection?'

'Who gave you those?'

'At the risk of sounding self-pitying – a bad habit I've been trying to break – nobody ever gives me anything. I took them.'

'When? Why?'

'Don't be stupid. You may think you're obsessed, pal, with Miss Return to Your Roots over there . . .' She juts her chin towards Riva, with a brief pause to assure herself that the sleeper's still breathing. 'Well, let me tell you, you know nothing – zero – zilch – *gornisht mit gornisht* – when it comes to real obsession. I've been on your trail for a long, long time.'

'So I see. But if you wanted to take your revenge and kill me, because of some ancient grudge against somebody who's been dust for 200 years, then why didn't you just do it last night at my house? Why come all the way out here? And why did you drag that poor innocent woman along?'

'First of all,' demands Anya, 'what makes you think I want to kill you? You've been watching too many sick films about psychopaths.'

'What else should I think?' demands Rosenbloom. 'I don't know much about etiquette back there in the shtetl, but even in these decadent times we don't feel a gun in the back is just a snappy way to say "please".'

'If I said to you,' replies Anya wearily, 'that I wanted you to stop what you were doing, stop everything, and drive miles and miles, into the back of beyond, just to be with me, you'd have told me to piss off.'

'Well, why couldn't you wait until after I saw Riva? We were only going to have an hour together.'

Anya leans forward and adds more coal to the fire.

'That hour together was just what I didn't want to happen.'

'Why?'

Anya looks at Rainbow and shakes her head. 'Come on, now. Stop pretending.'

Rainbow shrugs. 'You think I was trying to seduce her, don't you? Fling myself at her black-stockinged feet while the Ally

Pally sparrows sang a serenade. All because of this burning, incongruous passion. Well, OK, a few hours ago, I would have said you were right. I was madly – and that's the operative word – head over heels in lust. But it's pretty obvious where that ridiculous attraction came from. My dybbuk set out to drive me crazy, and she damned near did. I was just about ready to turn in my leather jacket for a Limnititzker housewife's headscarf, anything for a passport into that secret world of hers . . . But as soon as you – did whatever it was you did to get Kokos out of my head, I came to my so-called senses.'

For all those Sumerian wizards, Babylonian astrologers, Macedonian witches, Sephardic kabbalists and Irish Jesuits who have split every hair on their heads on the question Can demons feel pain?, here's your answer:
AYYYYYYYYYYYYYYYYYYYYYYYYYYYYYYYYYYYYYYYYYYYYY YYYYYYYYYYYYYYYYYYYYY!!! And no, that's not the wind wailing round the library windows.
How can she do this to me? Or, let's be clear-sighted about this, how can I do this to myself? These humans are clay remember, pliable clay. No, I'm wrong . . . they're twice as messy, and not half as durable.
I'm not stupid enough to let myself get carried away by righteous anger and reveal my presence. I swallow my fury, stifle my sorrow, and seek consolation by pretending it's all just another movie. Pass the popcorn.

'No, that's not what I thought.' Anya sucks at the insides of her own cheeks to suppress a smile. 'Sex didn't come into it. But it's a pretty entertaining idea.'
Rainbow seems affronted. Good; I hope she's writhing inside. 'What's so funny about it?' she demands. 'Especially with you tearing around like the wronged boyfriend in the last reel of *Some Came Running*, waving your wretched gun. Crazed with jealousy.'
'Jealous? Be serious. That's not what I call competition.'
Would you believe the chutzpah? The first time I met this

creature she was an unlettered half-caste peasant who smelt of stale sweat and dead chickens. Now already, she's had a wash and a workout or two, and read a few books and she thinks she's the answer to an Amazon's prayer.

'So what were you afraid of?'

'That history would repeat itself.'

'I'm sorry, I don't know what you're talking about.'

'Think about who she is. She's a ben Issachar!'

'I know. That's her maiden name. So what about it?'

Anya's losing patience. 'Stop being so obtuse.' Then she realises that Rainbow is, indeed, completely mystified.

'Didn't she tell you?'

'Who? Riva? Tell me what?'

'No, blast it. The dybbuk. Kokos. Didn't she tell you what happened? Why she came?'

'Of course. She told me all about you and Gittel, and how you called down the curse on Gittel's female line. Firstborn daughters of firstborn daughters and all that. But she didn't say anything about any ben Issachar.'

The Apostate almost chokes on her own laughter. (I wish she would, but fat lot of good it would do to a *gilgul*.)

Rainbow stares at her. Riva, meanwhile, in spite of the cacophony, sleeps on. I knew it; Anya has slipped something into her tea.

'I knew it,' Anya guffaws, in an unconscious echo of my unspoken words, 'I knew it! That overblown snob! Kokos left out the most important part of the story, didn't she. Just happened to forget to mention how she failed to do the job she was hired for, and got her comeuppance, good and proper, from the great wonder-rabbi Shmuel ben Issachar!'

I scream with rage. They take no notice, beyond a quick glance at the hearth, thinking it's just the wind in the chimney. What does that sleaze-bag of a *gilgul* expect me to do when I announce my presence to a quivering subject? Recite my entire career history complete with qualifications, pay scale, dates of promotions and dossier of official merit-ratings and reprimands? In our business, you work on the need-to-know principle. If

Anya thinks otherwise, she has no future at Mephistco. Her first freelance contract with the company could be her last.

Because I am – unlike Anya – neither amateur nor fool, I once again suppress my emotions for the sake of strategic advantage, and say not a word.

Just as well. Anya seems to be revving up to tell Rainbow her side of the story. It could be a long, long night.

I glance, speculatively, towards the window, where more bad weather has blown in from the North Sea. The sky's gone black. Maybe I should make a break for it, transit myself through the falling drops, and float on an oil-slick until morning. It would probably be more fun than listening to some self-deceiving *gilgul* spin her miserable yarn.

But caution keeps me here. If there are any factual errors (or, more likely, lies) I want to take careful note of them, and correct the record later.

'Do you want something to eat? You must be starving. I know I am.'

All of a sudden, the kidnapper turns perfect hostess. She goes to a shelf, brings back a box of matzos, tears it open. 'Here, have one.'

'Matzos?'

'It was Pesach the other week, remember? Don't worry, they're still well within the sell-by date.'

Which, I forbear to say out loud, is more than can be said for you, spook.

Rainbow takes one. 'Thanks.' And crunches it pensively, watching Anya do the same. 'Do you . . . ah . . . actually . . . um . . . get hungry? I thought you wouldn't . . . mmmmm need to eat . . .'

'Be serious. I'm Jewish, right?'

'Yes, but – '

'But you think ghosts don't get hungry. Well, maybe so. If I were, maybe I wouldn't.'

'Well, what are you, then?'

Anya seems not to hear this. She coughs on a shard of matzo. 'Sorry these damned things are so dry. I'm out of butter.'

'My Grandma Rosenbloom used to spread hers with chicken fat. But . . .' undeterred, 'you still haven't told me . . .'

'Chicken!' Anya makes a gagging motion. 'Don't say that word to me. In any way, shape or form, I've had it up to here with chickens!'

'You're not going to tell me, are you?' Rainbow reaches for the box, ravenous now, and helps herself to three more matzos. 'Got any jam?'

'No to the first. To the second, yes, but it's gone mouldy.'

'Why?'

'Because I've had it around for a lot longer than I care to tell you. Made it myself, with plums from a tree in another country.'

'Not that.'

'Not what?'

Anya is now standing with her back to the fireplace. I can see the nape of her neck go red.

Rainbow presses on. 'You know very well what. Not the bloody jam.'

'Your other question. I won't answer it because I can't. I just don't know.'

Rainbow, irritated: 'What do you mean you don't know? How can you not know what you are?'

The answer is lobbed back, at top speed and volume: 'BECAUSE I FUCKING DON'T! BECAUSE I FUCKING NEVER HAVE!!'

There's a stirring from the armchair. Rainbow and Anya both look towards Riva, who murmurs something in her sleep and turns over, huddled in her blanket, without breaking the stride of her dream. Whatever else her existential status, the Apostate is a damned good purveyor of surreptitious Mickey Finns.

'Relax,' says Anya, 'she'll be out for ages yet.' And flops back down on to the car seat.

Rainbow, slower than I am on the uptake, inches away from Anya, and looks appalled. 'I don't believe you did that.'

Anya shakes her head, and laughs softly. 'Calm down, Rosenbloom. It's perfectly harmless. Herbal and 100 per cent organic. You can buy the ingredients in any good health food shop. You start with – '

Rainbow reaches out a hand, and grabs Anya's wrist. 'Just stop it!' I can see her fingertips twitch slightly, as if surprised to have encountered warm flesh and solid bone. 'I don't want recipes. I want answers!'

Deftly, Anya twists her arm and catches Rainbow's hand in her own. Squeezes it, and lets it go.

'All I can do is tell you what I know.' She rises, moves the improvised drying rack of Riva's clothing to one side, feeds more coal to the fire, settles back and looks for the words in the flames.

21

'When somebody – I don't know – God, whoever – wrote my name and fate in the Book of Life, I think the pen must have slipped between two lines. Because I'm always neither one thing nor the other. Not quite a Jew – although the blood of my mother makes me as Jewish as any ben Issachar – not quite a Gentile. I didn't quite belong in the Jewish dorf – just as well, because horsemen came through more than once and left blood and burnt timbers behind them – and didn't quite belong in the hamlet where my father's people lived – maybe just as well also, because the crucifixes on their walls didn't save them when the cholera came and brought its own kind of pogrom. Not quite a woman – because I wanted to do things with Gittel that only a man was supposed to want to do; not quite a man – because I wanted Gittel to do the same things back to me.'

'It seems to me,' murmurs Rainbow, 'that it was Gittel who was neither one thing or the other. Not you.'

'Maybe so. But I didn't learn that until a long time after. And when Gittel cut my pride and my heart into pieces with her little sharp fingernails, and I let loose the dybbuk on her and got punished for it, I was neither one thing nor the other, once again.'

'How so?'

'Because when ben Issachar exorcised Kokos, and put her into the tree . . .'

That loudmouth! Tell-tale! Traitor! How dare she? I can't

wait until I'm out of here and then she'll feel the full force of my wrath . . .

'The tree? What tree? What are you talking about?'

'The tree in the forest, where he sealed up the dybbuk . . .'

'Kokos was sealed up in a tree?'

Is that just the trace of a smirk on the Rosenbloom face? The ghost of a twinkle in her eye? I'll make her repent it.

'Exorcising Gittel was not enough. The ben Issachars of this world are enthusiastic punishers – and I suppose he thought he was doing the rest of the human race a favour by getting Kokos off the scene. Anyway, for her the tree – for me a different penalty. Because the whole neighbourhood – thanks to Gittel's big-mouthed elder sister – knew exactly who had been behind the curse, although even the sister was too much of a prude to tell anyone the reason why.'

'What happened to you?'

'I'm still not sure. A nasty itch, for starters – ' and, as if reminded, 'ooh, could you scratch my left shoulderblade . . . just there? A little up the way . . . now over towards the middle . . . Aaaah, thanks, that's just right.' She settles back again. 'And then there was a kind of . . . blank space . . . where my death should have been.'

'A blank space?'

'I don't know exactly what happened to me. When the exorcism was carried out, and Gittel and her husband left the district a few weeks later, I dropped into a kind of daze. When the dybbuk disappeared was when – and only when – I knew my hopes of getting Gittel back had come to nothing. Stupid, wasn't I?'

Rainbow puts her hand on Anya's, leaves it there, says nothing.

'Then I woke up one summer morning – it was still dark, the birds were just starting their dawn chorus, and on that particular day there seemed only to be crows – and I felt very cold. As if it were January instead of August. So I went out, to find some sticks for a fire, and got myself lost. In my own forest. Couldn't find the way back, and the sun never quite rose enough to help me. So I just wandered off. When finally the daylight came, I was somewhere else I'd never been before.

'It took me a long, long time before I found a road back to the market town, and the dorf. And when I did, there was no one I knew there. As I said before, few people in that part of the world, in those days, made old bones. And all of them were gone. I looked in both the cemeteries, among the Christians and the Jews, and found the names of all my neighbours. In the Jewish place, I did what was right, and put a stone on each of the graves to show that someone had come to visit, that the occupants were not forgotten.'

Rainbow reaches out a finger, runs it along Anya's forehead and down her cheek. 'You don't look any older than I am. Younger, if anything. And 100 per cent alive.'

'I think I am. I don't know what happened.'

Well, I do. That wretched old ben Issachar did the cruellest thing possible to Anya – he put her, indefinitely, on hold. But why should I do her any favours and explain this, after what she's done to me?

'What did you do next?'

'There are some parts I just don't want to tell you; I think I'm probably afraid. Let's just say that I had a lot of time to learn things – about survival in terrible times, and camouflage, and new ways of living. About women like me – and you – who walk like ghosts through a world that tries not to see us. Talk about lost tribes – we could form a thousand of them. And all the while I was hunting . . .'

'For what?'

'For Gittel's line. The business was unfinished. And, in the course of that hunt, I spent some of the time in . . . the place where Kokos comes from.'

'Can you tell me about it? She's never said a word.'

'Nor should she. We have rules.'

What chutzpah! Listen to that big-mouthed *gilgul*, acting like she's a fully paid-up member of the team. What does she mean – *we*?

Rainbow, more politely, wonders the same thing, 'Well, then, are you some kind of a dybbuk now, too?'

Anya shrugs and sighs. 'I don't think so. As I said, I suppose I'm neither one thing nor the other.'

'So you've found us. Gittel's girls. Or me, anyway. The last of the line, and certain to remain so. So what are you going to do now? Take your revenge?'

Rainbow disconnects her hand from Anya's, rises, and goes to lean an elbow on the mantelpiece. She's so close I can smell her, and see the little nerve twitching in a secret place behind her ear, and hear her breathing just slightly faster than before.

'That was my original intention,' Anya confesses, looking up at her with a rueful smile.

'The sins of the mothers visited upon their daughters' daughters . . .'

'Well, I must admit, I tried. It was a long time, and a lot of travelling and enforced detours, before I caught up with your family, a couple of generations back. And when I did so, I didn't have any real . . . power. I turned up every so often, did what I could, with my limited resources. It never amounted to much, a few petty annoyances. An inexplicable chill, and some midnight noises, in your grandmother's Whitechapel flat when she was first married. Not strong enough so anyone would really notice . . .'

'Oh, but she did.'

'Really? How do you know?'

'She never stopped telling the story – and believe me, when my Grandma Gertie liked a story, she aired it often – of the weird goings-on in the place in Cable Street, and how she was sure the bedroom was haunted. She made my Grandpa move, three weeks after they'd arrived and half their wedding presents weren't even unpacked yet, and they lost their deposit to the landlord. I think that galled her more than the ghostly sound-effects.'

Anya brightens. 'I wish I'd known that. It would have boosted my confidence . . .'

'What else?'

226

'What?'

'What else did you do to my family?'

'Well, I made your mother sing off-key once. During an important audition. She could never figure out why – she'd rehearsed like crazy. Thought it spelled death for her professional future. In fact, she went off to a jazz club with other musician friends that very evening, to drown her sorrows, and met your father, who was playing in the band.'

'Not, perhaps, the punishment you'd originally intended.'

'Well, maybe all's well that ends well. Now I've met you.'

I cringe to admit it, but I've been duped. Hearing Anya's account, it has become clear that, when she turned up, in her rags and her stench, at Diabolexpo, she was reverting to an earlier self, complete with costume and an all-too-believable make-up job. From everything she says, it's clear this *gilgul*'s been on the scene for quite a while – there is no way she could have learned what she's learned, cleaned up her act and become who she is now if the only time she's had to do it in was the brief interval between our confrontation at the Mephistco stand and her appearance on the beach at Bournemouth.

One question: did she con Lil too, and all the rest of the team, or were all of them in on her little plot?

I feel like a bomb about to detonate. Hell hath no fury, etcetera and so forth. The mirror can barely contain me. A hairline crack runs down through the middle of the glass. But neither Anya nor Rainbow appears to notice.

Anya has risen from her seat, takes up a position facing Rainbow, at the opposite end of the mantelpiece.

Rainbow begins to edge backwards.

'I know how you must have felt – believe me, I've been there, too. Had my own heart broken by one inquisitive straight lady, way back in my desperate youth. I wish I could disown her.'

'Who? Your straight lady?'

'No, my heartless and sexually misguided ancestress. I know

she's my own flesh and blood, but I hope she got whatever was coming to her. And I'm sorry for the way she treated you.'

'Well, I'm not.'

'What?'

'If she hadn't got married and coupled with that whey-faced young man, one thing would never have led to another. You, in particular, would never have happened. And I'm glad that you did.'

'Why?'

Anya looks past Rainbow, into the coals. Her face is glowing redder than they are.

'Because I . . . like you. A lot. Even more than Gittel . . .'

'More than Gittel? But she was your lost love.'

'I think you're my found one.'

Now it takes courage to be that sloppily sentimental. But Anya's a better judge of character than she used to be, back in the old homeland. Like the plums for her jam, she knows when something's ripe for the picking.

So Clint's gun stays in its holster. Which soon comes off the shoulder anyway.

Next we get the usual nonsense: wordless dialogue, optical semaphoring, gauche laughter, ear-splitting silence. Sentences begun, then strangled at birth.

Not the sort of thing that turns a self-respecting dybbuk on: you'd never catch Lil and me, for instance, trying to swan-dive into each other's souls when the heavy breathing starts. (Not that you'd ever catch me doing any of it with that treacherous corporate stooge again. Her claw-prints are all over this Anya débâcle, and the only physical attentions from me she's likely to receive in future are a piece of my mind, the rough side of my tongue and my boot up her backside.)

If this were the movies, we'd now dissolve from first steamy kiss to bedroom scene. But Rainbow lives on the wrong side of the big white screen, and is a child of her time: she doesn't just look before she leaps, but holds a seminar on the pros and cons.

'OK, so . . . the attraction's mutual. I guess you know that.'

'No, not for sure. I've just kept hoping. But I can't read your thoughts. I'm not like Kokos.'

What presumption! You bet your boots you're not!

'That's just as well.'

And you, Rosenbloom, have the loyalty of a flea.

'But,' Rainbow continues, 'you're something . . . different. And frightening.'

'More so than that envoy from the other world who tried to colonise your mind? You didn't seem that scared of her. And I'm flesh and blood, at least. Look! Feel!'

She pulls her own shirt and T-shirt out of her jeans, seizes Rainbow's hand, and draws it underneath. Holds it there. Not that Rainbow is resisting. She gives her plenty of time. Rainbow takes it, long after Anya loosens her grip.

'See! Heart fluttering . . . nipples rising up to meet you. What more proof do you need?'

'How do I know you're not going to disappear?'

'How do you know that with any lover?'

'I mean . . .'

I know what she means. I've seen the movie, too – Rainbow and I watched it together, in Hampstead, on an Old Weepies double bill: the ageless heroine walks two steps out of the enchanted valley of Shangri-La and time's ravages hit her all at once. She crumbles into dust.

'You mean I'm suddenly going to be whisked off to some other dimension? I don't think so. But who ever gets a guarantee? Some lovers split after three days, some stay the course until they die. Either way, forever's not an option. Or do you usually bar women from your bed because of their mortality? If so, my track record's better than average, so far.'

'Mine won't be.'

'All the more reason, then. You know how it goes – had we but world enough, and time, this coyness, Lady, were no crime . . .'

Hmmph. Seduction by quotation now. You'd think she'd at least pick a female poet. Sappho wrote a few nicely pulsating ones, but I can't see Anya finding her way to Mephistco's archive to chase up the 2,000-year-out-of-print Collected Works.

But they seem to have other things on their mind than lesbian literary history. You can tell how preoccupied they are, when two dykes settle for old chestnuts by the seventeenth-century male metaphysicals. Rainbow picks up the cue: 'But at my back I always hear time's winged chariot hurrying near.'

They don't need chariots with wings to get themselves up the stairs. And I don't bother to find myself a reflective surface wherein to follow them – although no doubt the gleam in Rainbow's eye, or the slick of moisture on Anya's parted lips, would do at a pinch. I've seen it, heard it, felt it, tasted it all before.

OK, I admit it. I've learned my lesson. Amorous dybbuks should stick to their own kind. Rosenbloom was a mistake. And, for the moment, all I want is a little peace and quiet – although it's not all that quiet, thanks to the gaps between the attic floorboards left by the cottage's Victorian jerrybuilder: how Riva can snore on through all those goings-on I do not know.

Watching her sleep, however, is not the most stimulating experience I've had of late, although I realise that certain New York film-makers would have shot ten solid reels of it and begged for more. The night goes on and on and on. So what else did I expect? 'An hundred years should go to praise/ Thine Eyes, and on thy Forehead gaze./ Two hundred to adore each breast/ But thirty thousand to the rest.'

That's Rainbow, loud and clear. But struggling to find the breath for it.

Anya's response eludes me. Partly because the words are muffled by a warm, dense wall of flesh; partly because they are rhyming couplets of multiple hexameters, mouthed in an obscure Baltic dialect now lost.

The sun is well up over the water before they let each other sleep. I doubt we'll hear another word from them until it's lunchtime in Lithuania.

22

So while the Apostate's squaring the circle with the last of Gittel's breed, I turn my attention to the nearest branch of the familial tree of old Shmuel ben Issachar. The little dove is finally stirring in her makeshift nest.

I'm sorry, in a way, that my unorthodox matchmaking exercise has come to nothing. It would have been amusing to watch Rainbow striving to loosen Riva's rigidities, unbutton her inhibitions, slip off her certainties, rub away her prejudices with a gentle but persistent thumb.

Lil would be the first to say – and Nick would back her up – that I am never happier than when I'm banging my head against a wall. I always did like a challenge. I knew before I started that Rainbow had no missionary tendencies. It's not in her blood, as dyke or Jew, to go looking for converts. But if I were a free agent, I think what I'd do now is keep Rainbow hammering away at this lost cause just long enough to put the wind up those damned smug ben Issachars.

Riva's eyes open. She looks around her, dazed and sluggish, while her brain tries to piece together the blurred details and recollections that will tell her where she is, and – which she would rather forget – what brought her here.

She's not her usual self – the clothes are alien, if softer and infinitely easier on the body than her own, and her cropped head is bare. She sees her wig and familiar clothing, dry now, still hanging on the backs of chairs to one side of a dead fire. She pulls off the shirt and jeans, goes to the sink, and slaps cold water over her face and shoulders. Then she comes to look into the mirror.

We are eye to unseen eye. She studies herself; I study her back. The skin is young, but there are tired lines surfacing. Her colour's dreadful; Anya's little sleeping draught may have been harmless, but the day and night just past have taken a toll.

She fixes on the wig, her badge of office: chaste wife and mother of present and future pious men. It would be easy to dismiss her as nothing more than a minor accessory to ben Issachar's crime against me: these women stay in the background, mind their own business over the cookpots and the infant's cot, keep themselves out of public view.

But in her I see the carrier of the seed of all the wonder-rabbis that ever were: not the great Akiba nor Hillel nor Hananiah, not all the sages of Sura, Safed and Sefarad, could perpetuate the tribe if they lay with the earth's fairest, wisest, most fertile alien women: Jewishness comes only through the mother.

Without the Rivas of the world, no ben Issachar would ever have been born to learn the arts devoted to my undoing. So I'm not going to let those black eyes melt me.

If anybody ever let me have the contract on her, I'd dybbuk her but good.

But I realise now that nobody is likely to give me another contract, ever again.

Faced with this fact, a lesser entity might get maudlin, wallowing in memories of the long-gone glory days. (OK, so I'm guilty of psychic breaking and entering on a massive scale, and the occasional bit of arson, but I did deliver a few villains their come-uppances when nobody else could, and I once taught a woman how to fly . . .) But I'm spun of stronger metal than that: when you've spent a few thousand years wrestling with magicians determined to enslave you and entire religions devoted to your destruction, you develop ways of bouncing back.

And while I'm working hard at waking up my inner cheer-leader, Riva scans the room. She hears a cough from one of the

232

sleepers up above. In haste, she pulls on the rest of her clothes. She tries the front door, tugging at the knob until it almost comes away in her hand, before she remembers that Anya has pocketed the key; the door by the sink proves equally unyielding.

Then she sees Rainbow's cast-off shirt at the foot of the stairs, tangled in a heap with Anya's jeans. Above her head there is soft laughter, and the bedsprings once again begin to sing. She hisses her disapproval, then snatches up the denims, and digs the key from one of the pockets. She lets herself out, and bangs the door shut behind her.

I shift myself from the mirror to the window, to see what she does. For a moment Riva stands outside the cottage, blinking in the harsh sunlight; the air is well-scoured, after the night of rain. She tries the locked doors of the taxi, now streaked with grit and salt from the winds of the sea. Then she scans the barren landscape in all directions, crouches down in the shadow of the cab, and pees.

I can't resist the temptation; catching a Limnititzker, so to speak, with her knickers down. I transfer myself first to the salt-crusted wing-mirror, and then to the polished silver earring dangling from one of the lady's delicious little lobes.

'Do you know what they're doing up there?' I murmur. 'Can you picture it? Shall I tell you?'

If I expect her to be startled, I am disappointed. I'd hoped the shock would, at the very least, cause her to misdirect the stream and wet her shoes.

She finishes what she is doing, gives herself a resolute shake and lets the sea breeze dry her, rises slowly, pulls her dark blue tights up in an unhurried manner, and adjusts her skirt.

'Shazelsein!' she spits. A fine old Yiddish command, directing me to shut my trap.

'Typical of you Limnititzkers,' I remark. 'Holy as they come, but no manners.'

'To you, scum off the cesspits of Gehenna, no politeness is due.'

She unhooks the silver droplet from her ear, holds it in her palm, and glares down into it.

'You don't seriously expect to see me in here, do you?'

'I should hope not, dybbuk. Especially not on an empty stomach.'

The arrogance! But then I should have known it, shouldn't I? This woman inhabits several time-spans at once: she is no less at home with the whirling world of angels and demons than she is with the cordless phone and the digital clock. She brushes her teeth with fluoride, but spits to deter the Evil Eye. She may have travelled by jet to see her in-laws in New York or her cousins in Jerusalem, but there is a part of her that still lives in eighteenth-century Limnititzk.

I have made a serious miscalculation. I seek to recover my equilibrium, resort to taunts.

'Better high-tail it to the *mikveh*,' I jeer. 'You'll need a solid week of ritual baths when you get home . . . if you ever do get home. That Anya's a real nogoodnik. She might just decide to kill you, in case you spill the beans. Did you see yourself last night? Wearing that perverted creature's clothing? And with your *sheitel* off your head? You looked just like one of Them. Feh! You're contaminated. How will you ever dare enter your pious husband's hairy embrace again?'

There, that makes her squirm a bit.

'Big talk, dybbuk. But you're the one who's been contaminated. Your powers are waning. They've got you in a cage. Your game is up.'

'You know nothing about it.'

'I know quite a lot about it. Rainbow and I had a very interesting conversation, up at Alexandra Palace.'

I knew I should have found some way to follow that pair up to the pond. I must be getting tired: Anya's binding spell has packed more of a punch than I expected. A tactical mistake.

'Rainbow's all right,' Riva continues. 'Not such a bad person underneath. A shame about her . . . lifestyle. What a waste: she'd make a fine wife for an intelligent man.'

'Don't make me gag,' I say. 'Yours isn't the only way for a

Jew to live, in case you didn't know. For Rainbow, it would be suicide.'

'From an abomination like yourself,' she retorts, 'I can do without lectures on Jewish life.'

'Nor do I need such smugness from an upstart like you. No one even heard of the Limnititzkers till seventeen hundred and something. I've been part of Jewish life – and so have Rainbow and all her kind, and all the other heretics and deviants and dissenters – far longer than your little cult.'

'Aha!' she flings back at me. 'That's exactly why Limnititzkers have to survive in this world. To keep the Law alive.'

'And that's why there have to be heretics,' I reply. 'To keep asking the questions to override your easy answers.'

'Well, if you're such a fan of Rainbow's way of life, why did you try to do what you did to her? Pushing her at me that way. Disgusting. And bound to fail.'

'You don't know the first thing about the way I work.'

'I know plenty. For a start, I smelt your spoor on her when we danced together at the wedding. And I saw, when I looked into her eyes, that she was not quite . . . alone. I knew she needed help. Why do you think I told her those stories, the other night, about demons getting their comeuppances? I asked her, outright, at the beginning of our walk in the park, if she had a dybbuk in her. Then, when she began to tell me how it happened, and what you'd told her, about Gittel and the curse, the scales fell from my eyes.

'Because I've known that story since I was a little girl. Because – as you may not be entirely surprised to hear – How the Sage Saved the Bride from the Dybbuk is one of the best-loved tales in the Limnititzker lore; we tell it every year, with several other old favourites, on the anniversary of the great Wonder-Rabbi's death. I've always been dying to ask you – was it hot or cold in that tree? Did you get wet when it rained?'

Oh baby, if I weren't so trammelled, would I ever like to rev up and give this little sweetheart one cosmic klop on the jaw.

At that moment we are interrupted by the lovebirds, emerging into the light of day. They look at Riva, she looks at them;

everybody blushes so hard you'd think there were roses round the cottage door. I can't say I'm enchanted with this sugary scene. What am I supposed to do, dance a *hora* round their women-only wedding canopy?

'Listen, Riva,' says Anya, studying her shadow on the ground, 'I'm sorry about yesterday. I never meant to –'

Riva hold up a hand. '*Sha.* Don't mention it. We'll just forget all this happened, all right?'

'And I'm sorry, too,' puts in Rainbow, 'for getting you into this mess in the first place. You must hate me for it.'

'It was an interesting mess,' says Riva. 'And I don't hate you at all. Maybe it even did me good. Like travel, it broadens the mind. So don't worry. I'm not about to run off with you . . .' (I hear Anya's hiss of horror) 'but we might just manage to be friends.'

'I'll drive you back to London now,' says Rainbow. 'Your family must be frantic. And I guess you're missing your kids.'

'If you want to know the truth,' Riva tells her, 'this was the first unbroken night of sleep I've had in years. Motherhood is not an unmixed blessing.'

'What's that?' Rainbow indicates the object that Riva holds in the palm of her hand.

'My earring,' Riva replies. 'It was bothering me, so I had to take it off.' She closes her fingers over it. Everything goes dark around me.

'I'll just clean the muck off the windscreen and wing-mirrors,' says Rainbow, 'and we'll be off.'

'Hey! Hey, Rosenbloom!' I shout. 'How was your night of passion with the *gilgul?*'

But I am stifled in Riva's fist; I don't think Rainbow hears me. Riva, however, raises her clenched fingers to her lips, and hisses into them, 'Don't you dare call her that, dybbuk, ever again!' Then, in a louder voice, to Rainbow: 'I'm just going to walk along the path towards the dunes a bit, Rainbow. While we're out here, I might as well have a look at the sea.'

Liar. The indifference of Limnititzkers to the great outdoors is well-known; the only landscapes that interest them are the hills of a totally discorporeal Zion. What's she planning?

I soon find out.

'You think I'm some sort of kosher goody-goody, don't you, dybbuk?' she says into her fist. 'Well, I have a confession to make. I've always been a bit of a bad girl: I've disobeyed my father. "Don't look at those books," he tells me, when I go in to clean, "they're not for you. Just dust them." So, when the house is full, and my husband's away, and I give up my room to some guest like your Rainbow's Aunt Goldie – I spend the night in my father's study, and reading all the texts that weren't written for the eyes of women. And I've learned a thing or two.'

I'll bet she has. I know what's coming.

She's a true ben Issachar, that infuriating mixture of the wondrous and the terrible. She lifts her closed hand to her lips, which are like ripe peaches, and murmurs into the ivory cave of her fingers. I am warmed by an exhalation of spices and honey, but the words she speaks, as she flings the earring out to sea, cast me adrift in an ice-cold current.

There is a certain psalm, of multiple meanings and hidden potencies, which, when intoned with scrupulous precision, is particularly dangerous to our kind. She's learned it well, is letter-perfect, unfaltering; it sends me back, in some discomfort, to the place from whence I came.

23

When I get back to base, bruised and battered, I brace myself for a reception that will make the Day of Judgment look like a Sunday School picnic.

Oh, they won't go for anything so crude as physical torture. After they've scalded my ears with their abuse for a few weeks, and paraded my wreckage before the assembled ranks as an edifying example of what not to do and how not to do it, they will probably just turn me into a stone gargoyle on the roof of some Gothic cathedral. Pigeons will use me for a launch-pad, and the winds will slowly wear me to a stump, but the views will be terrific.

However, and not for the first time in this chronicle, I am wrong.

It takes me all the strength I have left to open the door into Contracts.

All the minions in the outer office take their eyes off their VDUs, and follow my limping progress up the room. I stagger into Nick Thumb's cubicle.

'Not now!' he bellows, without raising his head from the printout that spills off his desk and carpets most of the floor. 'I'm cross-checking the quarterly XPDs! Don't care what it is! Piss off!'

'Piss on your XPDs,' I croak, 'and give me a swig of that fizzy water fast or I'll disintegrate messily all over your in-tray.'

He looks up. The jets of vapour from his astonished mouth

steam up the glass walls of his cage; I kick the door shut behind me, for privacy, and lose my balance. He heaves himself from his swivel-chair, pulls a green bottle from his middle-management mini-fridge, spills most of its contents over me while struggling to insert it between my cracked and contorted lips. Then fusses and flaps, at a loss what to do next.

I come up choking. 'OK, OK. Thanks. The precautionary loosening of the clothing won't be necessary . . .'

'Kokos, I wouldn't dare.'

'I know,' I gasp. 'You're the only one I trust in this outfit. That's why I came here first.'

'You look . . .' He gropes for the apt phrase; it is considered bad form here to use words like 'hellish'.

'As gruesome as I feel. Those blasted ben Issachars . . .'

'Still pack a punch, do they?'

'You should see this year's model.'

'Oh, don't worry, dear, we have. Your progress has been properly monitored since your highly improper return to the field.'

'Well, thanks for letting the *gilgul* turn me into chopped liver.'

'Lil thought it would do you good to sweat a little . . . And you'll be interested to know that, as of today, you have just achieved the worst accident record in the division.'

This little jab in the ego is just what I need. I pull myself up to a sitting position.

'So I take a few risks,' I snap. 'That's what makes me an artist.'

'Tell that to the Review Board, baby.'

'Don't talk to me about those creeps, they'll have me in their clutches soon enough. I suppose I'm in for the mother of all court-martials.'

'In normal circumstances, you would be. Right now, Upstairs has other matters on what passes for its minds. The whole place is in an uproar. The latest word around the coffee-machines is that All Will Be Revealed tonight.'

'Tonight?'

239

'There's a big reception. Visiting Top Brass. And everybody, down to the gremlins in the Photocopying Department, has been invited – no, make that commanded – to attend.'

I tell him I'm not in a party mood.

'Sorry, mate. If you're on the premises today, you're coming, Security has its orders, on all the gates. Nobody leaves, until after the jamboree. So if I were you, I'd nip over to the Company Health Club for a couple of hours, tidy yourself up a bit, and see what they can do to lick your wounds.'

'I'm not a member.'

He rummages in a drawer, finds a slip and scrawls something on it. 'Here's a guest pass. It's in my name – so for pity's sake, don't disgrace me by messing around with any of the masseuses.'

'Well, hello there, stranger.'

I've been asleep, lulled by competent hands rubbing aromatic oils into my aching shoulderblades. I wake to someone xylophoning up and down my spine, and to the discovery that I am no longer the only customer in the massage room.

Lil, propped up on one elbow, grins at me from under a towelling turban. She is being kneaded and punched like bread dough by a Valkyrie sporting the corporate logo tattooed on a bicep.

'Good, isn't it? I've been watching you sleep.'

'I love being spied on by the enemy,' I mutter, and turn my face the other way.

'Come on, we're all girls together here. Koke. No office politics.'

'Office politics!' I shriek, rising up like a cobra. With a karate chop to the nape of my neck, my masseuse gets me back where she wants me.

'Mmmm, interesting,' muses Lil. 'I see that love-bite from Diabolexpo hasn't altogether faded yet . . . How long has it been, now?'

'Not long enough. Go away.' Something very interesting is being done to the soles of my feet. If only she'd leave me in peace to enjoy it. 'You're polluting the atmosphere.'

There is a slight intake of breath from the Valkyrie. All girls together we may be in here, but she knows full well Lil's position in the corporate hierarchy. This is not the way the workers usually speak to a queen bee.

'Oh-oh. It must be all the toxins coming out. And just what do you mean by enemy, anyhow?'

'I suppose you sent me that *gilgul* as a friendly gesture, then, to lend a helping hand on the Gittel job.'

'The Apostate? Nothing to do with me: in fact, I spent six hours fighting that decision in a totally futile meeting with Topaz and three top-level gorillas from Resource Deployment with cottonwool in their ears and Closed For Lunch signs on their brains.'

The Valkyrie smacks her on both haunches. 'Turn over.'

To my relief, Lil seems to have abandoned her ceremonial tail.

Staring up at the ceiling while work proceeds on her thighs and knees, Lil continues. 'She must have wormed her way into Topaz's confidence, maybe gave her a new recipe for ginger biscuits or something, who knows?'

'She also works both sides of the blanket: that binding spell she slammed me with had the Opposition's fingerprints all over it.'

She throws a meaningful look to the two masseuses. They nod and gather up their jars and sponges; the tattooed one pauses in the doorway. 'Give us a shout if you need anything,' she says as she goes, with a smile altogether too knowing for my taste.

'Freelance double agents would be the least of your worries,' says Lil, 'if you knew what was happening Upstairs.'

'Isn't power sexy?' I jeer. 'All those secrets . . .'

'Don't taunt me. I've had a really horrendous time while you've been away cavorting with your Jews . . .'

'Save your breath. I know all about it. The loneliness of the high corporate peaks. Uneasy lies the head that wears the crown. It's what they pay you for.'

She mutters something into her towel. It sounds like 'Not much longer . . .' But I don't press her.

'Anyway,' she says, 'you won't be in the dark after tonight.'

'Is it absolutely necessary for me to . . .?'

'Yes.'

We both adjourn to the sauna. I suspect Lil would like to make further efforts towards reconciliation. So, I confess, would I. She may be a back-stabbing, double-dealing, power-hungry twister, but she's one of my own kind.

However, I think, to borrow her own phrase and tactics, I'll let her sweat for a bit.

Afterwards, in the changing room, everyone shoots sidelong glances at Lil. They know she knows something. I for one will not give her the satisfaction of even seeming to care. But even I, no fan of fashion statements, have to admit I'm impressed with her battledress: a kimono made of silk and moonlight, with sleeves of butterfly wings.

'Very pizazzy, pal. And to think,' I say, brushing mud from a faraway marsh off my boots, 'that I knew you when your idea of power-dressing was a tool-belt round your hips.'

Party time. The conference room, despite its lofty ceiling, imposing works of art and impressive dimensions, feels like Saturday night in the Dodge City saloon – smoke-filled, hot and jittery.

I scan the crowd. For the first time, after a stint in the field, I think to myself 'Home sweet home'. Sipping champagne and nibbling canapés, we make a rich and handsome multitude, whose costumes and countenances have given life to 100,000 human fantasies, esoteric texts, carved misericords, cathedral drainpipes, forest shrines, amulets and allegories. Here, milling around the caviare, dwells all the menace and the glamour of the Unseen World.

Near the champagne supply, I spot Lil among a gaggle of boy wonders from Upstairs, each one taller, more tanned and more athletic than the last. Behind her, we get a tantalising glimpse of our unknown guests of honour: the bushy-tailed Fox Ghosts from Kyoto, back again.

Soon an authoritative clinking of knife on wine-glass demands our attention. There is a sudden, anxious hush. All speculations expire: this is it.

The Big Boss speaks.

Not in person, but via a closed-circuit television screen that fills an entire wall. The face remains in shadow.

We receive the news (clearly no surprise to the highest ranks in the room) that our entire organisation has been acquired by the Japanese.

A pause: the speaker, though absent from our midst, has a fine grasp of the audience. The murmurs – of surprise, dismay, muted terror, mutiny – are allowed to run their course. The phrase 'I told you so' is heard simultaneously from different portions of the crowd.

A sharp, commanding clearing of the highest-ranking throat indicates that the speech is not yet finished. Silence falls again.

There will, of course, be changes. Economies of scale. Maximum use of state-of-the-art technology in place of costly and often error-prone personnel.

Everyone will, as per standing Union agreements, receive outplacement counselling, redundancy payments. Pensions will, of course, be protected.

Security codes covering delicate operations have – even as we stand here – been altered. Departing staff will be required to clear their desks and hand in their entry passes by midnight tonight.

Everyone is thanked for their attention, their loyalty and their cooperation. The bar will remain open for another twenty minutes. Good luck to you all. Have a nice eternity.

We retreat into Lil's office: Lil, Nick, me. Lil shuts the door on the sounds of *Götterdämmerung* in the corridor, and unlocks her drinks cupboard.

'Might as well demolish this stuff; I'm not leaving it behind.'

243

'You mean you've got the boot along with the rest of us?' Even Nick's surprised.

'Yes. The only difference is, I knew it was coming.'

'Thanks for keeping us so clued in,' he snaps.

'Can you imagine what they would have done to anyone who spilled the beans?'

'Why you?' I demand. 'Madam High-Flier.'

'My brief but meteoric rise,' sighs Lil, 'was part of the writing on the wall.'

'Why?' asks Nick. 'I thought it was equal opportunities in action.'

Lil snorts. 'Gender doesn't mean a thing to this hard-nosed bunch: their contempt for all of us is perfectly impartial. We're nothing but a bunch of museum pieces: machines can do everything that we can do, only faster and cheaper. That's why I was promoted: they needed a good engineer to put in the technology.'

'So why get rid of you now?'

'The system's virtually glitch-proof: three technicians can run the whole thing. I designed it myself.'

I can tell from Lil's face, she can't decide whether to be diabolically proud of her achievements, or mortally ashamed. For that flicker of uncertainty, I begin to like her again, better than I have since the days of the Great Succubus Strike. This doesn't mean I won't make her jump through a hoop or six before I let her know it: in the craft of dybbukry revenge and forgiveness are merely two sides of a single coin.

'And what do we all do for a living now?' sighs Nick, wreathing himself, and the rest of us, in a chilly, mournful mist. 'We might as well just lie down and call in the exorcists.'

It's amazing how fast you can dance when the bad cowboys shoot bullets at your boots.

'Hey, wait a minute.' I hear my own voice breaking the gloomy silence. 'I have an idea.'

So what's new? You can't spend all those centuries working my particular client group without learning something from your subjects about survival. It comes with the territory, along with storytelling, family arguments, and all those bottomless pots of soup.

I sketch out the whole scenario in seven minutes flat. They listen. Think. Laugh. Look at each other. Shrug their shoulders.

'So what do we have to lose?' asks Nick.

'OK,' says Lil. 'Let's do it.'

24

After the End

W hy is this night different from all other nights? Because on other nights Rainbow Rosenbloom and her lover Anya dine alone, and go to bed eagerly and early. On this night, they will stay up late, and dine with guests.

Why is this night different from all other nights?
Because Rainbow's house – usually a women-only zone – now contains the Crown Prince Michael and his beloved Noah, along with a few favourite colleagues from *Outsider*. Plus Naomi, Mary-Catherine and the full flotilla of Rosenbloom aunts. Nevertheless, those of the aunts possessed of spouses have excused the latter from attendance: Tottenham Hotspur play at home tonight.

Why is this night different from all other nights?
Because polite Jewish matrons of a certain age now uncomplainingly sit cross-legged on the floor to consume their dinners. Only Lila – nicely suntanned and rested from her extended holiday – remarks that a dining table sometimes comes in handy.

Why is this night different from all other nights?
Because Minna has been forced to admit that she has finally tasted sweet-and-sour stuffed cabbage more delicious than her own. Because Molly for once refrains from remarks on how a

nice girl like Rainbow should get married, and has only priase for every dish that Anya produces, from mushroom-and-barley soup to lokshen kugel. Because Becky doesn't start any fights with her sisters about politics, being far too interested in what's coming out of the kitchen. Because Goldie stays awake start to finish, and – although she of course eats only the little snack brought from her own strictly kosher larder – declares that every dish she sees looks and smells just as good as the ones made long ago by old Great-Grandma Rosenbloom, rest her soul.

Why is this night different from all other nights?

Because Rainbow has cleaned the flat, under Anya's all-seeing, dust-detecting eye. This will not happen often.

Why is this night different from all other nights?

Because on this night, for the first time in some 200 years, Anya the Apostate feels ever so slightly tired. A few threads of grey have appeared in her hair. Because time now once again begins to move forward for her – no faster, let us hope, than for any less well-travelled mortal.

Why is this night different from all other nights?

Because on this night all of Rainbow's separate worlds collide. And because there is, once again, an invisible guest at the feast. But this time she is not sitting on Rainbow's shoulder, but observing the celebrations through a windowpane. And this time the visitor is not alone: Nick and Lil and a couple of other old comrades are at my side.

We do not announce our presence: this is only a flying visit, a sentimental detour at my request.

With our histories in our heads, and a few lucky charms and useful phone numbers sewn into the hems of our garments, we are in transit, from the barred and shuttered Mephistco Plant Number Three to the scene of our new venture. A little band of optimistic refugees.

Our destination, should she discover it, will come as no surprise to Rainbow Rosenbloom. In a way, it's all due to her that we have found this outlet for our particular talents.

I, Kokos, am bursting with ideas for plots: name a human comedy or tragedy I haven't seen played out a thousand times. And who better than Lil for engineering special effects that will make the most jaded audience sit up and take notice. Nick, of course, is a genius at that all-important art of drafting contracts: when it comes to making deals, he wrote the book.

I look forward to the moment, at some London press show, when Rainbow first sees my name on screen as the credits roll. And, if Rosenbloom knows what's good for her, she'd better give our first picture a rave review. Or I really will come back to haunt her. Count on that.

Selected Titles from Seal Press

EGALIA'S DAUGHTERS by Gerd Brantenberg. $11.95, 0-931188-34-2; $16.95, cloth, 0-931188-35-0. A hilarious satire on sex roles in which the wim rule and the menwim stay at home.

LOVERS' CHOICE by Becky Birtha. $10.95, 1-878067-41-9. A collection of stories that charts the course of black women's lives and relationships with insight, poetry and intelligence.

THE FORBIDDEN POEMS by Becky Birtha. $10.95, 1-878067-01-X. Chronicling a journey of loss and mending, Birtha again exhibits the strength of her vision and the richness of her language.

ALMA ROSE by Edith Forbes. $10.95, 1-878067-33-8. This first novel by a gifted lesbian writer is filled with unforgettable characters and the vibrant spirit of the West.

DISAPPEARING MOON CAFE by SKY Lee. $10.95, 1-878067-12-5, $18.95, cloth 1-878067-11-7. A spellbinding first novel that portrays four generations of the Wong family in Vancouver's Chinatown.

OUT OF TIME by Paula Martinac. $9.95, 0-931188-91-1. A delightful and thoughtful novel about lesbian history and the power of memory. *Winner of the 1990 Lambda Literary Award for Best Lesbian Fiction.*

HOME MOVIES by Paula Martinac. $10.95, 1-878067-32-X. This timely story charts the emotional terrain of losing a loved one to AIDS and the intricacies of personal and family relationships. *Finalist for the 1994 Lambda Literary Award for Best Lesbian Novel.*

ANGEL by Merle Collins. $9.95, 10-931188-64-4. A stirring novel that centers on several generations of women and traces the struggle of the Grenadian people to achieve political autonomy.

MARGINS by Terri de la Peña. $10.95, 1-878067-19-2. One of the first lesbian novels by a Chicana author, *Margins* is a story about family relationships, recovery from loss, creativity and love.

NERVOUS CONDITIONS by Tsitsi Dangarembga. $10.95, 0-931188-74-1. A moving story of a Zimbabwean girl's coming of age and of the devastating human loss involved in the colonization of one culture by another.

SEAL PRESS, founded in 1976 to provide a forum for women writers and feminist issues, has many other books of fiction and non-fiction, including books on health and self-help, sports and outdoors, mysteries and non-fiction anthologies. Any of the books above may be ordered from us at 3131 Western Avenue, Suite 410, Seattle, Washington 98121 (please add 15% of the book total for shipping and handling). Write to us for a free catalog.